About the Author

Lexie Winston has been an astronaut, rock star, princess and time traveller. In her dreams. But none of the dreams have lived up to what becoming an author has been like. She gets to live in a world of pure imagination, and her heroines get to do the things she's always wished she could.

When not writing books, Lexie is a mother of two gorgeous teenagers and the wife to a patient and understanding man. They live in Western Australia and are lorded over by a black toy poodle. She loves camping, reading and if her iPad was stolen, her world would explode. (It has the kindle app on it.)

And check out my website at lexiewinston.com

And you can find all my links at
https://linktr.ee/LexieWinston

Glorious Gluttony

Gangs, Guns, and Glory

Galaxy Circus

(Sci-Fi Reverse Harem Series)

Apprentice

Stagehand

Whisperer

A Night Most Wicked - Galaxy Circus Novella

Broken Promises

(Dark Poly Romance Series)

Secrets Kept

Lies Untold

M.I.T.H.O.S

(Contemporary RH)

Spies Like Me

Coming 2022

SUPERFICIAL GIRL

Part 1

LEXIE WINSTON

First published by Neighpalm Publishing in 2022

Superficial Girl - Part 1: Neighpalm Industries Collective

Mobi format: 978-0-6487933-8-0
Print: 978-0-6489412-2-4

Cover design by Lexie Winston
Edited by Inked Imagination
Proofreading - Elemental Editing

❋ Created with Vellum

Content Warning

Please be advised there is drug use and attempted rape in this book.

Chapter One

Jacinta

The best thing about owning a club is the owner's VIP booth. Up here, overlooking the teeming masses, I feel safe and protected. Being a social butterfly has not come easy to me as of late, and I don't doubt that my kidnapping has something to do with it. Although I'm surrounded by acquaintances—because, let's be real, I don't consider most of these leeches my friends—I feel all alone. Tonight is the first night of our twenty-seven years on this planet that I'm not celebrating my birthday with my twin brother. Don't get me wrong, I'm thrilled he's at home with Harlow and the others and that they're moving on with their lives, yet I can't help but feel a little bit jealous.

Yes, I know jealousy is what caused problems

when Harlow first came into our lives, but it's not something I can just turn off. Deep-rooted fears of being left alone or being second best have plagued me all my life, as my therapist could surely attest to.

I've gotten better with how I deal with that green-eyed monster and the fears that keep it fed, but it occasionally rears its ugly head, and today, it's riding me hard. I glance around at the people who are here to celebrate my birthday with me. They are all familiar faces who laugh and say the right things to my face, but once I turn my back, they have no problem dissing me. Their eyes fill with pity when they think I'm not looking, and although they outwardly share encouragement, it's their whispers that tell the truth about how they feel.

I take another sip of my drink as the few people in my booth carry on a conversation around me, something about two of Hollywood's biggest leading men, but I don't have it in me to listen. I probably should since Declan represents both of them, but then I spot Hope's red head moving through the crowd like a lighthouse beacon warning ships away from the shore. She smiles and exchanges words here and there, but there's no stopping to engage. She's a woman on a mission to reach me.

Her costume tonight is Medusa, featuring a cool snakeskin bodysuit with flowing gauzy panels and a snake headdress. She looks fierce, which is exactly what I tried to envisage for myself. For years, Jax and I wore matching costumes, so tonight is the first night in years that I've worn something that's completely my own. I decided on Wonder Woman, wanting to channel a little of her power. Plus, who doesn't love a magic lasso? Though the one on my hip certainly doesn't have the magic I wish it did.

Hope holds a tray of drinks that she places on the table before putting her hands on her hips, glaring at the woman sitting beside me like she wants to turn her into stone. A mediocre daytime soap actress, Kerry Star is always hanging around in the hope Declan might see her and decide she would be perfect for his next blockbuster. The first thing she asked was when Dec would be joining us. Her face fell when I told her he was home with his girlfriend, which gave me a shady hint of glee that probably makes me a terrible person in some people's books. In mine, it just makes me a good sister.

"Move. You're in my seat."

Kerry gasps when she hears Hope's order, though she has no right to. The stupid girl is probably going to push the issue.

"I've been here for a while now. Jacinta and I are in the middle of a conversation!" I can hear the annoyance in her tone despite the music, which is loud even though it's muted by general club standards.

Shit! We are?

"Yes, but now you're done." Hope waves a

hand, and a security guard appears behind her, making Kerry jump to her feet.

"Okay, okay, no need for that." She shuffles out of her seat and looks for somewhere else in the booth to sit, but no one moves. Hope stares each and every one of the others down. "You're all done. Take a hike and find someone else to sponge off of. This tab is closed."

Everyone starts to argue with her, but she stands her ground, glaring at them.

"Is there a problem here, Ms. Summers?" The security guard steps up, and I just smirk when everyone looks at me because they have failed to remember that Hope is now a Summers too.

"No, it's fine. They were all just leaving," she answers. He crosses his arms and adds his weighted stare to Hope's, and the people surrounding me practically shrivel up. It's a mass exodus from my booth as they all rush away without a backward glance.

She high-fives the guard. "Thanks, Dean."

"My pleasure," he says with a grin, giving us both a wink before returning to his place at the top of the stairs that lead to the VIP area.

Hope's giggling as she sits down. "Did you enjoy that?" I ask her, already knowing her response. As someone who found herself part of our family because she formed a genuine connection with my brother, then the rest of us, she's always taken a harsh view of the sycophants that only seek to use us.

"Fuck yes. You know I've always hated the Summers' clingers. I know it's part of the deal, but I'm not changing who I am now. I can be nice for business, but this is social, and that crap doesn't fly with me." She waves a hand, and a waitress wearing a black cat costume, like all the other female staff, comes over to clear the mess off our table.

"Such assholes, happily drinking on your dime and just as happy to stab you in the back at the next function you don't attend. I already heard whispers of you having a falling out with your family because not one of the brothers is here to celebrate your birthday. I think those two are fueling that." She points a manicured finger at Lindy and Rowena, my PA and new designer, who are flirting with a couple of B-grade movie stars at the bar. "I doubt any of them realize we all attended a funeral this morning, so they can be somewhat excused, but those two, they are just stirring up trouble. Why haven't you fired them yet?" she asks, moving the tray in front of us now that there's more space. I smile and thank the girl who's wiping down the table, pulling a twenty-dollar bill from my cleavage and passing it to her. She thanks me without flinching over where it came from and heads back to the bar. I guess they have seen worse. At least it's not sweaty.

"What are these?" I ask my adopted sister,

ignoring her question about Lindy and Rowena. I'm not entirely sure I know the answer. Honestly, I've chased off my brothers' girlfriends faster than I've cleaned up the mess that is my work life. Have I really been that burnt out for so long?

Hope frowns, and I can feel her weighted stare, but she's out of luck. I feel her sigh more than hear it, then she reaches out, grabbing the four shot glasses. She puts two in front of me and two in front of her before going back for the cocktail glasses. The cocktail glasses are actually conical chemistry beakers, each one filled with a green liquid and what looks like a gummy eyeball floating in it. It's also smoking, which is a nice festive touch.

"That one is called a Zombie Brain." She points to one that's full of white liquid with red running around the inside of her glass, and I wrinkle my nose. She shifts her finger and points to the other glass. This one is full of black liquid with a gold kind of haze floating through it. "And those are called Black Magic. As for these, they're the club special tonight—Mad Doctor. It's sour apple flavored, and it's delicious. I had one while I was checking on a few things for Jaxon downstairs." She places the smoking concoction in front of me and picks up her Zombie Brain. "Come on, let's forget about everything and just have a good time tonight. We'll worry about the rumors and speculation tomorrow. Your dad has the new head of PR working up a statement for the press since we've been so close-lipped on what happened. The press has been respectful, but that's over now. You guys are about to become cannon fodder for the media once more."

My stomach lurches at the thought of the press harassing us. I'm *so* over all the attention. Once upon a time, I would have smiled and waved and enjoyed having all the cameras on me, but I can see how that was a reaction to the lack of attention from my mother when I was younger. It was toxic attention, not the right kind, and it did more harm than good.

"Let's drink these, then you and I can go down on that dance floor amongst the lowly peasants and blow off some steam." Hope's clearly excited about dancing, and even though the thought of being surrounded by all those people, with them touching me and watching my every move, fills me with dread, I can't let my new sister down.

"Woo-hoo, let's get this party started!" I plaster on a smile and grab my drink. Clinking them together, we toss them back. The coconut taste is a surprise, and I feel my eyebrows jump. "Oh, that wasn't so bad," I say, and she licks her lips, catching a drop she missed.

"No, they were delicious. They go in the drink again column. Let's try these." Again, we clink our shot glasses together, and I physically brace myself. There aren't many black liquors, so I'm pretty sure I know what this one is going to taste like. Sure enough, when I throw it back, the distinct taste of anise hits my taste buds, but there's something else that slightly tempers the abrasive taste.

"Oh, that one wasn't horrible either," Hope says, looking at the shot glass before sticking her tongue in it, trying to get a bit more of the residue.

"Hope! How much did you have to drink downstairs?" I ask, giggling while she tries to tongue her shot glass. She stops and looks sideways at me before putting the glass down, a sheepish smile on her face.

"I may have had two Mad Doctors, but they're fucking delicious. And so was that."

"I think it might have been Baileys that gave it the hazy color, and you're right, another for the again list," I tell her before picking up my beaker. The dry ice has stopped smoking now, so I can take a sip without worrying about hurting myself. The sour apple flavor is a tart contrast to the licorice from the sambuca, and my tongue rebels, not entirely happy with what I'm putting it through. After a couple of sips, it chills and happily accepts the refreshing, cold beverage.

"How are things going at the house? Are you enjoying your sabbatical? I feel like I haven't seen you and Harlow since the kidnapping," Hope says, taking a sip of her Mad Doctor. Before I can answer, she continues, "Apart from Jaxon, the guys have finally started coming back to work, but it doesn't seem like it's going to last all that long. I think there might be more than just Holden making a career move. When I was down in HR the other day, finalizing Cole's employment, I heard a couple of people talking about more interviews for big positions in the company."

I'm people watching instead of looking at her, but the hurt in her voice makes me turn to her once more. Sure enough, she's looking wounded and put out, and it suddenly occurs to me that Hope has been holding everything together at work while the rest of us try to recover from what happened. She hasn't had a chance to examine her own feelings because she's been making sure we all have companies to come back to at the end of the day.

I reach for her hand and scoot closer, resting my head on her shoulder. "Oh, honey, I'm sorry you're feeling left out. It wasn't our intention. You've been in the city dealing with Neighpalm every time this has come up in conversation. It wasn't planned, and I guess we all assumed someone had filled you in. I'm actually surprised Dad didn't say anything to you. I know he's been going in a couple of times a week."

Hope's hand tightens in mine before she pulls away. "Yes, but he's as busy as I am, so we barely even see each other. With Nana and Poppy off on an extended vacation to visit with Ben, and you guys dealing with Willow Castle and the zoo, there just hasn't been time to sit down and catch up. So imagine my surprise when I heard that not only are we opening applications for Neighpalm Couture and the new Neighpalm Cruise Lines, but there's rumors being whispered of a Neighpalm Entertainment and an amusement park we might have purchased."

"Babe, we're not hiding anything. I'm not sure how HR heard about that. We certainly haven't said anything to anyone, so they must have an outside source. Nobody should know about it because it's a surprise for Harlow that Declan's revealing tonight. I only just found out about it yesterday because Oliver let something slip when Harlow wasn't around. Nana and Poppy are back tomorrow, and we're having a party at Dad's. I'll make sure we fill you in on everything that's been going on. I promise we'll do better. It's just been a lot, you know?"

She's still frowning, but she shakes it off. "Okay, I'd like that. I haven't been home in weeks. I haven't even had a chance to move all my stuff in or get the furniture into storage. I was going to keep my apartment, but Nana convinced me I didn't need it since I can use the family suite at the hotel when I need to stay in town."

"Come on then. Let's blow off some steam, like you said, and tomorrow I will help you arrange this week. Harlow and the guys will be so pleased to see you, and if we get time, I can show you what we've been doing over at their place."

"Okay, sounds good to me," she says, finally

smiling again. I breathe a sigh of relief and finish my drink before standing up. "I'm just going to use our private bathroom to freshen up before we hit the dance floor. You good to wait here?" I ask, and she waves me off.

"Absolutely. I might see if I can find a man to take home tonight. I really could do with some stress relief, and if I can convince them to leave the mask on, all the better. There's nothing more illicit than a one-night stand with a stranger." I leave her eyeing the masked crowd below us and head toward the employees only exit. My brother has an office back there, and attached to it is a bathroom. Nice and quiet and private, exactly what I need.

Moving through the crowded VIP area, having people I know wave and touch me on the way past, makes me want to vomit. Thinking about going downstairs with Hope is going to require a little more than liquid courage.

When the employees' door closes behind me, the sudden quiet is a little disorienting. Sound-proofed for my brother's sanity, it's a sudden shock I hadn't been expecting, so I lean my back against the door as I get my bearings. My drinks have gone straight to my head, only having drunk water prior to them.

Finally, I push up and walk down the corridor to my brother's office, grateful that the boots that go with this costume have chunky heels. I key the combination into the touchpad next to his door and push it open when the green light flashes. The familiar scent of my brother greets me when I walk through the door, and I have a small moment of guilt that I quickly shake off before heading to his bathroom. A few minutes later, when I'm washing my hands, I finally lock eyes with my reflection, not at all happy with what I see looking back at me.

Chapter Two

Jacinta

Before me is a woman who's clearly suffering from some kind of trauma—survivor's guilt or PTSD or something. I can see it in the terrified look in her eyes, and I have no clue how no one else sees it too. Maybe it's because I've become adept at projecting the same self-centered, confident woman I've always had to be. But I'm not. I've reverted to that scared teenager I was when I realized my mother had used me to break in and kill someone.

All that therapy I had afterward, where they assured me none of it was my fault, is gone, and left behind are so many feelings and thoughts that I can't control. How can Jaxon and Harlow even look at me after everything they've been through? Peter made them take drugs and fuck at gunpoint! Jaxon got shot and almost didn't make it. I nearly lost the other half of my soul. I ran away like a coward, but I should have stayed and helped them escape too. I didn't, and they paid the price.

Reaching into my bustier once more, I drag out a little plastic bag full of white powder and a dollar bill, laying them down on the marble sink in front of me. My nervous habit of chewing my lip comes back in full force while I stare at the baggie. I tried to convince myself I don't need this. That I could go out into that crowd and enjoy myself tonight. That I could fake it until I make it, and no one would be any wiser to the turmoil inside my mind.

A week ago, I'd been forced to attend a fashion industry award show. I wasn't able to avoid it because I was supposed to present a Neighpalm Couture sponsored award. Although I didn't want to leave my brother, he insisted he was fine. According to him, it was time to start getting our lives back to normal, but if this is normal, my new normal, then I don't fucking want it.

Normal had officially left the building. The thought of going out in public and being surrounded by people who really are no better than strangers was terrifying. How many other people out there have thought about using us for our money? It's only going to be worse now that the news of being the heirs to the Bucătaru fortune is about to break. How do I ever trust any kind of human interaction again?

I'd put on a smile and gone. Granted, I was escorted by a couple of the security guards that have become our norm for the time being, something to make Dad feel better, but I hadn't been able to stop shaking during the limo ride there. The guard who had sat in the back with me took note and poured me a large glass of whiskey. I threw it back without hesitation before asking for another. The man didn't even raise an eyebrow. He just poured the drink for me. By the time we arrived, I was feeling looser and more confident. Luckily, my award was early in the evening, and I was still doing a good job of pretending to be sober when I presented it.

After that, it kind of went downhill. I drank copious amounts just to keep the whispering demons at bay. The guards were able to keep me from making too much of a fool of myself, and I made sure they got a bonus from Dad. Getting a drunk heiress to her suite in the hotel probably wasn't part of the contract, but they did it without any complaint or drawing unwanted attention.

A conversation from early on in the night was vividly stuck in my mind. I was using the bathroom and overheard the models talking about a casting call they had attended. I managed to catch their first scandalized words when the door opened.

"He wanted you to do what?" I was taking a moment to hide out, trying to calm my nerves after having to play nice with the editor of some popular fashion blog. He was a

complete asshole, but he was an asshole with a lot of sway over industry minds. Those who didn't play nice often ended up on his shit list, which could be a career's kiss of death.

"He said that I could walk in his show if I let him fuck me in the ass." The other voice sounded blasé, like it was an everyday occurrence, and I didn't doubt it.

"And did you?" The first voice had lost a little of the scandalized tone, now sounding more curious.

"Sure. I mean, why not? He has all the good drugs too, and he gives you a little party favor once he's gotten his rocks off."

"What did he give you?"

"A little baggie of coke." I heard a sink running, then it turned off again.

"Oh, nice. People say it's good at calming nerves. I've thought about trying it before I go on a casting call. I always get super nervous and end up tripping or something. I've tried dexies, but they just make me twitchy and paranoid."

"Yeah, it's great. I use it before a show too. It helps me block out all the eyes on me and lets me focus on what I'm doing. I also don't get hungry, so that's a bonus too. Helps me keep my figure looking like this."

"So, was the sex good?"

"The guy has a small dick, so it makes anal easier, and he likes to call you Mommy while he slaps your ass and fucks you. Thankfully, we popped an X beforehand, and he pinned me against a bed while he was doing it, so I could muffle my laughter in the blankets." The door opened again as the two women walked out, leaving me alone.

The next day, I snuck upstairs to the sex room at

Willow Castle and took one of the bricks of cocaine that had been rewrapped and returned to the safe after Jaxon and Harlow's ordeal with Peter. I wasn't sure why they didn't flush it down the toilet, but I was kind of glad they didn't. Back at home, I had put some of it into some small baggies. I wasn't sure why since I had no plans to actually use it, but something in me felt a little better with the knowledge that I had it ready just in case. That same something, though I couldn't pinpoint what, had made me slip one into my costume tonight.

I'm no stranger to drug use. Drugs are widely available in the fashion industry, not to mention in the music and film industries as well. My brothers and I have been around it all our adult lives, and I know some of them have indulged from time to time, but I always avoided it. I used to bear the brunt of my mother's meth rages, not that I knew that was what they were at the time, but I always swore that I would never be like her. I rarely drink to excess, preferring to be in control around the vipers that surround me all the time, but hearing those women talk about the lack of nerves and being able to block out everyone's eyes really resonated with me. It sounded like exactly what I needed.

I open the little bag and tap a little bit out onto the marble counter. Opening the drawer, I scratch around, looking for something to help me cut it into lines. The only thing I can find is a comb, so I grab it and run the toothed edge through the powder a couple times, getting rid of any lumps, before flipping it over and working the fine white powder into a line. It's only a small amount since I don't want to overdo it my first time. I could end up hating it and curled into an even bigger anxiety-ridden ball at the bottom of a bathroom stall out on the public level.

Picking up the dollar, I roll it into a straw and, pushing my hair behind my back, bend over. Sticking the straw up one nostril, I block the other and inhale, running it along the length of the line. The powder coats the inside of my nostril, the burning sensation bringing tears to my eyes until it slowly numbs. I breathe in deeply before breathing out. While I wait for something to happen, I clean up. I don't need more rumors floating around about me. Leaving the dollar rolled, I tuck it and the baggie back into my top. I don't know how long a coke high will last, especially because it's my first time, but I may need more later. It's still early, and I'll be expected to hang around for a good portion of the night.

Using a nearby folded washcloth, I wipe the sink, removing all traces of coke residue, before folding it and leaving it on the sink in case I need it again. I can feel the exact moment the coke starts to work. My body coils with anticipation, and all the nerves and guilt and other overwhelming emotions just seem to drift away, leaving me feeling confident and alert and ready to face the world. I look at myself in the mirror, and a small smile creeps across my face. Now, I finally feel like I match my costume. Turning away, I exit the bathroom into my brother's office just in time. Hope has the door cracked, peeking in, a relieved look on her face.

"There you are! I was getting worried for a moment." I should probably feel guilty about worrying her, but I don't. I feel exhilarated and like pre-kidnapping me—confident and ready to blow off some steam with one of my only real friends.

"Sorry, just giving myself a pep talk. Trying to convince myself not to tell all those people out there what I really think about them."

Hope's worry leaves, and she rolls her eyes. "I know. It's a minute-by-minute struggle. But we should be okay down on the dance floor. The music is way too loud to talk. We can just lose ourselves for a little while."

"I want to grab another one of those drinks while we're down there. They were delicious," I say as we get back to the employees only door and exit back onto the VIP floor. The music assaults my senses, and my heart starts pumping harder in anticipation. I feel fucking amazing. "Woo-hoo!" I throw my hands up and cheer as we make our way through the throng of dancing celebrities, past Dean, and onto the floor with the plebs.

We beeline to the bar, which is so filled with costumed patrons, the bartenders are running off their feet to keep up with one of the busiest nights of the year. We've always thrown amazing Halloween parties and are one of the hot LA nightspots.

I catch the eye of one, and when they finish up with the person they're serving, they head toward us. I hear grumbles all around me, and she smiles and points. "They're the bosses, guys. They get top priority. What can I get you ladies?"

"Hi, Katie, can we get two more Mad Doctors?" Hope asks before I can.

"Sure can. Have you both got a ride home tonight?" she asks as she mixes some green liquids and other things in a shaker.

"Hope here is on the prowl, but our security will bring a car when we're ready to leave."

She drops a couple of small pieces of dry ice into the bottom of two clean beakers. "Okay, well, shout out if you run into trouble, and we can arrange something," she says as she pours the contents of the shaker over the dry ice. The drink immediately starts to smoke, and I can't stop myself from grinning. It's such a fucking cool effect. "Remember to let it stop smoking before you start drinking," she warns us before waving goodbye and going back to the patrons.

Hope and I take our drinks and head to the dance floor. Stopping at a small round table, we put our drinks on it while we wait for them to stop smoking. I don't like to take drinks onto the dance floor. There's nothing worse than being bumped by someone and wearing whatever they had in their glass. I hate spending the rest of the night sticky.

The lights are bright, the smoke is thick, and the music is pumping. I feel myself start to sway along to the rhythm, my heart synching with the bass heavy track that the DJ is currently playing. People brush past me, but I feel none of the anxiety that has plagued me in public since our ordeal. I feel like I can rule the world, and I can't wait to join the writhing masses and lose myself to the pulse of the music.

It's too loud down here for us to have a decent conversation without shouting, so with silent agreement, we people watch. I scan the crowd, looking for a familiar face, but I don't find anyone I know, which makes me happy. Of course, all of my so-called friends are too good to be down here dancing with the "poor and non-influential," and I can't tell you how much I love it. I love the fact that I can go out there and not be expected to perform any differently from any of the others.

My eye briefly catches on a sexy, dark-haired man wearing a Batman costume complete with mask. A small smirk lifts his lips as the two of us eye fuck each other across the room. I don't know what it is about the man, it's not like I can see his body or anything hidden beneath his armored costume, but his eyes are a shade of blue I've never seen before. They're like the Caribbean Sea, bright and mesmerizing, framed with thick black lashes. He winks at me before turning and disappearing into the crowd. I try to see where he goes, but he quickly gets swallowed up. Shaking off my disappointment, I check on my drink.

It's finally stopped smoking, so I drink it down, causing Hope to throw her head back with laughter. Shrugging, I gesture to the dance floor, and she nods, quickly doing the same.

Once she's done, she places her beaker back on the table and grabs my hand, dragging me into the crowd. I brace myself for the onslaught, but none of the feelings that hit me are negative. It feels good to join the crowd, and when I start moving my body in time to the music, I feel in sync. We're all like-minded people trying to have a good time, moving to the same rhythm, even if only for a short period of time. I throw my hands into the air, dancing to the primitive sexual beat, the crowd around me worked up into a frenzied, chaotic mass of moving limbs and twitching bodies.

My body tingles every time someone brushes across my exposed skin, and in this costume, there's a lot of skin to brush against. A quiet moan, unheard by anyone but me, leaves my lips, and I feel my nipples pebble. Closing my eyes, I toss my head back and revel in all of the sensations, my mind uber-focused on everything that's happening around me. The brush of a hand, the slide of a leg along mine, the hard push of a body against my back. Nobody makes unwanted advances when you're just one with the crowd. It's fucking magical.

When I open my eyes, I see that Hope has found someone to grind against. The guy has his thigh between her legs, and she's riding it with a blissed-out look on her face, all inhibitions having gone down the drain with the Mad Doctors. Smiling, I turn back and move farther into the crowd. Hope is a smart girl who knows how to look after herself. She'll use our car and our hotel suite if she decides to have a booty call, and she has her own set of security guards who are outside with mine, knowing we're safe in the club with in-house bouncers looking after us.

The crowd gets thicker as I move farther into the wall-to-wall bodies and sensation overload. Everything feels amazing, and I can only imagine what an orgasm would feel like while riding this high. I'm tempted to find someone to grind on myself, but there's also a very large part of me that has my heart set on a group of certain someones, and until I know whether or not something may come of that, I'm reluctant to go in search of a one-night stand. I guess the wait is my fault though. I did tell Jace I needed to get my head on straight and that I couldn't start anything while the stalker situation and inheritance thing were up in the air. I've made no promises to anyone, which has to be why they're holding back.

A hand suddenly snakes around my waist,

jolting me out of my thoughts, and I'm yanked back into a hard body. Once I get over my initial shock, I relax back into him, and we rub against one another, losing track of time until panic starts to creep back into my body. From one moment to the next, my emotions race from focused euphoria to tangled nerves and guilt-induced anxiety. Shaking myself free from my dance partner, I push through the crowd, not looking back to see who it was, though the black, armor-covered arm had given me a fairly good clue.

I get a few dirty looks and curses as I carve a path to the bathroom, my heart racing as the panic dictates I find somewhere with not so many people. I get to the back of the club and find a line to the female bathrooms. Looking around as anxiety rides me hard, I spy a storage room and dart toward it. I just need five minutes of peace to get myself together.

That will do. It has to.

Chapter Three

Jacinta

Closing the door behind me, I breathe a sigh of relief as the music becomes muted. I finally have a little taste of the space I need.

Pacing back and forth across the small space, I shake out my hands as I try to calm my breathing and my racing heart. The comedown is brutal and quick, and I finally admit, thanks to the new onslaught of negative emotions, that I can't go on like this. It's time to admit that it's affected me more than everyone thought. I need some extra sessions with my therapist. I haven't been honest with her the last couple sessions, and I know she sees it, but she's waiting for me to fess up.

I bite my lip, and my gaze drifts back to the door. The thought of going back out there almost forces my Mad Doctors to make a reappearance. I can't do it on my own. I should leave. I should find Hope and tell her that I'm heading back to the hotel, but it's not even midnight, and I really should be here when the stage show is on. My mind is filled with all the *shoulds*. How did I get to this point in my life where it feels like so few of my choices are actually my own? How have I lived for nearly thirty years, but so much of it still isn't *mine*?

My hand drifts across the top of my breast, and I look down, seeing the rolled up dollar bill inside my cleavage. Maybe I'll take another hit. Just for tonight, I'll use the coke to get through. It's not like I'll need it again. I'll make sure I avoid any big occasions like this until I can work through it with my therapist.

Happy with my decision, I pull out my supplies and look around for a clean surface to set up my line.

There aren't many options, but there is a metal sink at the back of the small room that they must use to fill mop buckets. It has a flat metal section that must be for draining stuff. I hurry over to it and tap out some of the coke, a bigger pile this time. I don't have the comb, so I just stab at it with the rolled up bill, hoping it will get rid of any lumps. Then, using the long side to form it into two lines, I snort the first one. Just as I'm bending over to snort up the other, the door opens and Batman slips in. Fuck! Oh well, I'm caught now, so I quickly snort the second line before wiping my nose with the back of my hand and glaring at the masked man.

"Don't you know how to fucking knock?" I snap, and he closes the door and storms over, trapping me between the sink and his body. He grabs hold of my hair and yanks my head to the side just as the coke starts to flow through my body. The moan that leaves my mouth is slightly pornographic.

"Don't you know it's polite to share?" he whispers in a husky voice before attacking my mouth with his in a hot, demanding kiss. His tongue explores every inch of my mouth as he holds my head hostage. Instead of panicking like I probably should, with his hard body fencing me in, I melt against him, feeling safe and protected for the first time since I escaped from Peter. This kiss feels like he's laying claim to my body, and the taste of him is wild and addicting. Just as I reach up to wrap my arms around him, he rips himself away from my mouth. Those piercing blue eyes behind his mask feel like they can see deep into my soul.

Without a word, he bends me back, using my hair to control my movement so that my breasts lift up to him like an obscene offering to a god. They're barely covered by the Wonder Woman bustier, the rounded globes highlighted in the dim lighting.

"Stay there," he orders, letting go of my hair to grab the baggie of powder and the dollar straw.

Tapping out the last little bit of powder across

my right breast, he forms it into a line with a hand much more experienced than mine. With his eyes locked on mine, he bends over and snorts the powder from my breast. My panties become even damper with desire while my mouth goes dry at the sexy sight. He throws the straw to the side then runs his tongue along my breast, cleaning up the residue, before yanking down the top of my bustier and latching his hot mouth around one of my nipples. A moan leaves my mouth, but just as quickly as it happens, he pulls away and grabs hold of my hair once more. His blue eyes are lit with fervor, and I watch as his pupils blow out, leaving only a tiny ring of blue.

"Say stop, and I'll let go, pull up your top, and walk away. We can go back to the dance floor and pretend like this never happened. But I think you need this. I think you want me to take away your control and make this decision for you. I think you crave having someone take care of these needs for you. So what will it be? Do you want me to take care of you?"

Those words in that husky voice hit every one of my buttons, and all I can do is groan and nod my head as much as he allows me with his tight grip.

"I need the words. Do you want this?"

"Yes." The word is a quiet sigh that falls off my lips. My body is taut with anticipation, and my eyes are hooded with desire. I want what this man is offering, damn the consequences. Maybe he can finally silence all the nasty voices inside my head. I don't even care that he's a perfect stranger. It might be better that way.

He leans closer and brushes his lips across mine, a soft gesture, before whispering, "Good girl."

Suddenly, he spins me and pushes me over the sink. I hear the clink of him undoing his belt buckle, the noise loud in the room. He pulls my hands behind my back, and I feel him wrap his leather belt around them, securing them tightly. He then spins me back around to face him. My hands are securely fastened behind my back, pinned against the sink, leaving my heaving breasts on display. A small smirk lifts his lips.

"Hmm, more party favors." He leans in and licks a long line over each nipple. They're so tight now they ache, and his attention feels so good, another loud noise slips from my mouth unbidden. "I like pulling noises like that from you. Don't be shy now." He brushes another light kiss across my lips before returning his attention to my nipples. My mystery companion licks, sucks, and uses his fingers to pluck at them until I'm just about sobbing, then he pulls back, leaving me aching and close to begging when the cool air brushes over them.

He kneels and shimmies down the blue skirt of my costume, taking my panties with him so that my bottom half is completely naked to his eyes. I should feel self-conscious and exposed, but all I feel is sexy, wanton, and desirable. I desperately want to run my hands through his hair and pull his face to exactly where I need it, but I can't. I'm completely at his mercy.

He licks his lips and gently lifts my left leg, dragging it up and over his shoulder, opening me up to him. I can feel my desire trickling down the remaining leg, and he runs his tongue up my thigh, trying to catch it before it can go any farther. This time, it's his moan that reaches my ears, and when his shocking blue eyes lock with mine, I see my need reflected in them. As much as he acts like he's in control, I think he's hanging on by a thread.

Without another word, he runs his tongue through my folds, and my other knee buckles. He wraps his large hands around my waist and holds me in place as he thoroughly works my pussy over with his mouth. The tension in my body ratchets higher with the tease of his tongue across my clit in light brushes before going back to my folds, thrusting his tongue as deep as he can. It's kind of depraved, but he has no hesitation about shoving his face into my wet, needy pussy. It's almost like he wants to be coated in me.

Pulling back, he sinks two fingers deep into my channel, and I clench around him as another ragged moan leaves my mouth. Slowly, he thrusts them in and out while he pays special attention to my clit. Arching my back, I moan at all the sensations that are battering my body. Every touch feels amazing, like nothing I've ever felt before or could possibly feel again. I want to bottle this moment so I can always have it. Just as I feel myself about to tip over the edge, he pulls away.

I scream my frustration, and he chuckles as he removes my leg from his shoulder and stands up, his hands going to his pants and his eyes meeting mine.

"It's almost like you thought you were in charge, but I can guarantee you're not. I'm in charge of your pleasure, and you will come when *I* allow you to." His husky voice holds a threat, and I shudder with anticipation. "If I wanted, I could take my cock out right now and get you down on your knees so I could fuck that pretty mouth of yours. Or I could stroke it myself and paint that soft, silky skin with my release, denying you yours." He slowly draws his pants down his thick thighs, showing me that he's going commando. His long, girthy length glistens with precum, and my mouth starts to water. I wouldn't be opposed to getting down on my knees, but the thought of being denied my orgasm makes me cry out, begging him.

"Please." I sound desperate and breathy, and he chuckles as he runs a hand up and down that thick length.

"Oh, I do believe hearing you beg is my new favorite sound." He bends down and pulls a condom out of the wallet in his pants before ripping it open with his teeth and sliding it over his cock.

Grabbing me by the waist, he spins me, using a large hand to gently bend me over the sink, kicking my legs farther apart with his. He slides his hand into my hair before gripping tight and pulling my head back just a little.

"I'm going to fuck you so hard, you're going to be feeling me for days." He slowly releases my hair and runs a finger down the length of my spine before clasping my hip. I feel him line himself up, and with a smooth movement, he forces himself deep with one thrust. I gasp at that invasion and the slight bite of pain as my pussy adjusts to the intrusion.

His hands clench my waist hard as he takes a moment to adjust, leaving what I'm sure will be bruises tomorrow morning. I feel the brush of armor against my back as he leans in and runs a wet tongue along the same path his finger just took, but I'm done waiting. I need him to move, and I'm not above begging.

"Please, I need it," I all but sob, and I get that wicked chuckle again before he pulls back and thrusts deep. My body, which is already teetering on the edge of an orgasm, trembles with the sensation, but he doesn't stop there. He sets a punishing pace, giving us both what we need. My focus narrows as I zero in on all the sensations flowing through my body. I desperately want to pluck at my nipples, but my hands are tied. I bite my lip at the feeling of his long deep strokes, my breath becoming a hiss. Wanting more, I arch my back further, giving him a better angle, and sure enough, he starts to hit the hot button on the front wall of my pussy. Over and over again, he slides against that spot that makes my eyes roll back in my head. I push back against his thrusts, needing something else, hanging on the cusp of an explosion that I'm unable to reach.

"Please, I need more!" I cry out, and one of his hands slides around my hip to my clit. With one last vicious thrust, he pinches it, and I fly off the edge. A hot, searing bolt of pleasure courses through my body, and my scream echoes around the room, his guttural groan joining it in harmony. His cock throbs, and my channel fiercely clasps him in release, unwilling to let him retreat just yet as my orgasm continues to rack my body.

I'm not sure how long we stand there, but the soft brush of a kiss across my shoulder brings me back to the present, as does the feeling of loss when he pulls himself free. I remain still as he moves around behind me, mourning the brush of his pants against my thighs when he pulls them back up. After a moment, I feel his hands on mine, releasing me from his restraints before rubbing some sensation back into my arms. His hands drop away, and I use my now free arms to push myself off the sink while the shuffling sounds tell me he's putting his belt back on. Dazedly, I feel him turn me around, then he hands me a couple of napkins he grabbed off a nearby shelf. I slowly clean myself up as he bends down and helps me back into my clothes. When he stands, he pulls my bustier up, covering my breasts and putting me back to rights. He then smooths back my hair before lifting my head so my eyes can meet his.

What I see there has me shrinking back. Gone is the heated, lust-filled look, and in its place is cold, calculating anger.

"Next time you want to get high, I suggest you lock the door behind you. You're lucky it was me that walked in, not someone who would sell a photo of the spoiled heiress doing coke to the press." He releases my hair and steps away while a chill starts to fill me. He sounds so annoyed, and I don't know how he snapped so quickly.

"I'll be seeing you around, Jacinta. Oh, and happy birthday."

Without a backward glance, Batman leaves the room, firmly closing the door behind him, and I sag against the sink, my strung out body still enjoying the echoes of my orgasm despite my racing mind. *Oh my god. Who the hell was that? He obviously knew who I was. Did he target me? What was I thinking?*

Panic sets in, and all the alcohol I've had to drink returns. I whirl around and violently vomit into the sink. Tears stream down my face as I keep retching until there's nothing left to bring up. How could I have been so fucking stupid? Finally, I'm done. Shaking and weak, I run the water, cupping my hand under it to wash out my mouth. I rinse and spit a couple of times until the sour taste is not as intense on my tongue.

My eyes drift to the empty bag and the rolled note on the sink. Swiping it onto the floor, I scream. I'm not sure if it's anger or frustration or if I'm actually terrified. My tangled, confused emotions are warring with the other part of me that feels like I could take on the world. I pace back and forth, tearing at my hair, my mind unable to form a single coherent thought, until the door opens.

Hope hurries in. "There you are! I was getting worried, and I was searching for you in the bathrooms. I stopped a guy wearing a Batman costume. I thought I'd seen you dancing with him earlier. He pointed me to the storeroom. Is everything okay?" she asks softly, and her eyes widen when I look up at her.

I can feel the tears running down my cheeks, and a sob bursts out. "It's all too much."

Comprehension fills her face, and she comes over, wrapping her arm around me. "Oh, babe, I'm sorry. I should have known this would have been too soon after everything. Come on, let's grab you a bottle of water, then we can go."

I cling to her, and as much as I should insist that she stay and have a good time, I'm not going to. I'm grateful I have her because I'm not sure I could make it out to the car without having a panic attack.

"We'll go out the back door so you won't have to fight through the crowd. Come on. After a good night's sleep, you'll feel much better. Then we can talk about making an appointment with your thera-pist in the morning." My new sister's soft voice and loving embrace are just the right amount of gentle-ness that I need. So, without any complaint, I let her lead me out of the storage room to the back door, helping me into our waiting car. Two of our security guards silently join us in the back while the other two get in the front of the limo, one acting as a driver.

"Is everything all right?" one of them asks, and Hope quietly assures him it is, laughingly blaming copious amounts of alcohol. When the guard seems reassured, the limo falls into silence.

By the time we get back to the hotel, I've chewed a hole in my lip and picked off all the gel polish from my nails, unable to sit still in the loaded silence. The elevator ride up to our room is much the same, with Hope instinctively knowing I'm not ready to talk about anything. She helps me out of my costume and grabs the old, soft sleep shirt that belongs to one of my brothers.

Once I have it on, I climb into my bed.

"Do you want me to stay?" she asks, but I shake my head.

"No, I'll be fine."

I hear her sigh. "Okay, but we *are* talking about this in the morning," she threatens before wishing me good night and closing the door.

As my eyes finally drift closed and the tension leaves my body, the memory of that man—his face in my pussy, and his tongue on my clit—slams into my mind, and I drift off to sleep, wondering what I had ever done to him to make him act so cruel afterward.

Batman

Fuck! What was I thinking, following Jacinta Summers into that supply closet? I'd observed her on the dance floor for a while, trying to figure out her angle. Why would she, one of the richest women in America, be mixing with everyday people on the main level when she could be up in the VIP level surrounded by people kissing her ass? But the look on her face as she danced, unburdened by notoriety, as just another person, was simply breathtaking. Anonymity awarded by blending in with the masses. Her face was joyous, and I found myself drawn to her, unable to stop myself from joining in. When I wrapped my arm around her waist, she leaned into me and went with the flow. Our bodies became one as we moved in synchronicity to the throbbing beat, our surroundings fading away until it felt like it was just the two of us.

When she left the dance floor, I followed, wanting to make sure she was okay. Alright, I was a little curious too. We had been enjoying ourselves, but I could feel her body get stiffer and less fluid, then all of a sudden, she was struggling to get out of my arms. Some men might get upset that what had felt like a prelude to sex was now over, but I was more concerned. Had she seen someone in the crowd that frightened her? I knew she had recently been through family trauma, so I decided to play the protector for a moment.

It wasn't hard for me to trail her. While she had to shove and push her way through, everyone parted when they saw Batman coming through. But just as I saw her disappear toward the bathroom, someone bumped me, spilling their drink all over me. It took me a couple of moments to dodge the drunk asshole spoiling for a fight, and when I finally did catch up to where she had gone, she was nowhere to be seen. Once I was pointed to the supply closet by someone in the line for the ladies' room, I continued on.

When I saw her bent over that line of coke, fury flowed through me. This fucking woman who has every goddamn advantage in life was throwing it away on drugs, alcohol, and partying. How could she be so shallow and self-involved even after she went through such a terrifying ordeal? Instead of taking time to reassess her life choices, there she was, flaunting her bad decisions.

I had no intention of doing anything but taking the coke away from her then leaving, but she snapped at me. The fire in her eyes tipped me over the edge, sending all my blood directly to my dick. The mouth on the bitch was just asking to be punished. Before I knew it, I had her in my arms and my mouth on hers. She melted against me, her firm breasts pressing into my chest, returning my kiss with as much passion as me, and I instantly knew that this girl would be the death of me.

Snorting the coke myself probably wasn't my finest moment, and I know it will come back to bite me in the ass, but I wanted to be on an even playing field. The way she looked at me, my hand in her hair as I snorted the coke off her magnificent tits, made my cock weep with excitement. She looked at me like I was her next hit, like I could give her a high like no other, and I just couldn't help myself.

"Hey, excuse me. Did you see my friend? She was wearing a Wonder Woman outfit, and I think I saw her dancing with you before." Hope Summers grabs me by the arm, her brow furrowed. Thank God she doesn't recognize me under my mask.

"Yeah, she's in the supply closet across from the ladies' bathrooms," I tell her before pulling away and continuing my trek through the club. I need to get out of here. I need to clear my head, but the drugs are still clouding my judgment.

"Is she okay?" I hear Hope call after me, but I don't answer. If I do, there's a chance she might figure out who I am. I'm counting on the fact that Jacinta won't want her sister to know about her drug use. If she does tell her about the sex, I'm hoping they'll both just write it off as a one-night stand.

I'm such a fucking idiot. I didn't think about the consequences of my actions. I let my primal nature take over and made the biggest mistake of my life. Despite how fucking amazing the sex was. Despite how she was putty in my hands, pliant and willing and everything I could want in a partner. Despite all of that, it still boils down to her core character and not wanting anything to do with the spoiled, pampered princess who wouldn't know how to take responsibility for anything, let alone her own actions.

There's also the problem of her being my boss.

Chapter Four

Jacinta

When I wake the next morning, I feel rough. I roll over in the big bed with a groan and contemplate pretending like the world doesn't exist today. But we're having a family thing this afternoon to celebrate my, Jaxon's, and Harlow's birthdays. We decided that we didn't want to do it on the same day we buried the people who had caused us so much heartache. It's not going to be huge, but I still can't get out of attending since I'm one of the guests of honor. Not to mention, I don't want to miss celebrating Harlow's birthday with her for the first time.

As I lie there, my eyes closed tight against the invading light, I think back to all those weeks ago and what a fucking bitch I was to her. I let my insecurities make bad decisions, and I almost missed out on knowing what an amazing person she is. I was so angry at the time, but I will forever be grateful to Dad, Nana, and Poppy for not making excuses for my shit.

Punishing me and making me take some time out to evaluate my life was the best thing that could have happened to me. It made me realize all the people I'd considered friends were no more than users, hoping that being in my orbit could be good for their own careers. I also learned that I much prefer the hands-on design part of the business to the everyday running crap. I was more than happy to hand it over to someone else, and Molly and Emma have been doing an amazing job as temporary CEOs. It's time to find a bright and shiny college graduate for them to mentor, because I will not be returning to the role, ever.

All the applications are in, and we have a Monday morning meeting set for the three of us and Nana to go over all the applicants. Basically, between the party and the impending meeting, my "me time" is over as soon as I convince myself to get up.

Hauling myself out of bed, I make my way to the shower in the suite. An ache between my legs reminds me of what transpired in that storage room, and when I catch a glimpse of myself in the mirror, I shudder at the sight. I hadn't removed my makeup before collapsing into bed, so it's smeared rather unattractively across my face. My black hair is a mess, and my blue-green eyes look like they have sunk into my skull. My normally pale skin looks almost unhealthily translucent. Fuck, I require high maintenance before I can present myself at home without questions being hurled at me. A little roughness is understandable since I was supposed to be celebrating last night, but this… *this* cannot be explained to my family.

Sighing, I reach into the cabinet and pull out some Tylenol, popping two of the pills out. I dry swallow them before pulling my shirt over my head. When I got undressed last night, I realized that Batman must have pocketed my panties, which is somewhat horrifying. A stranger is wandering around with my used underwear! It's kind of fucking creepy, but I also let him do those delicious things to me, so I don't really have any room to complain, do I?

Another loud sigh fills the quiet bathroom before I can stop it. Shaking my head free of the memories, I turn on the shower and hop in when it gets to the right temperature. I stand under the stream of water, hoping it will wash away the onslaught of feelings those memories have created. Shame and guilt are two of the most prevalent, but mixed in there is *longing*—longing for another no strings attached, drug-fueled fuck in the dark where all I have to do is feel. No need to worry about consequences or gossip because no one knows but the two of us. No need to worry about the morning after because neither of us want anything but to get our rocks off before going our separate ways. I can even handle the disdain, to be quite honest. It's not like I don't feel the same way. Self-loathing is becoming a familiar emotion.

I'm not sure how long I spend in the shower, but by the time I get out and dry off, Hope is banging on the bathroom door. "Hurry up! We need to get moving if we're going to get to Dad's on time. The car is waiting for us."

I open the door and push her out of my way. "Okay, don't get your panties in a knot. I won't be long." I move over to where my bag is and pull out a long-sleeved maxi dress from one of Couture's lines and some underwear. Dropping my towel, not caring about Hope being in the room, I quickly pull on my underwear, but not before she can gasp and point at my hips.

"What the fuck is that?" she asks. Frowning, I look down. Sure enough, five perfect round finger-print marks decorate each side of my hips, showing exactly where Batman was hanging onto me last night. Fuck! I almost snort with laughter at the look on Hope's face—her eyes are comically wide, and her mouth has formed a perfect circle—but I pull the dress over my head, ignoring the giant purple elephant in the room.

"Jazzy!" she growls. "When you disappeared, I thought you were getting some air or peeing or something, but you were doing *so* much more than that. Was it Batman? Did that man hurt you? I thought you were overwhelmed by the crowds and the funerals and everything yesterday. Should I have had security chase after him? Do we need to pull up the security footage?" Hope's voice is all panicked as she fires question after question at me while I towel dry my hair, brush it, and pull it into a low ponytail at the base of my neck.

Finally, I face her once more. "No, it's fine. Batman fucked me so good I'm still feeling him this morning."

After a loud breath that seems to help her stuff her concerns down, Hope's worry turns to glee, and she raises her hand for a high five. "Yes, bitch, good for you!"

Rolling my eyes, I slap her hand before searching for my shoes and slipping them on. I gather up all my crap, shove it in my bag, and zip it up.

"Who was he? Are you going to see him again?" she asks as I pick it up and put it over my shoulder before pushing her out of my room. Her bag is already by the door, so she picks it up before we leave our suite. The cleaners will be in there sometime today to put it back to rights for the next time we need it.

"We didn't take the time to exchange names," I explain as I press the button to call the elevator. "And we certainly didn't exchange numbers afterward, so there is very little chance I'll be seeing Batman or whatever his name was again."

Hope whistles as we step in and make our way down to the lobby and out to the valet parking where our car and security are waiting. The neighboring suite had been reserved for them, so they must have been up and out the door pretty quickly to get down here without us running into each other. Or Hope's just so organized she knocked on their door before coming to get me. That's the more likely scenario.

"Well, ain't that a shame. Anyone who gives you good enough dick that you're still feeling it the next day is definitely worth a repeat performance."

I give her a wane smile and climb into the back of the car, nodding my thanks to the security guard holding it. He isn't one of the men who was sitting in the back with us last night. He must have been in the front. He's unsuccessfully trying to smother a smirk, so I'm guessing he overheard what Hope just said. He's a tall, well-built Asian man, with shiny black hair tied back in a ponytail much like mine is. I'm going to go with Japanese. He climbs in behind Hope and pulls the door closed before knocking on the dividing window. I get a wink when he sees me looking at him, then he starts talking to the other guard who had already been seated when we arrived.

Hope's elbow nudges me in the side before she leans in. "Now that one is a tall glass of deliciousness too. I wouldn't mind being the seaweed to his sushi roll."

I tear my eyes away from the gorgeous man. "Fuck, Hope, you can't say that! You sound like a racist."

She rolls her eyes. "Fine, what about the taco to his meat, the bun to his sausage, the ice cream to his pickle?" she says a little too loudly.

I frown at the last one, which, to me, sounds like nothing I want in my life. "Huh?"

Before she can answer, a cultured, slightly accented voice does.

"I believe she's suggesting that she'd like me to park my rocket in her docking bay." He looks at the other guard who's not even hiding his grin and raises an eyebrow. "Wouldn't you say so?"

"Sounds to me like she'd like to be the sheath to your sword or the holster to your gun," he says, joining in.

"Indeed?" the original man says blandly, and Hope blushes bright red as the two of them burst into laughter, no longer able to control themselves.

"I'm so sorry. You weren't meant to hear that. My ears are still recovering from last night, and I must have been speaking louder than I thought."

The man is kind enough to wave off her apology, which saves things from becoming even more awkward. "Don't be. I can't deny that I haven't made the same kind of innuendos about women." The guard is gracious enough to let it slide, and I can't believe I've been so rude to the men hired to protect us. I don't know any of their names, which feels like a massive slight considering these guys are probably going to learn more about me than I'd ever wish them to.

"I'm sorry. I don't believe we've been properly introduced. I'm Jacinta, and this is Hope." The two men exchange a glance, and I can feel Hope staring at me with a concerned look on her face.

She grabs my hand and gives it a squeeze. "Jazzy was fairly out of it when you were all introduced to us. Her brother had just been shot, and his recovery was still up in the air. You'll have to forgive her for not remembering."

I feel my pale skin blush bright red, and I look down at my hands once the embarrassment makes it too hard to look at either of them. "Oh my god, I am so sorry," I apologize, flushed with shame. I always make it a point to know the names of the people who work with our family. When I meet a new employee, I like to make it clear that I don't think I'm above them or anything like that. They're doing something for us, and I appreciate it. You never know when you'll end up making a special connection with someone—like Mrs. Heyton.

"It's okay, Ms. Summers. Trauma like that isn't easy to recover from," the second guard says gently, and when I look up at him, he's smiling. He's a plain-looking man. I wouldn't say handsome, since his nose looks like it's been broken one time too many, but his eyes sparkle with laughter. "I'm Simon, and this is Riku. We were instructed to blend in with the background unless it looked like you needed us. I guess it shows how good we are at our job. Yesterday was the first time that we had gone out with you to any event. You've had others on your detail in the past. We were all rotating, but your dad decided he wanted the guards to get to know the person they were assigned to."

"Yes, Simon and I are permanently guarding you now, Ms. Summers, and Franklin and Charles in the front are responsible for the other Ms. Summers." Riku's gorgeous voice sends a shiver down my spine, but I hold myself still, showing no outward signs of it. I've had about all the embarrassment I can handle today.

Hope rolls her eyes. "I'm Hope, she's Jacinta, and the other one is Harlow. You can't go around calling us all Ms. Summers! It's just too confusing. Anyway, now that we all know each other, I'm going to cram in some work before we get home. I have a few things I need to catch up on before tomorrow's board meeting."

That catches my ear. "There's a board meeting tomorrow?" I pull out my phone to check my emails, and sure enough, there's one advising me of it. "Shit. I've been so busy at Willow Castle and trying to get some new sketches together, I must have missed the notification."

"It's in the morning before your other meeting

to discuss all the applicants. According to the agenda Poppy sent out, I'm introducing everyone to Cole, we're going over all the applicants for the CEO for Cruise Lines, discussing the purchase of the amusement park, and appointing a team to manage that." She stabs at the email on her phone screen.

I feel sick. So much has happened recently, and I haven't really stuck my head up for air. I squeeze Hope's hand. "I'm sorry, Hope, and I'm going to have to apologize to everyone else as well. I haven't really been all that present for the last month."

"Babe, it's understandable. It was nice seeing you cut loose and have fun like that. Maybe we can do it more often. I think Cole has set up some more functions for us all to attend so we can be seen out and about. I'm guessing the theory is it will help get rid of all the rumors flying around about our family."

Any calm I'd managed to grab slips from my grasp when she says that. Whatever these *functions* will be, they mean I need to be around people again. That means having to plaster on fake smiles and pretend that everything is good, exchanging hugs and air kisses with fake people when all I want to do is run screaming. Simon and Riku have fallen back into silence, and I know they're paid to keep their mouths shut, but there's no way that I'm going to show them the freak-out that's happening on the inside.

I sit quietly for a moment, the only sign of my agitation a tapping foot on the thick carpet floors, but as Hope's finger flies across her phone, sending messages and emails, I can't sit here any longer. I slide along the bench seat and open up the little fridge along one side of the vehicle. Inside is a well-stocked bar with glasses and ice. I pull one out before closing it and reaching for the bottle of whiskey that's sitting in a little cabinet next to it. A generous splash goes into the glass. Simon and Riku quietly watch with no judgment in either of their eyes, but Hope is suddenly much too disinterested in her phone.

"Jazzy, what are you doing?" Hope asks carefully as I screw the lid on the bottle and slide back into my spot, drink in hand.

"Just a little hair of the dog." I force a smile on my face and lighten my tone. Hope studies me for a moment, and I pray she can't see the desperation I feel in my eyes. Soon enough, she looks down at her phone again, and I breathe a sigh of relief. When I look at the guards again, Simon has taken out his phone too, but Riku is still looking at me. His gaze is so penetrative, I feel like he can see into my soul and can see all the ugly, frayed, terrified pieces of me, so I look away.

For the next few minutes, I stare out the window, but that hardly helps. I can still feel his eyes on me, so I down the rest of the whiskey, the hot burn warming my cold insides enough for me to relax a little bit. I place the glass down and grab a pillow that's tucked into a corner. Putting it under my head, I close my eyes, blocking out that penetrating gaze. Yes, I'm a coward. If I ignore him, maybe I can ignore everything else churning inside me just for a moment. I'll deal with it as soon as we get home.

Maybe.

Chapter Five

Jacinta

When I get home, I realize I won't be dealing with it either. The driveway is lined with cars.

Frowning, I climb out of the limo, followed by Hope and our guards. Now that we're home, I imagine they'll disappear. I'm not sure where. I think they are staying in the staff accommodation with Josh, Doug, and Clem—Harlow's zoo employees. As we enter through the front door, I hear laughter and music floating down the central hallway that leads to the main living area. Despite it being the first of November, it's California, so the day is sunny and warm. I'm sure they've set up the patio for entertaining. It sounds like a lot of people are out there, and I'm not quite ready to smile.

"I'm going to head up to my room and put my

things away. I'll be down in a moment," I tell Hope, going left into what is now only my and her wing. The boys and Harlow have been living at Willow Castle for a few weeks despite it being a construction zone. I think that might be another reason why I'm feeling all out of sorts and anxious. I haven't ever been apart from my brother. Even college, with us being twins, was done together.

It's not like I haven't seen them practically every day, but I'm no longer able to climb into his bed when I have a nightmare. He's not there at breakfast or swimming laps in the indoor pool when I need him. It's jarring.

Honestly, I'm sure my difficulty adjusting speaks to deeper issues than just our recent trauma, but how am I supposed to deal with that? It feels like when one issue is uncovered, there are already five more waiting to pile on. I thought I was getting better and becoming a stronger person since I buried the hatchet with Harlow and accepted her as my sister, but my circumstances are just too cruel. Apparently, I'm not deserving of some peace.

"Okay, will you take my bag too, please?" she asks and hands it over. I take it, grateful that I'm going to get five minutes alone to get my head into the right gear.

I hurry through the downstairs entertainment area of our wing. There are a few folded blankets, and all of the big relaxation pods are in front of the TV instead of over by the wall where they normally stay. I know Harlow and the guys spent the night here watching horror movies since their theater room is next on the renovations list. Seeing evidence of them being here perks me right up, so it's with a little more pep in my step that I run up our stairs to my bedroom. I drop Hope's bag in front of her room before entering mine.

The McCallister brothers are moving in so they're closer to the zoo construction and because I think my Nana is trying to weave some of her matchmaking magic. We agreed that they could have the whole third floor to themselves, while Hope and I would have this one, with us all sharing the downstairs for now. My brothers have moved all their personal stuff and left behind furniture, so it's all ready for the McCallisters to move in. I think that's happening sometime this week.

Stepping into my room is stepping into my sanctuary. All my worries melt away like a snake shedding its skin. Dropping my bag inside the bathroom near my laundry basket for Mrs. Heyton, I step up to the window that overlooks the backyard, trying to see who's actually here. I see Dad, Kai, and Thomas over by the grill with beers in hand and smiles on their faces. It's the most relaxed they've been for a long time. Everyone has been carrying around this thinly veiled worry for so long. I think yesterday's funerals finally let people bury some of those feelings with the people responsible for them.

The pool has been winterized, a cover now over

it, so there's no one in it. Growling, I slam my hand against the window in frustration. Damn it, I'm going to have to physically go down to see who else is here. That makes me feel queasy, so I go over and sit down on my bed.

My leg bounces up and down, my feelings manifesting physically. The whiskey from the limo hasn't numbed me enough. My eyes slide to the drawer where I hid the coke. Maybe a small hit will help? It certainly did last night. *I'll just use it once more, then I'll return it to the safe.* Striding over to my desk drawer, I pull it open, grab one of the little bags, and clear some space. I need to get this done before anyone comes looking for me.

I get everything ready, and soon enough, I'm snorting up the powder. I feel the now familiar burn at the top of my nasal passage, and I sniff hard as my eyes water. When I'm sure the desk is clean and all evidence of my self-medication is gone, I straighten out my dress and wipe my nose with the back of my hand. *There. All good now.*

Taking a deep breath, I leave my room and make my way downstairs. The coke kicks in just as I'm leaving my wing, and I feel a smile spread across my lips as my anxiety and nerves float away on the breeze. I feel fucking amazing.

The party noise gets louder as I move through the house, seeing evidence of visitors scattered all over the living area, but I make it to the back patio without being noticed. I take a moment to see who's here, clinging to anonymity while I have it. Of course all of my brothers and Harlow, Nana, Poppy, and Dad are here, but I can also see Chuck and Melinda, Josh, Clem, and Doug. There's also the McCallister brothers, and I smirk when I see that Hope is as far away from them as she can possibly get. Molly and Emma are chatting with Lindy and Rowena, though I'm not sure why the latter are here. I'm assuming they weaseled an invite from Dad who is too kind to say no. Jake, Thomas's agency friend, is in what looks to be an intense conversation with some of our security guards who have joined the festivities, and lastly, my eyes lock on Jace, who's standing with Alex and Shane. All three of them have beers in their hands, and their eyes light up when Jace nods in my direction.

A small amount of nerves and guilt return. Guilt because of what I did last night with a stranger even though these three men have made their interest obvious, and tiny excited butterflies. I smile at the three of them, but before I can do anything else, my twin notices I'm here.

"Jazzy, there you are! I thought I was going to have to come up and drag you down." Jaxon strides over to me and yanks me into his arms, hugging me tight. "All good?" he whispers for my ears only, and I nod my head, unable to answer with how tightly I'm pressed against his chest.

He pulls back and looks at me carefully, and I have a moment of panic that he's going to know, but he just smiles and drags me out of the doorway. Greetings are shouted at me from every direction, and it's not long before Nana grabs me and drags me over to where Emma and Molly are still pinned down by Lindy and Rowena.

"It's a rescue mission," she whispers out of the side of her mouth, and I smother a chuckle.

Emma and Molly stand up, and both of them give me a hug, Emma whispering in my ear, "Kill me now." I can't smother the chuckle that bursts out of me this time.

"Why are you so happy?" Lindy asks, raising an eyebrow as I sit down at the table. Before I can answer, Jaxon comes over and hands me a glass of champagne, giving me a kiss on the cheek.

"Thanks, bro," I say to him as Hope and Harlow join us. Harlow's champagne glass has OJ in it, so she must be having mimosas, but Hope's is full of sparkling golden champagne. I clink glasses with both of them.

"Happy birthday to my sisters," Hope says loudly, and everyone cheers. I down half the glass before putting it down in front of me.

"How was your night?" Harlow asks, taking a small sip before placing it back on the table.

A blush colors my cheeks, and Hope snorts. "I'll tell you later," I whisper out of the corner of my mouth just as Lindy pipes up again.

"What happened to you last night, Jacinta? I

saw you head downstairs to dance with the public, but you didn't come back up to the VIP."

Harlow reaches for her glass and takes another sip, hiding her smile. *Bitch is going to let me deal with this on my own.* Straightening my spine, I plaster my public Jacinta smile on my face. *I can't stand this woman, and she's one of the reasons I'm grateful I'm not running Couture anymore. I know her contract is coming to an end, which must be why she's making nice with Molly and Emma.* I'm about to deliver an epic slap down, but Hope jumps in.

"We had a blast dancing the night away. The dance floor on the public level is *so* much better than the one in VIP. Everyone lets loose and doesn't care what anyone else thinks."

"You totally missed out," Rowena says, a smug grin on her face. "There were so many celebs in the VIP area, like Sean Walsh, Jarred Reed, Cayden Storm, Hayden Christie, a couple of members of Sanctuary of Chaos, and even Selena Cross and Evangeline Masters."

Hope snorts. "Declan has most of them on speed dial, and Evangeline is one of Jacinta's closest friends. All those celebs were there because one of the Summers invited them. Sanctuary of Chaos reached out to me for an invite. They were back from tour and wanted to blow off some steam. I was happy to put them on the list. They're great guys."

"Who are you talking about?" Holden comes over and leans in, giving Harlow a kiss, his hand pausing on her belly for a moment. They share a secret smile, and my killer gossip instincts kick in.

I stand up. "Oh, Hope was just schooling Rowena on how all of last night's VIPs were there by invitation from us, which Lindy should have known anyway. Who wants another drink? Harlow?" I ask, heading for the temporary bar that's been set up on one side. I pour the three of us some more champagne, but a hand on my arm startles me, and I knock one of the glasses over.

"Shit," I hiss, grabbing a cloth to wipe it up while giving myself a moment to get my breathing under control.

"Are you okay, Jazzy?" Jace's Southern drawl brings a shiver down my spine like it always does, and goosebumps erupt on my skin under his hand. When my eyes meet his unmatched ones, they're shadowed despite the smile that's on his face. I hadn't realized until this moment how much I had missed him. We'd spent a whole week hanging out and drawing and doing shit together when we were in Prague and afterward at Chuck and Melinda's. I wouldn't hesitate to say that apart from Harlow and Hope, Jace is probably my best friend. But that's not all I feel for him, and I don't think it's all he feels for me. My head just really isn't in the right spot for any kind of relationship, let alone the complicated one I think he wants to entangle me in along with the two men standing at his back.

"Oh, hi. I, yes, I'm okay. You just startled me," I tell him, my breathing coming a little bit faster. Over his shoulder, Alex and Shane are looking at me with the same kind of laser focus. I had only seen them briefly after the kidnapping because I wasn't sure if I wanted to see the pity in their eyes when they looked at me. To my relief, all I see now is concern.

"Hi, guys." Even to my own ears, my voice sounds breathy. Alex and Shane reply, but I don't hear it because Jace has pulled me into a tight hug, pressing a kiss to my head.

"I was so fucking worried. Thank God you're okay. You *are* okay, aren't you?" He pulls back and studies me hard, so I put a fake grin on my face and wave a hand.

"Of course! Nothing a few good therapy sessions won't sort out. Now, tell me about you guys. How are you all? Are you excited for your first show, Jace? Emma and Molly showed me some of your designs, and they are freaking gorgeous! I can't wait for the world to see your line. Everyone is going to want to steal you from us." I tuck my arm into his and turn him so that Alex and Shane aren't left out of the conversation.

My tongue just about falls out of my mouth when I get a good look at the couple. Alex's golden blond hair is longer on top than normal, and he's got it styled over to one side. His gorgeous, tall model body wears anything and everything well, but he looks particularly snazzy today in a pair of slacks and a polo with a popped collar. In contrast, Shane's slightly shorter form is stockier but just as nice, and he's wearing simple jeans and a shirt. His gray-streaked brown hair is combed back, held in place by something, and his beard has been trimmed short. They make such a delicious couple, and Jace's ice-blond boyish looks and black-rimmed glasses fit in perfectly. They would belong on the cover of any magazine.

A shiver shudders down my spine, and I can't control it. All three of them see it, and the worry changes to something very different.

"You look gorgeous as always, Jacinta." Shane's gravelly voice is a whole sensation on its own to my heightened senses, and I involuntarily squeeze my hand on Jace's arm. He chuckles quietly.

"You certainly seem to be radiant." Alex is frowning slightly as he looks closely at me, and my pulse speeds up, but he quickly shakes it off. "To think you went through such a harrowing ordeal only weeks ago. You look like you've just returned from a spa." His over-the-top compliment makes me smile.

"Are you guys going to New Orleans with Jace for the launch of his line? Have we booked you to walk in it, Alex? And you to photograph it, Shane?

I'm afraid I'm a little out of the loop now that I've handed the reins over to Emma and Molly."

Before they can answer, a voice interrupts. "Why is Jace getting a show while nothing has been booked for me?" Alex's and Shane's faces blank at the sound of Rowena's voice, and Jace's body tenses behind me. "Do I need to sleep with you too to get somewhere in this industry?"

Chapter Six

Jacinta

I spin around, but before I can answer, Harlow and Hope are there. "I think you need to leave now, Rowena. All those glasses of champagne are making you stupid." Harlow gestures off to the side, and Riku steps up from somewhere. "Riku, can you please see that Rowena and Lindy are escorted home? Is there someone who hasn't been drinking?"

"Simon and I haven't had anything yet. We'll see that they get to where they need to go," he says quietly, and another shiver rolls down my spine. Damn it, I'm so sensitive to certain stimulation at the moment.

Rowena and Lindy are both spluttering excuses, but Harlow hasn't finished yet.

"Those kinds of allegations border on sexual

harassment, so I would be *very* careful which little bird you let whisper in your ear." Rowena blushes bright pink, and her eyes float to where Lindy is standing off to the side. "I would keep your head down and work hard. Without an eye for fashion, even I know Jace's designs are divine. I've had the honor of wearing them. So far I haven't seen anything you've come up with. Is there a reason for that?"

"Rowena hasn't approached us to present anything yet. We haven't even seen a basic sketch," Molly happily calls out across the patio.

"Off you go then, and I suggest you put in some hard work this week. We're already halfway through your trial period." Nana joins the group that has drawn the attention of everyone here, which breaks through the enjoyment that I had. My skin starts to itch with all the focus now on us. I pull away from Jace, grab the two glasses of champagne I poured, and hand them to my sisters. Harlow hesitates for only a second, but it's long enough for me to see and to remember what I was doing.

"Go now. I'm bored," I say, shooing them away, and Lindy looks ready to put up a fight, but Riku and Simon gently take each woman by an arm and lead them away. I see the moment the fight leaves both of them in favor of panic. *Good, let them sweat.*

The gathered people disperse, and the itch fades a little. "Guys, I have something I need to talk to Harlow about, but I promise I'll come find you when I'm done. I do want to hear about how you all are and what you've been doing." I kiss each of them on the cheek, and by Alex's and Shane's surprised looks, they weren't expecting it. I linger a little longer with Jace though.

"I've missed you," I whisper into his ear before pulling away. I quickly refill the glass I had knocked over before making a beeline for my secret keeping sister.

"Come with me, you sneaky bitch." I pull her away from the crowd and into the corner near the covered hot tub. When my twin sees what I'm doing, he excuses himself from the conversation he was having with Miles McCallister.

"Is everything okay here?" he asks when he gets to us.

I take a long drink of my champagne, chugging over half of it, as I try to get my thoughts into order. Tapping my foot, I raise a perfectly mani-cured eyebrow. "Is there something you want to tell me?" I ask, looking between the two of them before locking my gaze on Harlow's. But my impe-rial bullshit doesn't work on her. She just smirks, wrapping an arm around my brother and hugging him close to her. Gah, I love seeing them all loved up.

"So that's how it's going to be, is it? Who's asking? Jacinta Summers or Jazzy, my kind, loving, and wonderful sister who hides behind a wall of stuck-up derision?" Harlow doesn't pull any punches, which is exactly what I normally need. Right now, I just want her to give up the goods.

"Well, I'm not entirely sure, to be honest. If you two have been keeping secrets from me, then there's a good chance you're talking to Jacinta Summers."

"Does it make a difference that you're the first person I'm telling after your brothers?"

I wave my hand impatiently. "Yes, yes, fine, get on with it."

"You're going to be an aunt," Jaxon tells me.

"I knew it!" I exclaim, and Harlow nods, smiling serenely.

"Yup, something good actually came from that whole clusterfuck. I mean, it most definitely wasn't planned, and it's sooner than I thought it would happen, but we're happy."

She rests her head on Jax's shoulder as I squeal and throw my arms around her and my twin, spilling my champagne everywhere. I bounce up and down with excitement, the real kind that has nothing to do with the cocaine euphoria. "Oh my god, two babies!" I shout, unable to lower my voice, and of course that brings the patio to a very abrupt silence.

"Did I hear right?" Hope shouts, scrambling to her feet. "Are you fucking pregnant, Harlow Summers, and you didn't tell me?"

Hope's curse has Harlow cringing and turning to face her with a resigned look on her face. "In my defense, I've only known for five days. I told the guys yesterday, and I was going to tell everyone today," Harlow calls back, and Nana jumps to her feet.

"Brad, Howard, come here right now!" she calls over to the grill. They still haven't heard the commotion and are oblivious to everything that is going on now.

"Chuck! Chuck!" Melinda adds.

"What is it, Mom?" Dad asks as he, Poppy, and Chuck leave Thomas and Kai at the grill.

"Babies!" she announces, clapping her hands, and Chuck's mouth drops open.

"You told them? I thought we were going to tell Maxine first. It's been all I could do not to tell anyone today."

Everyone's eyes turn to Melinda, who rolls hers at her husband. "No, you idiot, you just did."

"You're pregnant?" Emma asks Melinda, wide eyed with surprise.

"Yeah, I think the night of the gala. We gave up on having children years ago, and just when we decided to foster another little one, I found out I was pregnant. It's our little miracle," she says, cupping her belly. Dad and Poppy congratulate Chuck with hearty slaps on the shoulder, but when Chuck pulls away, he looks confused.

"Well, if you hadn't said anything, why were we talking about babies?" Everyone's eyes swing back to my sister who sheepishly waves a hand.

"Me."

The group gets back on track, and suddenly we're surrounded by people wanting to wish Harlow, Jaxon, and all of the guys congratulations.

Once everyone crowds into the same corner of the yard, it's all too much for me. The itch becomes an out of control throbbing, and I start to feel sick and anxious. Stumbling away, I hurry back inside and up to my room to catch my breath, only for a moment. Not even the happy news is enough to distract me from my insecurities.

I slam the door behind me and go straight into my bathroom. Twisting on the cold water, I cup my hands beneath the stream, letting it pool before splashing my face. It doesn't help, and I find myself in my room, pacing back and forth, trying to slow my breathing while I wring my hands in agitation.

"Come on, Jacinta. Everything is fine. It's all family downstairs. They don't want anything from you. They don't need you for anything, and they love and accept you for who you are, not what you can do for them. Snap out of it, bitch."

I grab my cell and call my therapist, scheduling an appointment for this week. It's time I spoke to someone about what happened. I can't go on like this. It's not fair to anyone.

Once that's done, I breathe a sigh of relief. Okay, one step forward. It's a small step, but it's a good one. I cross over to the window and look down again. The grill is no longer manned, so I'm assuming lunch is being served, which means I need to go back downstairs.

The thought of this makes goosebumps rise across my skin, so I scratch at them while I contemplate my next move. If I don't go down, they're going to know something is wrong. Before the kidnapping, I could fake it until I made it, the consummate actress putting on a smile to show the world I was fine. Now, I just don't care enough. All of that superficial shit means nothing to me. It's fake, an act, and not how I want to live my life.

But my family can see right through all of that anyway. How the fuck am I going to hide this from them? They don't need to be worrying about me. Harlow and my brothers have enough stress on their plates with the zoo, Veronica, and now Harlow's pregnancy!

Again, my eyes drift to where I'm keeping the coke. Okay, one more hit, just to get me through lunch. People should start leaving after that, and I'll be okay once everyone is gone. I rush through the process, making two lines in the hope that the feeling will last longer. A noise on the stairs has me scrambling to put everything back in the drawer and wipe my nose with my hand.

"Hey, is everything okay?" Harlow's frowning when she walks in carrying a bag. "Are you upset about the baby news?" She sounds small and unsure, and I feel like the biggest bitch in the world, but I also don't know how to explain why I'm up here. But then her bag gives me an idea.

"No! I'm thrilled with the baby news. I can't wait to meet my niece or nephew, or maybe both. I mean, Jaxon and I *are* twins." I grab her and hug her again before pulling away. Her mouth is open in shock, so I guess she hadn't considered that yet. I start to chuckle before going over to my closet.

"No, I came up here because I remembered your gift," I tell her, going into it and bringing out a bag.

She recovers from her shock and sits down on the bed, smiling. "Oh, good, because I have this for you. If you had waited until I'd given it to you, you would have found out about the baby then." She holds out the bag, and we do a swap. I'm excited to see what's in mine, and when I pull out the clothes that are in there, I actually cackle. Harlow has given me three auntie-themed shirts.

One of them says, *Auntitude. If you don't know what that is, mess with my niece or nephew and find out.* The other one says, *Fuantie. The fun aunt, cooler than Mom. Professional advice giver, expert storyteller, spoiler of children, best person in the whole world.* Then the last one is a shirt with a matching baby onesie. Mine says, *Aunt with all the sass,* and the onesie says, *I get my sass from my aunt.*

Then there's a baby-sized T-shirt that has two pictures on it. There's a wooden rocking horse with the words *Your aunt* over it, while the other picture features a dabbing rainbow unicorn. Above the second photo, it says, *My aunt.*

"I fucking love them, and I can't wait to wear them. My niece and whatever that is in your belly are going to be the most spoiled and loved babies in the world." I can't stop the tears of joy from forming in my eyes. I grab her around the neck and pull her to me, hugging her hard. "I love you so much. I'm so sorry I was such a fucking bitch to you. Please forgive me," I ask her, a little sob sneaking out.

"Hey, hey! What's all this? That's water under the bridge. We're solid, and I love you too. What brought all this on?" She pushes me back and looks at me closely. Shit!

"Oh, nothing, just feeling a little emotional. My twin is going to be a daddy. I just can't believe it!" I practically jump off the bed and into my bathroom. That won't make me look any more normal, but I need to keep her from staring at my pupils. Splashing water on my face, I get my shit together, and when I come back out, Harlow has lost the worried look. She's smiling like she doesn't have a care in the world which is a nice change. She seems to be embracing this Earth goddess mother thing already.

"Yeah, we're all kind of still floating on shock and surprise. I mean, who would have thought Peter's crazy ass scheme would work? I'm sure once reality hits us and we realize we're going to have two babies under one roof as well as trying to get the zoo up and running, everyone will go into freak out mode. Well, maybe not Kai. He's already in Daddy mode, so maybe he'll hold us all together."

We're both chuckling by the time she finishes, because she's not wrong. It's certainly going to be fun in their house for a while.

I point to the other bag. "Open mine! It's not much, since the guys kind of stole all the thunder with your gifts this year."

She pulls out the gorgeous leather halter that I had gotten for her new horse and the mono-grammed grooming set. "Just a little something for the other new addition in your life."

"Thank you! They're gorgeous." Her eyes are bright with happiness, and she gives me another hug.

"Well, come on. Let's go downstairs. I'm sure everyone will be looking for us if they have to wait much longer." I leave my bag on my bed, but she brings hers with us and puts it by the table in the foyer.

"So, how was last night?" she asks as she tucks my arm into hers. We walk down the corridor together, which gives me a little wiggle of warmth. It's silly, but this is a little moment of sisterhood, something I hadn't realized I needed.

"Ah, yeah, it was fun. Hope and I drank too much and danced for hours," I say, leaving out the

Batman detail. She doesn't need to hear about the hot as fuck and equally mortifying experience.

Before Harlow can respond, we make it back outside where a long stretch of tables and chairs have been set up, the former piled with copious amounts of food. A couple of hired staff members are bustling around, directed by Mrs. Heyton.

"Ah, *wunderbar*, you are here. I thought I was going to have to send someone on a rescue mission," she jokes. "Come, come, all this food needs to be eaten, and my two girls are too skinny."

Chapter Seven

Jacinta

She nudges Harlow toward a spot between Thomas and Kai, then she directs me to one between Shane and Alex. Food is being passed around, and the happy sound of laughter and conversation is an added balm to my frayed edges. All in all, I feel pretty fucking good now, and I don't hate the feeling.

"Hi," I chirp as I sit between the two men who have been on my periphery for so many years. Now that I've stepped back from the CEO role at Couture, there's nothing professionally stopping me from pursuing a relationship or something with these three sexy men if they're open to it. To be fair to them, maybe I should see my therapist and sort out everything else in my life before I commit to a real relationship. There's nothing stopping me from some harmless flirting though.

"Hi, gorgeous." Alex gives me a kiss on the cheek, more forward than he's ever been, followed by a cheeky wink. "That dress is perfect on you."

"Thank you, it's one I designed myself." I watch, bemused, as Shane starts to add food to my plate before passing it down to Jace on his other side. Alex goes over to the drinks station and pours another glass of champagne before returning and placing it in front of me. A giddy feeling of warmth rushes through me. I like being cared for. It's a new thing. Not that my family has never cared for me, but any men who have been in my life romantically usually want me running around after them.

"We were just talking about Jace's show and what a wonderful idea it was to hire an antebellum style home to show off all his gorgeous ball gowns," Shane says in his gravelly voice that makes my nipples pebble beneath my dress. There's no bra to hide it, and when I look at Alex, he's peeking at my breasts. Instead of hiding my reaction, I pull my shoulders back enough that he can get a good look. His gaze rises to meet mine, and his eyes widen minutely before a small smirk rises on his lips. He closes the distance between us.

"I have the same reaction every time he says something to me too," he whispers. His hand caresses my dress-covered leg before going back to his food.

"The house is gorgeous, and it has these two curving staircases that descend from a balcony to the backyard. Then there's this path through these fabulous old trees. They're overgrown, creating this kind of natural arbor. I thought we could set up chairs on either side and have the models come down the staircases then use the path as the runway. It's going to be an amazing backdrop for those dresses."

"Yes, and I get final say in the models, don't I?" Jace leans forward so I can see him past Shane.

"Yes, of course. We can have a call next week."

"Good. I want healthy, realistic models to wear my clothes. Not models who are only skinny because they exist on coke and mineral water," he grumbles, tearing apart a roll and running it through his gravy.

"It's so exciting. I saw his menswear designs, and I will totally look incredible in them." And that right there is one of the things I love about Alex. He's one hundred percent sure of himself. He knows he's hot, and he's not afraid to tell you about it, but not in an arrogant, stuck-up way. It's completely adorable, like an overenthusiastic golden retriever.

"You'll have to audition too," Shane cautions, and I wave my hand.

"Actually, he won't because he's on a part-time retainer with us. It's part of his contract to be in it. Hayden Christie is the same. Having the two of them is like having the superstars of the modeling world, and we'll have all the who's who of fashion scrambling for an invite."

Alex preens, and Shane, Jace, and I exchange an amused glance. This is fun. I like being included in their circle. It makes me feel warm and wanted.

The clinking of a fork against a glass draws my attention to the head of the table. Dad, flanked by Emma and Molly, is standing, looking the happiest I've seen him since the first day Harlow joined our family.

"Welcome, everyone, and thank you for coming to celebrate the births of Jaxon, Jacinta, and Harlow. It is made even more special by the fact that it is our first with Harlow. These last few months have been a bit tumultuous with everything that has happened, but I'm happy to say we have weathered the bad times, and I hope there are only sunny days ahead of us."

"Here, here!" calls Poppy.

"So, not only are we celebrating birthdays, but we are also now celebrating impending birthdays. Congratulations to all of you who are expecting a child, which brings me to *our* announcement." Dad's grin turns a little sheepish, and he blushes bright red, as do Emma and Molly. "Seems like there might have been something in the water at the gala because we're expecting too."

Nana gasps. "Another baby?" She looks between Emma and Molly. "Which one of you?"

Dad becomes even redder, pointedly not looking up, while Molly messes with her napkin.

Emma is the brave one who answers Nana. "Both of us." There's a shocked silence before the table erupts.

"Oh my!" Nana leaps to her feet and practically runs toward the three of them to give them her congratulations.

"Holy shit, how did that happen? I thought you were infertile after the mumps?" Holden asks.

His question is almost drowned out by Oliver's. "Dad, you are a stud!"

Rolling my eyes, I wait for my turn to congratulate the happy throuple.

Dad shrugs, and Emma looks embarrassed. "I guess they got the diagnosis wrong."

"We never used condoms because we didn't think there was any chance of this happening. I guess that kind of bit us in the ass."

"But we're just rolling with it. Emma and I always wanted children but hadn't gotten around to it yet. We couldn't be happier about having them with a man like Brad." Molly fusses between her two partners like she's trying to reassure everyone.

While I watch on, I examine my own feelings. Am I okay with this? I wait for the rolling feelings of jealousy, but unlike how I felt when Dad told us about Harlow, there's nothing like that. All I feel is happiness, much like when Dad offered Hope a place with our family. These announcements mean more sisters… or brothers, but I will deal with that if they are boys. Our family is going to be big and beautiful and full of love, and I can't wait for it.

A hand on my leg jolts me out of my thoughts. "Are you okay?" Alex whispers in my ear, and when I look at him, there's an intent frown on his face. I guess he's got good reason to be concerned. He saw the fallout of the whole Harlow debacle firsthand. God, I was such a bitch during that shoot.

"Yeah, I'm awesome," I tell him, leaning forward to brush a quick kiss on his lips. His eyes widen in shock before I stand up and walk down to my father and his girlfriends. I give them all a huge hug, telling them how excited I am for them.

Dad holds me at arm's length. "Are you sure you're okay with this?" he asks carefully, and I squeeze his hands.

"Yes, Dad, I promise. I know that I haven't had the best track record, but I'm super happy about this. I can't wait to meet my new sisters."

"Or brothers," Oliver pipes up, and I drop one of Dad's hands to flip him off.

"Let's hope not. There are enough boys in this family. Let's hope it's two gorgeous, precious girls so that it evens up the numbers in this family. Then Dad would have five daughters and six sons."

"And two grandchildren." Kai swings his arm around Harlow's shoulder and kisses her cheek with a resounding *smack*.

"With Chuck and Melinda's baby, we're going

to have five babies to love," Thomas points out, and Nana claps her hands gleefully.

"Oh my goodness! This is so exciting. We haven't had babies before since you were all children by the time you came to us. This is going to be quite the learning curve."

Dad has lost his red cheeks, and now he's looking a little green. It's all I can do to smother my laughter.

"Don't worry, Dad. You've got this. You and the guys can all go to birthing classes together." That shuts up my brothers, putting deer in the headlights expressions on their faces, but Kai, of course, is totally unfazed.

"I've already looked into nearby classes. Veronica is having a C-section, so I won't need to know for her, but I want to be there when Harlow has our baby."

It's just like him to be enthusiastic about something new. This is a big challenge for all of them, but I guess he's had longer to get used to the idea of the whole dad thing. I think it's only just hitting the other guys that they will all be dads to their two babies.

I watch Emma and Molly crowd around Dad and marvel at all the love I feel right now. It's like everything is right with the world, like I'm almost bulletproof. Nothing can touch us now that we are such a tight, united force.

I go back to my seat, but by now everyone is

finishing up their meal. To be honest, I'm not all that hungry despite barely eating. I take another sip of my drink and push the food around on my plate.

"Jacinta, we were wondering if you would like to come over for dinner this week. I overheard that you're coming into the office tomorrow for some meetings, and we thought you could come to our place for a meal afterward." Jace sounds hopeful, and I can't deny I've missed him. The couple of days he and I spent together in Prague, then Connecticut, were fun. It was nice to not have any pressure on me. I could be myself, and Jace seemed to be attracted to that side of me. It doesn't hurt that he's sexy and sweet too. His accent makes my toes curl inside my shoes. We got so drunk that night, we were spreading gossip to give Harlow an alias. Making out on the dance floor was so much fun, but that's as far as we got. He put the brakes on because neither of us were really in full control of our faculties. I'm kind of glad he did because so much is still up in the air.

"Yes, we'd love to have you come… For dinner, that is. Shane is an excellent cook." Alex winks with a cheeky grin.

A hand on mine startles me, and I slosh a little bit of my drink over the glass. "Ignore Alex. But yes, it feels like forever since we got to see you. You haven't been around the last few times we've been at Couture headquarters or your other building. I've been picking Jace up from work because he doesn't have a car, and I usually go right past the building on the way home from my studio." There's no judgment in Shane's tone. It's just like he's sharing a piece of his day with me, and the lack of pressure is refreshing. It makes it easier to stay in the moment with them.

"No, I've been working exclusively from home. Well, actually, exclusively from *their* home at the moment. Willow Castle needed a complete overhaul. I set up in one of the offices there, so I can work and supervise all the people coming and going in the process. Harlow is busy with the zoo reconstruction, so she doesn't have time for the inside. I offered to take care of it. We pour over Pinterest together, then I make it happen. It's different from fashion, but I have to say that I like the design aspect of this too."

"What fun!" Alex claps his hands. "I can't wait to see what you've done with the place. You should make a YouTube series or blog about it. I can just see you branching Couture out into interior design."

I hold up a hand. "Oh no, slow your roll, cowboy."

"I'd love to show you how I can ride," Alex whispers out of the side of his mouth, and I can't stop the small blush that I feel wash across my cheeks because his comment brings up thoughts of these three men wrapped up in passion, and that is *not* lunchtime appropriate—especially a lunch with family attending.

"Oh, um, yes, well, that would be… Um, what I mean is I would love to come to dinner." I clear my throat, all flustered from Alex's suggestive comment and the dirty thoughts now full frontal in my mind.

"Fabulous. I'll pick you both up at the end of the day then," Shane suggests. It's kind of nice to have decisions taken out of my hand.

We chat for a little longer about what they've been up to. Alex tells us a hilarious story about a photo shoot he was at for a boutique gin company. The director of the advertisement drank so much gin between takes that he fell asleep behind the lens of the camera and forgot to call cut. Alex and the girl he was shooting the ad with ended up stuck in the middle of a lake in a rowboat, and neither of them knew how to get it back in.

Shane tells me about how he's been invited to join a group of photographers in a new campaign for Hawaiian Tourism. When he says the dates, I do a double take.

"Oh, hey, that works well. Jax's new hotel has its grand opening that weekend. Do you think we could book you to do the official press photos for that too?" Catching Hope out of the corner of my eye, I wave her over.

"The sex hotel?" Shane asks, sounding much too interested, and I roll my eyes and smile.

"Yes, the sex hotel. Poor Jax. I think he wants it to be called the Intimate Indulgent Hotel or something better than the sex hotel, but I think he's stuck with it."

Hope finishes her conversation with Harlow and comes over to us.

"Hey, I haven't had a chance to speak to you all yet." The three guys stand up, and the four of them exchange hugs and kisses in greeting. I love seeing them get along with my family. Even though we haven't really started anything between the four of us yet, the way they fit into the Summers' jigsaw puzzle makes me hopeful and optimistic that if we ever do get this relationship off the ground, I can have the kind of love my siblings, dad, and grandparents have found.

"Hope, Shane was just saying he's going to be in Hawaii for a shoot when Jax's hotel opening is happening. Have we booked an official photographer for that yet?"

"No, I don't think so. I'll check with Cole tomorrow, but that's a great idea. Will you do that?"

Shane shrugs. "Sure, as long as it doesn't clash with what I'm doing for Hawaiian Tourism."

"If you send me your schedule with them, I'll make sure Cole works around it. Actually, you should probably meet him. We use you for so much of our press that you're basically our unofficial official photographer." We all laugh at Hope's words.

"And it would be good for you to have a working relationship with him."

"Is this Cole Chambers? He used to do PR for Elite Model Management, which is who Hayden Christie is represented by, right?" Hope nods in answer to Shane's question. "I've met and worked with him. He's a great guy."

"Yes, but both he and Hayden have jumped ship after some nasty gossip surfaced about one of the talent scouts guaranteeing models positions if they gave him a blow job." I screw up my nose at Hope's words. The fashion world can be so fucking nasty. "Declan is now representing Hayden, and Cole is our new PR guy, which was a lucky strike for us. I think he's going to do great! He's a hard-ass, but he has contacts everywhere and really knows what he's doing."

"If he's so great, how come he wasn't able to put a spin on the scout's bad press?" I ask, and Hope frowns at me. Okay, yeah, I guess I realize how that question could sound kind of bad, but I totally didn't mean it that way.

"He didn't think that kind of thing should be covered up and didn't want anything to do with a company that condones it. Apparently, the scout was only the tip of the iceberg. There's a whole underage sex scandal that's going to rock the modeling world once the exposé hits the papers this week."

"That company is *nasty*. I was offered representation from them once. I had a meeting with the owner. He was touchy feely and implied that if I wanted to succeed, I should bend over for him. I politely declined and got out of there as fast as I could. Thankfully, I already had an offer from Declan. Maybe if I hadn't had other options, I would have done what he suggested too." That last little bit is said quietly, and there's no question as to whether Alex feels ashamed of what he's admitting. "The modeling industry is full of beautiful people trying to hit it big. Every day, more and more people leave their homes for LA in the hope that they will be the next big thing."

"Look at me. I took a chance on Neighpalm Couture. I hadn't quit my job back home or anything, but I only had a hundred bucks to my name after I paid for my hotel and airfare to get out here," Jace points out. "If you had said no, I was tucking tail and going home to save up to try again. Not everyone is so lucky to have a backup plan, even a small one."

"That's so true. It's why we try to keep things above board on our end. But there are so many things out of our control, like the number of models that have eating disorders and drug problems. I wish we could help them all, but we just can't. It's why I have a policy to only hire models with healthy bodies. I want curves to show off our clothes, none of these stick-thin coat hangers that everyone else uses. In order to give people their best chance at success, we need them to give us their best too."

"What would be better is if you used real women, not models," Hope says, and I shrug.

"I know, and maybe that's something we need to look at doing, but that's not going to fix the problem. Unfortunately, it's endemic to the industry, and I'm not sure it can ever be fixed. The best we can do right now is spread the word about our hiring policies so that the models who want to be healthy and employed know that they can find an opportunity with us. The others, well, until they recognize that they need help, I'm not sure what we can do for them."

The words have a grim finality to them, or at least they do to me, maybe because of what I'm going through. I don't want to be this mess for the rest of my life, but maybe I, like the industry that gave me life for so many years, am just irreparably broken.

I don't know if it's a boost from the cocaine, the euphoria of the baby announcements, or the presence of these men around me, but I don't know if I'm willing to accept that.

Chapter Eight

Jacinta

Eventually, everyone drifts home. Harlow and her guys return to Willow Castle, and the McCallisters to their B&B. Nana insists that Jace, Alex, and Shane stay the night, but they manage to gracefully turn her down with explanations that they all have work in the morning. Riding the last burst of energy that the warm and fuzzies have given me, I offer to see them out. It totally has nothing to do with wanting just a few more minutes of basking in the comfort they give me.

Their car is parked in a darkened corner of the yard, and when we reach it, Alex maneuvers me until my back is to the car so the three of them can surround me. My heart starts to race, and I can feel my breathing pick up, but I'm not entirely sure if it's from panic or desire.

"We just want to make our intentions clear." Alex takes the lead, sounding more serious than I've heard him all day. "Now that the stalker has been dealt with, we fully intend to pursue you."

I start to shake my head, but he holds up his hand, silencing me. "No, we know you told Jace that you didn't want to start anything, and he said there were more reasons than just the stalker, but we don't care. This whole thing has shown us that life is too short to let it pass by without taking what you want from it. We want you, Jacinta Summers."

I look between the men, my heart still racing. "But why? You seem to have a pretty good thing going with the three of you."

"While we do have a great thing going, and Jace has made that even better, we're greedy, Jacinta. We want more, specifically you. We always have." Shane surprises me by being the one to answer. He's always been the strong, silent type, so I wasn't expecting him to admit that.

"I know you've thought about it, and I know that you're not opposed to the idea of a poly relationship. You told me you wish you could have what Harlow has with your brothers. How they're such a tight-knit, loving unit. How Harlow loves them for who they are and not for what they can give her," Jace adds, my drunken ramblings from Prague coming back to bite me in the ass.

"We can give that to you." Alex grabs my hand and squeezes it. "We *want* to give that to you, so this is your official notice, because we aren't taking no for an answer."

Shane frowns at his boyfriends before gently saying, "What Alex means to say is that we hope you will give us a chance."

"Think about it and let us know how you're feeling tomorrow at dinner," Jace suggests before each of them gives me a gentle kiss on the lips. There's no tongue and no real pressure, just a light dusting that has me chasing their mouths, causing them to chuckle. Feeling my cheeks pinken again, I step away from the car as Shane takes the driver's seat with Alex next to him and Jace in the back.

"Drive carefully." I wave as they leave me without another word and a lot to consider.

I walk back toward the house, but movement in the shadows has me jumping, a small scream letting loose as Riku melts out of the shadows of the house. "Holy fuck, I didn't see you there." Now my heart is beating for an entirely different reason. I hold my hand over my chest like I can stop it from leaping out. "Were you eavesdropping? What were you doing standing there?"

"Ms. Summers, I'm still on duty, and I'm supposed to keep you in sight whenever you leave the house. Those are my instructions, unless you're in the bathroom or in a building belonging to your family. I'm sorry I scared you. That was not my intention, and while I did hear your conversation, it's none of my business."

My heart rate slows, and my breathing starts to return to normal while I look this bodyguard up and down. He's dressed in cargo pants and a black shirt that stretches across his chest, with Senshi Security printed on one defined pec. He's wearing a gun holster, which I only notice because he discarded the jacket that was covering it earlier.

He's got this calm way about him that projects an aura like nothing can bother him. He seems all disciplined and regimented, and it makes me feel like ruffling his feathers. What would he be like if someone got under his skin? Does he maintain this solemn warrior thing he's got going, or is there something more explosive hidden deep?

"Tell me, Riku, when you were contracted to work for my family, were you told about my sister and brothers' relationship?"

"Our company was briefed about the unique relationship, yes," he replies as we start walking back to the house.

"And it doesn't bother you that my sister is in a relationship with six other men or that my father is in a relationship with two different women? Because not many people are that open-minded. Sure, they may smile and say they are to your face, but they are really spreading malicious gossip behind our backs."

"That's a very jaded way to look at life, Ms.

Summers. I think you'll find that most people really don't care about you and your family enough to have an opinion one way or another."

I pat him on the shoulder as we climb the front steps. "You poor, naïve man. Just you wait! Most of us have been out of the spotlight for the last month, but the press is champing at the bit for the story. A press release is going out tomorrow, then you and Simon will really be earning your wages. Anyway, you didn't answer my question. Does it bother you? Did you hear what those three men were proposing? Are you going to be able to protect me while knowing I may be in a relationship with three men? Or are your preconceived prejudices about monogamous relationships going to stop you from protecting me to your full capabilities?"

My hand is on the door handle, but he puts his own over it to stop me from turning it.

"Maybe it's you who needs to adjust your preconceived notions about people. What's to say that I don't come from a less than traditional family myself?" He actually sounds a little annoyed, but I kind of like that despite feeling a little embarrassed by his accusation. No one ever stands up to me besides my family, so I like men with a little bark and bite.

I'm feeling bold and slightly turned on, so I decide to play with fire. I push Riku against the wall next to the door and crowd into his space.

"You are right, my apologies." I run my finger

down the center of his chest, feeling his sculpted body under the tight shirt. "So it won't bother you to guard me while I'm visiting with them, knowing that I'm probably having sex with the three of them... at the same time?"

His Adam's apple bobs as he swallows before he clears his throat and shakes his head. "Of course not, Ms. Summers. What you do in your personal life has no bearing on me or the way I conduct myself."

"That's good to know, Riku. I appreciate the fact that you don't let your personal opinions cloud your professional life." I push away from him and open the door, allowing him to grab it as he follows behind me. "So... Do you come from a less than traditional family?"

"No, I don't, but we were raised to be open-minded and tolerant, which thankfully made it easier for my sister who came out as gay when we were teenagers. She and her wife just had a baby, and my parents adore their granddaughter and daughter-in-law."

We pause in the foyer. "Oh, that must be nice. I can't wait to be an aunt! And I guess a big sister too. All these babies coming into our family is exciting." My mind is racing as Riku smiles and digs into his back pocket, pulling out his phone case. He opens it up and pulls out a business card, handing it to me.

"This is my sister's business. She owns a baby

boutique if you need to think about baby supplies and gifts for your loved ones."

Taking it, I cock an eyebrow in surprise. "Well, that is handy. I want to outfit Harlow's nursery, which is next on the list. Maybe I'll check out her store to see what she has." Then something occurs to me. "I wonder if Emma and Molly will be moving in now that they're pregnant. I should ask Dad."

I start to make my way down the corridor, but Riku snaps out a hand and grabs me by the elbow. "Why don't you wait until you've got him alone? That's not the kind of thing you want to bring up in front of a lot of people."

I frown down at his hand before I recognize what he just said. "Yeah, okay, you're right. I'll ask him when I get him alone." My skin prickles under Riku's hand, which is warm against my skin. He releases me and steps back.

"Forgive me for putting my hands on you." He bows his head. "I shouldn't have done that."

"It's fine." I wave off his apology and hide my disappointment. "You were right. I wouldn't have stopped if you had just asked me to."

"Are you going back to join the party?" he asks, and I think about it. I promised Hope that I would take her over to Harlow's and give her a tour, but it's too late now. We'll have to do it another time.

"No, I think I'm just going to head to bed. I'm tired after last night, and I still want to go over the intern applications. It's even more important now that we get the right one since both Emma and Molly will be taking time off in nine months. Tell everyone where I've gone, will you?" He inclines his head. "I'll see you in the morning?" I ask.

"Yes, your father has arranged for both Neigh-palm helicopters to be here in the morning so that security can come with you, Harlow, and Hope. Apparently, everyone is going in for the board meeting in the morning."

"I still think it's sexist that only us girls have security. The guys could be a target as much as we are."

"They do. Each of them has a temporary body-guard, but they only use them for public engage-ments, so they aren't staying here at the house like us and Hope's security."

"But Harlow doesn't have full-time security," I complain, though I'm not trying too hard. Honestly, I see the benefit of having Riku and his partner.

"She does. They're just staying over here, allowing your family their privacy at night. Your brothers insisted that they can take care of her when they're all home, so her security only works during the day."

"Well, okay then. Good night, Riku." At this point, there's nothing else I can say. Did I really need him to explain my sister's security detail? No. Honestly, I think part of me just didn't want to separate from him. He's attractive, but there's part of me that says it's more than that. I don't know what I want from him yet. I guess that's a problem for future Jacinta.

"Good night, Ms. Summers. Sweet dreams." His voice is velvety smooth, and his goodbye is like a benediction. He waits for me to close the door on my wing.

Breathing out a sigh, I lean against the door once he's out of sight. Having that man as my security is going to be a study in not sexually harassing my employees. I've never felt attracted to anyone working for me before. Well, apart from Jace, but he doesn't really count because we have a friendship as well. And Alex and Shane don't technically work for me, just *with* me, kind of. But Riku is going to be working very closely with me, guarding my body, practically my shadow. I need to remember to keep it professional because he's mouth-wateringly gorgeous, and I bet when he does finally let go of the overly formal, stick up his ass security guard persona, he's like fire. Still waters run deep and all that jazz.

Pushing off the door, I make my way to my second-floor bedroom, exhausted and ready for bed. Today was fun and a lot easier than I thought it was going to be thanks to my secret stash. The coke really helped me keep my shit together, but I know I have to be careful not to rely on it. I won't need it tomorrow because I'll be at work. Since it's familiar territory, nothing will cause me to feel anxious. The interviews will be a piece of cake, and with Nana, Molly, and Emma's help, we should be able to find a good fit for our branch of the company. Maybe I'm a fool, only time will tell, but I'm optimistic that I can make it through the day without needing that extra help.

Stripping off my dress, I use the bathroom before climbing into bed. It feels amazing. I find my body relaxing with the familiarity, and before I know it, I'm out.

Chapter Nine

Jace

"Do you think we did the right thing?" I look back over my shoulder as the car heads down the driveway. In the dark, I can just make out Jacinta walking back toward her house. "I think she was surprised. Maybe she's not ready. She could still be traumatized."

"Of course we're doing the right thing," Alex admonishes me. "What better way to get over what she went through than to get under someone else?"

Shane snorts. "I'm not sure that's quite how the saying goes," he rumbles quietly, his eyes on the road.

"Even if it isn't, it's how it should go. I'm sick of waiting. I've been patient. I stepped back like you suggested, Jace, after you came back from Prague, but everything is out there now. I couldn't care less about her money before, and I couldn't care less now even though she's got more. I want *her*, preferably between the three of us, and I'm not waiting any longer. I want to sweep her off her feet and show her that she belongs with us."

Alex's hands have been flying through the air with enthusiasm, and he just about smacks Shane in the face. Shane snatches it out of the air, kissing his hand before placing it back in his lap.

"Settle down, Romeo. You don't have to convince the two of us. You know we feel the same way, but I think we need to approach this carefully."

"What do you mean?" I ask, leaning forward a little so Shane's eyes can meet mine in the rearview mirror.

"We have to be careful how we approach this. Jacinta seems... skittish. Like one wrong move could send her running."

"Really? I hadn't noticed." Alex turns around in his seat so he can see us both.

"Babe, I love you, but you can be self-involved," Shane says gently.

I think back to our interaction today, and now that he mentions it, she did seem off. "You know, you're right. She wasn't as carefree as she normally is. It kind of felt like she was putting on an act."

"Oh? Do you think she wasn't happy about all the pregnancies?" Alex does this thing where he purses his lips when he gets all gossipy. Shane tells him his lips look like an asshole, and Alex usually replies with something like, "Well, I guess you won't mind kissing them then." He's got that look on his face now, except I trust him enough to know this is just relationship gossip. Ya know, the kind where you and your partners sit down and dish through everything you're thinking about the party you just left or whatever scandal your friends have gotten involved in. It stays within our little group, so it's harmless, and it feeds the beast that is Alex on the trail of a juicy story.

"No, I don't think so. She seemed genuinely happy about all of that, and she was telling me about the shirts Harlow bought her. Says she can't wait to wear them or decorate the baby's room at Willow Castle." I think back to one of the conversations we had at lunch today. "She even mentioned something about needing to expand Couture to include children and maternity lines."

Alex claps his hands. "Yes, that would be so cool! I could model in the ads with the kids. I'd make an awesome father." He puffs out his chest a little, and I raise my eyebrows.

"You want kids?" I'm kind of surprised, though not unpleasantly. Alex is sweet and funny and kind despite any of his flaws.

"I want a hundred of them!" he announces, and Shane chuckles when he sees my face.

"Alex is an only child." Well, that's not hard to see. "And he feels like his parents did him a disservice by not providing him with childhood company."

"Well, I would debate that. I wouldn't have minded being an only child," I mutter, but Shane still hears me.

"Oh, some days I feel the same way, especially when my brother calls me to ask if he can borrow money for his latest get-rich-quick scheme."

"My sisters aren't that bad, but the two of them are always sticking their noses into my life. Setting me up with their coworkers is like their sole purpose in life apart from their own families. The two of them are so blissfully happy, and they want me to be too, but they have terrible taste in potential partners. They must have used up their one good decision with their own partners."

"See, that's what I want. I want a house filled with noise and laughter, not one that's cold and unfeeling where the only noises you hear are the servants going about their daily tasks."

From what I understand, Alex's family is upper class, and he was raised by nannies. They think he's wasting his life modeling, so they basically disowned him. It's so far removed from my life that I have no clue how to relate to it.

When Harlow first introduced me to Alex and Shane, I admit I was a little bit starstruck. Alex Winters and Shane Silver are one of the powerhouse couples in the fashion industry. I thought they were doing Harlow a favor by taking little ole country bumpkin me under their wing. I'd stay a night or two, then find my own place, and that would be my brush with fashion royalty.

But that first night, after Harlow had gone to bed and we'd all consumed a decent amount of alcohol, one thing led to another, and I found myself waking up sandwiched between the two men. I thought maybe I was a hot fling, something for them to amuse themselves with while they waited for Jacinta.

I'd had every intention of finding my own place, but a couple of nights turned into weeks, and before I knew it, I'd become part of a throuple. And I'm fucking thrilled. There's so much more to these two men than what people see on the outside. People see Alex as shallow and not very bright, but he actually fusses over us like a mother hen, making sure both Shane and I have everything we need mentally, emotionally, and physically. He's the first one to ask us how our days were or to wrap his arms around us if he thinks we need a hug.

And Shane? That saying about still waters running deep was made for him. He's intelligent and kind and gentle. No, he's not the most demonstrative of men, but he shows he cares with small gestures and gentle touches. And in the bedroom, well, the teddy bear becomes a grizzly, and if he asked me to call him Daddy, I'd gladly do it.

I wasn't sure whether they'd ever be happy with just me or if they'd keep that dream of Jacinta joining them. Honestly, I was starting to think that maybe the three of us could simply find that happiness in each other, but then I'd gone to Prague with the Summers family.

I finally understood their obsession, and I had fallen in love. Jacinta is nothing like she's portrayed in the media. She has depth, and she's kind, loving, and protective of her family, with a wicked sense of adventure and humor. I'd never been in love before, though I'm pretty sure now that what I have with Shane and Alex is love too. By the time we returned to California, I would have happily laid my life down for her.

We had a few moments while we were away, but she made it clear that her life was complicated, so those stolen moments were all we had.

When she was kidnapped, I wanted to storm the Summers' place and demand that they let us be involved. Alex had to literally sit on me while Shane chimed in as the voice of reason. Once they were found and Jaxon was in the hospital, there was nothing that could have stopped me from going to her.

But when we arrived, she was like a robot. Sure, she said all the right things, but the light in her eyes was gone. The reality of almost losing her twin and Harlow had sucked the life out of her, and I could tell she blamed herself—survivor's guilt from having gotten away. But if she hadn't, they might never have found the other two.

As we drove away from the hospital that day, the car was quiet, all of us lost in our thoughts until Alex broke the silence.

"One month," he announced suddenly.

"Huh?"

"She gets one month to recover, then we make our intentions clear. I am not going to let that woman get away, and I think if we gave her the chance, she would."

Both Shane and I were in agreement, and it was a done thing. Our throuple was going to become a quadruple.

"Dinner tomorrow has to be perfect. I'm going to cook." Alex pulls out his phone and starts to google recipes. "What do you think she likes?"

"Chicken tenders and fries," I say absently, earning a glare.

"Are you telling me sophisticated heiress Jacinta Summers loves kid food?"

I shrug. "Yeah, and mac and cheese or tomato soup and grilled cheese. She likes the food that reminds her of all the good times growing up in her family. If you made her shepherd's pie or lasagna, she'd think it was the best thing ever."

"You really got to know her while you were away," Shane muses, and I nod.

"Yeah, we spent almost every day together. We didn't want to get in the way of Harlow and the guys. They were dealing with a lot, so we kept each other busy. She's so much fun. I've missed her, and I'm worried we'll never get back there again."

"Full court press," Alex mutters.

Shane chuckles. "Sports terms now?"

"That woman is *not* getting away from us. I want her locked down and moving into the spare bedroom at our place within the next couple of months."

Shane whistles. "Jacinta better watch out! Alex is on a mission."

Alex flips him off, and I laugh at their antics.

"You may be out of luck. She loves her family home, and I have a feeling you're going to need a crowbar to get her out of it."

"Well, we can move there or something. I'm not sure, but if we can knock her up, we can tie her to one of us permanently."

"What the fuck?" Shane shouts and swerves slightly on the road before getting control of the car again. "Are you serious? Don't you think that's a little like… entrapment, especially with what happened with Veronica?"

"As a heart attack. I want that woman, and I want the two of you, and if one of us has to get her pregnant to do that, I am all for it. I plan to tell her all about it. I'm not going to hide it, so I am nothing like that crazy bitch."

"Slow your role, baby daddy. Let's try other things first before we go to the 'knock up a woman' plan," Shane cautions Alex, but I start to think about how I would feel.

Do I want kids? Yes, absolutely. Can I see

myself having them with Jacinta? No question about it. My cock gets hard just thinking about it, then my mind starts imagining the three of us working toward that specific goal, and it throbs inside my pants. "I'm in."

Shane's head swings around, and his eyes bug out. "Really?" He quickly turns back to look at the road.

"Yeah, I want that so badly. You have no idea. I'm in love with her. I'm in love with both of you too. I never knew being in a relationship could be like this. I know it's quick, and I don't expect it to be mutual, but it's the truth."

Before I can say anything else, Alex is unbuckling his belt and throwing himself into the backseat with me. His mouth collides with mine as he kisses me passionately, his hands plucking at my clothes.

I feel the car swerve onto the edge of the road, and out of the corner of my eye, I see Shane get out, then the back door opens. He hauls Alex off me only to replace him. Shane's kisses are different from Alex's. They're rougher, his beard tickling my lips and cheeks. His tongue is more aggressive, and he holds me with a harder grip. It's delicious.

"We feel the same way. We just didn't want to scare you," Shane says breathlessly as he pulls away. The three of us are breathing heavily, and the car is starting to fog up.

He cups my face and gives me one more kiss before pulling away. "As much as I'd like to continue this, there's not enough room in the backseat of the car for the three of us."

"Well, get back to driving! The quicker we get home, the quicker you can join us." Alex tugs me back against his body.

Shane groans and adjusts his cock in his pants. "You're going to make me suffer on the way home, aren't you?" He climbs out and gets back into the driver's seat as we buckle back in. Once we get moving, Alex's hand tackles the button and zipper on my pants before he reaches in and grabs hold of my dick.

"Sure am," he says before he leans down and takes it into his mouth. I groan as I feel his wet mouth engulf the head of my cock, and my hands slide into his hair as my head drifts back against the seat.

"Drive fast, Shane," I mutter as Alex starts to bob up and down. I guess our conversation can continue later.

Chapter Ten

Jacinta

The next morning, I wake up bright and early, excited to go to work. I throw back my blankets and speed through my shower. I even feel good about getting dressed for the day, which is something that I haven't been able to say lately. It's nice to put on something a little fancier than jeans or shorts and a T-shirt, which has practically been my uniform for the last few weeks. Slipping on a pair of fuchsia Jimmy Choos that have a four-inch heel, I smooth my hands over my black pencil skirt before studying myself in my floor-length mirror. I have a fitted sleeveless shirt on, my long black hair is tied back in a sleek pony-tail, and my lipstick matches my shoes. I look good and ready to take on the world, and I feel *amazing*.

Huh, maybe all I needed was to put on my figurative armor to face the world.

A knock on my door has me calling out, "Come in!" I move over to my drafting table and stack some of my designs in my portfolio bag. I'm putting my laptop in its case as my twin steps into my room.

"Oh, hey!" I'm surprised to see him. I know they went home last night, but I guess they needed to come over to catch the helicopters into work.

"Hey, I just wanted to check in on you. See if you're okay. You disappeared last night before I could," he says, leaning against the doorframe.

"Yeah, of course. Why wouldn't I be?" I ask, putting my laptop and portfolio bags over my shoulder before going to my desk.

"You did all the right things and reacted the right way about all the baby news yesterday, but I also know that you are a flawless actress." I freeze at his words, some of the excitement fading away. "Look at me, Jazzy, please."

Sighing, I place my bags on the desk and turn around. I close the distance between us and wrap my arms around him. "Jax, I promise I am okay with all of this. In fact, I'm thrilled for all of you. I actually want to speak to Dad today and see if he's going to invite Emma and Molly to live with us. It's all so quick, but it just feels right. They're a part of our family, especially now, and they should be here with us too."

He hugs me back, and I feel the tension drain

out of him with my words, which makes me equally pleased and guilty. Pleased that he still cares enough to check in on me, and guilty for the exact same reason. He should be thrilled about what's happening in his life, not worried about me being upset about it.

"It makes me so happy to hear that," he tells me as we pull apart. "Harlow said you liked the things she gave you?" He's totally fishing, but he wouldn't be the brother I know and love if he gave up that easily.

"I love them! I can't wait to be an auntie and a big sister. I know I'm getting at least one niece, but I'm excited to find out what the other babies are. Are you guys going to find out? I wonder if Dad and the girls will."

Leaving Jax, I head into my closet to grab my handbag.

"I'm not sure. We haven't really discussed it. It will go to a group vote, I guess. We all know what Oli's vote will be, but I guess we'll have to see how everyone else votes." I smile at this, glad to hear that they're working together as a family.

"I love that you guys put things to a vote. It must make decision-making easier." I pick out a cute Jimmy Choo bag to go with my heels before shoving my phone, lipstick, and some gum into my purse. When I come back out, Jax is standing by my desk, and my heart starts racing. Fuck, I don't want him to open the top drawer. I stride over as casually as I can and shove my portfolio and laptop at him. "Here, can you take these things downstairs and pour me a coffee? I just need to find the business card Riku gave me last night. I think it might have fallen under my bed."

He takes my bags and raises an eyebrow, walking backward to the door. "Your bodyguard Riku? What would he be giving you a business card for? We've already hired his company."

Well, that's certainly news to me. Riku owns the company that we've hired. Huh, the man is full of surprises. I shake my head and wave my hand.

"His sister owns a baby boutique, and I mentioned I was excited to be outfitting the nursery for you guys. He gave me her card and told me to give her a call, says she has some unique things there."

"Oh cool. He's a nice guy. It would be good if we could support his sister's business. It's always nice to pay it forward, and he *is* looking after your whiny ass after all."

He winks and hightails it out of my room before I can respond. I breathe a sigh of relief, followed by a chuckle. *That ass.*

I grab the card from my bedside table before hurrying back to my desk. I need to hide the coke in a better place. Pulling open the drawer, I gather up the remaining baggies and hurry back into my closet. I grab an old handbag off the shelf and shove them in, but I find myself pausing before I put it back. *Maybe I'll take one with me just in case.* So I grab one little bag then put the handbag back on the shelf and shove another in front of it. *There, no one will find them.*

Finally, I go back to my desk and put the little baggie in my handbag. All the tension washes out of my body at the thought that it's there just in case. Of course, I won't need it. I'm only going to work, into meetings with people I know, and everyone else works for me. I'm the boss, the one in charge. I will be fine. Or at least I'll keep telling myself that.

Picking it up by its cute little handle, I head downstairs. The living room is a hive of activity, with Harlow and the rest of my brothers having breakfast with the rest of my family. Mrs. Heyton is bustling around, pouring coffee for anyone who needs it and prepping travel mugs for the ride in.

"Jacinta, *meiner kleiner schmetterling,* there you are. I have your chamomile tea ready for you." Mrs. Heyton bustles back into the kitchen as everyone says good morning to me.

"Wow, don't you look amazing!" Harlow says as she gets up and gives me a quick hug. "We good?" she whispers in my ear, and I squeeze her extra hard.

"We're great. Thank you, I'm feeling great."

"Those shoes and that bag are gorgeous." Hope sighs, pointing at them. "I've never been able to pull off that pink. It clashes with my hair." She tugs on her red locks in frustration.

"Ahh, but they come in other colors. I think there's a couple more pairs in the wardrobe. Why don't you grab them for yourself while we're there?" I suggest, taking the to-go cup of tea Mrs. Heyton returned with. "Thank you." I give her a kiss on her soft cheek, and she pats my own.

"*Bitte schön*. Can you girls each take a mug of coffee for your bodyguards, *bitte*?" Hope and Harlow nod, but I scrunch up my nose and hold up my handbag in one hand and my tea in the other. Mrs. Heyton rolls her eyes, but before she can say anything, there's a knock on the glass door. Riku is standing on the other side.

Holden lets him in with a smile. "Morning, man, just in time for coffee."

Mrs. Heyton holds out two more travel mugs from the sideboard.

"For you and Simon," she tells him, and he gives her this gentle smile before speaking in rapid German. Their conversation is so fast that I can't pick it up with my small smattering of the language, but I see Harlow smile and nod.

"Did you actually understand that?" I ask, and she smirks.

"Yup, remember what I said about languages being my thing? German is one I picked up as well."

"Well, what are they saying?" I ask her.

"Basically, he's telling her thank you, then he explained that when you're just going to the office, you'll only have one guard, and it's Simon's day off. He'll only join when you go out in public." She turns to me. "I think that's the same for all of us."

"Alright. Is everyone ready?" Dad stands up, draining the last of his coffee. "Let's get moving." There's a mad rush as everyone grabs everything they need. Kai and Thomas have already left, checking on the helicopters, and Harlow is the only one who seems to have her shit together. She throws her faithful backpack over her shoulder and strides out the door without a care. I check that Jax still has my other bags, and when I'm sure he does, I grab Hope, and we power walk after her. When we get there, Thomas and Kai are running last-minute checks, and Hope's and Harlow's security guys are there, already holding the to-go coffee courtesy of their charges.

We split up into two groups. Harlow, the guys, and her bodyguard take the one with Thomas flying it, and the rest of us take the other.

Once settled, it doesn't take us long to get into the air and make our way to Neighpalm headquarters. When we touch down, we split up. Emma and Molly are making their way to the Couture level, and the rest of us are heading to the board room on the top floor for our meeting.

As we get settled around the table, Hope clears her throat, drawing our attention to her. "I told Cole to give us an hour before he comes in. That gives us time to discuss anything we need to before he joins us."

"That was smart, Hope, thank you." Poppy pats her on the shoulder as he passes her to take his seat at the head of the table. While he's retired from everyday Neighpalm business, he's still chairman of the board and leader of these meetings. Nana and Dad take a seat on either side of him as the rest of us spread out around the table, pulling out laptops and notebooks. Today is Harlow's first board meeting and Hope's first one as a member of the board, not the PR representative. She and Holden sit next to one another so they can give a Records report.

"Okay, let's get the ball rolling. The agenda should be in your emails. Business reports first. Dec, let's start with you. Anything to report for Productions?" Poppy opens the floor, and Nana is poised to take the minutes of the meeting. We've always kept everything in the family so that we can discuss things without having to worry about loose lips. Hope was the only outsider ever allowed to attend. Cole, the new PR guy, will be the second.

"Productions is doing well. We've recently signed Jarred Reed, Cayden Storm, and Hayden Christie to our talent management branch, and we've just wrapped filming on Sean Walsh's latest film. No major hiccups apart from Selena Cross lying to us about her riding abilities, but Maxine was able to jump in and help us out with stunts for that movie. Both movies will be releasing in the spring, so we'll run a media campaign in the lead-up to that. I'll arrange a meeting with Cole to spearhead that. We've also got a lot of applicants for the Ninja Starfish reality show. We'll start filming auditions for that in December with the guys and Holden acting as judges."

"Excellent. That's good news. Alright, Kai?" Poppy turns to my bronzed brother, who casually leans back in his chair. His long hair is looking a little shaggy, and he's dressed in shorts and a Neigh-palm Energy Drink T-shirt. Apart from formal events, we can't get him to put on a suit.

"Product development has just come up with a new flavor, which will be launching in the summer, as well as announcing our new X Games team. The Blaze twins have come on board, but I'm still scouting one or two more. I want a fresh look for the new flavor, but I haven't hit the right combo yet. Tyler and Tristan are coming in to talk to me next week about some options. I want their input. I don't want to put together a team that doesn't get along. We saw the fallout of that with Ninja Starfish, and I don't want to go through that with one of mine." I see various heads nod around the table.

"That's smart, because that was a fucking disaster." Holden groans, taking a sip of his coffee. "But I've promised them full control of choosing when we run that comp. Dec and I are just there to guide them."

"Smart decision on both your behalf," Dad praises Kai and Holden, and even though they're grown men, they both puff up slightly. Dad has never been stingy with praise, but they lap it up anyway. I mean, I'm the same damn way, so it's not like I can blame them for it.

"Who's next?" Poppy looks down at his agenda before turning to Hope and Holden. "Okay, you two, what's going on with Records?"

"As you know, I've taken over management of Ninja Starfish. They're one of our biggest sellers at the moment, so I want to personally get them back on track. Hope is overseeing the rest of the business." Holden looks to our new sister, who smiles and takes over.

"Apart from Ninja Starfish, everyone else on the label is doing well. No scandals or drama to report. Sanctuary of Chaos has just finished their world tour and are taking two months off. Daisy Dallas has just signed to play the lead role in a new movie and will be writing the soundtrack for it. Both Wicked Sins and N3D Fusion are touring right now. I have a few demos on my desk that our talent scouts would like me to listen to, and the new band that Holden signed is hitting the studios this week. I've got Stanley Brown lined up to work with them, and Chester's going to come in and give them some moral support."

"Good thinking, Hope. Having someone like Chester Mercury take an interest in them will be a big ego boost. Thankfully, the fallout from Giselle didn't destroy his relationship with us." Dad sounds relieved.

"Excellent, it seems like you two have got everything under control." Poppy takes control again, seamlessly moving from one facet of the business to the next. "I'm happy to report that Neighpalm Air is going strong with no problems. Our acquisition of Northwest European Airlines went smoothly, and we have transitioned them under our banner. The only bump in the road is the Veronica situation, but that seems to be under control for now. Once the baby arrives, the case for the attempted murder charge will go ahead. Forrest and his team are dealing with that. We've also paid all her roommate's medical bills and promised her a job once she recovers. If she no longer wishes to be a flight attendant, we will find her another role or offer her a generous severance if she chooses to work somewhere else."

"I wouldn't blame her," Nana adds, pausing her typing as she speaks up for the first time. "I'm not sure I would want to associate with the people almost responsible for my death."

The room breaks out into noise, and I jump in my seat. I wasn't expecting such a strong reaction, but my brothers all voice their arguments until Nana holds up a hand to quiet them down.

"Sorry, I worded that wrong. *Indirectly* responsible. I'm not putting the blame on any of you, that's firmly on that woman, but it was her obsession with you that pushed her over the edge."

Kai and Thomas grumble a little more, but we get the meeting back on track, and Oliver, Jaxon, Harlow, and I all give our reports on our businesses. We're just about to move on to new business when a knock sounds on the door.

Hope stands up. "That must be Cole, perfect timing."

Chapter Eleven

Jacinta

When the door opens, Hope is blocking my view of the newcomer, but I hear them exchange a friendly greeting that makes my ears prick up. That voice sounds familiar, but I can't quite put my finger on it. It's not until Hope steps out of the way, giving me a good look at the devilishly handsome man who has fucking dimples when he smiles, that I feel my stomach plummet. His eyes meet mine, and I stare in horror at the familiar Caribbean blue that's as bright now as it was in the club. Fucking hell. He'd known who I was the whole time. It's not like Wonder Woman wears a mask.

His gaze hardens before moving on, dismissing me like dirt, as Hope introduces him to my brothers, Harlow, Nana, and Poppy. Dad has already met him, having been involved in the interview process, but everyone else greets him warmly, welcoming him to the Neighpalm family. Finally, he and Hope get to me.

"And this is Jacinta Summers. She's head designer for Neighpalm Couture and has recently stepped down as CEO due to other commitments popping up in her life."

"Ah, yes, the Count Bucătaru heirs. Ms. Summers, your reputation precedes you." He reaches out for the hand I hold out to him. I will not let this asshole intimidate me. I eat men like him for lunch.

"Mr. Chambers, I wish I could say the same, but I know less than nothing about you." Hope gasps at the shots fired, and his hand briefly tightens around mine as a sly grin crosses his face.

"Oh, I guess that puts you at a disadvantage then." Our hands are still clenched when Hope steps in, knowing that this could all turn to shit if she doesn't do something.

"Okay, great! Now that we know everyone, why don't you take a seat, Cole, and we'll continue our meeting." She gestures to a seat on the other side of the table, but he pulls out the vacant one next to me and sits his ass down on it. I feel myself stiffen as he opens up his laptop and shuffles some papers in front of him.

What the actual fuck? What is this man's game? I'm pretty sure he's not going to out me for my drug use because he's got no leg to stand on there. It wouldn't look good to his new employers if I shared that the only reason he knows about it is because he snorted coke off my tits before fucking me like he owns me.

Taking a couple of deep breaths, I slowly relax my body muscle by muscle. I don't want him to know that his very presence bothers me. After a few moments, I have my shit together enough to tune back into the conversation. If he wants to play games, he can bring it, because I am an expert game player. My confidence kicks in, and I feel more like me than I have in months. *Finally, a challenge.*

"Cole, we've just discussed each of the businesses. Grace will forward you the minutes of the meeting. Let's move on to our new acquisitions." Poppy does something to his computer, and all of our own laptops start dinging. "We've had some interesting resumes handed in for the position of CEO for Cruise Lines. As much as I would have liked to keep it in the family, I understand Hope's and Jaxon's positions. I've sent you a list of the top five front runners that Jaxon, Brad, and I have weeded out. Have a look and speak up if any of you know anything about these five applicants."

"I can't help you with that because I don't know anyone." Harlow laughs as she leans back in her chair, but the rest of us read through the information Dad has provided. I'm consciously aware of every movement Cole makes next to me, so much so that it takes me a little longer to assimilate the information.

Thomas is the first to finish, tapping a pen against his lip in thought. "They all look like good candidates, and I don't think I've heard whispers or bad things about any of them."

"Can I ask a question?"

Poppy smiles at Harlow before he answers. "Of course you can. You have as much right as anyone at this table."

"Why appoint an individual? Why not appoint a team? That way we're not relying on one person. It's a big job to take on. I know how daunting it is to be on the ground level of building a new branch of the business, and without your help, and Clem and Doug, I would be a mess."

Poppy's eyebrows jump in surprise as he considers what she said.

"That's actually a smart idea. A team would be a good idea. It also makes it so that they are all accountable for the decisions they make instead of one person being responsible for it all. It would relieve the stress and probably make a more cohesive business structure." I feel a shiver course through my body at the sound of Cole's voice. Fucking hell, why am I having such a visceral reaction to this man?

"So, what, offer them all the position?" Oliver asks, leaning forward.

"Yes, make it a CEO team. You would need to give the leadership model a trial period to see if they could work well together. You may need to replace one or two until you get a unit that thrives as a team, but eventually, you would find the right combination." Cole shrugs. "It also gives you a chance to see how well they gel with the family. After all, it is your business, and you are handing it over to strangers. You would want them to be people you liked, not ones you clashed with."

I snort, unable to stop the sound from slipping out, and everyone looks at me. "If only we could do that with all our employees."

Dad frowns. "But we do. That's why everyone is given a temporary contract before being offered a permanent position. You did that with Jace and Rowena."

"Yes, but we don't necessarily get rid of the ones we don't like either. Look at Lindy. I've put up with her for years. Not to mention Veronica, Raquel, or Cecelia. I never liked any of them. If it had been up to me, they wouldn't have made it past their trial periods. Maybe then Kai and Thomas wouldn't be stuck in the situation they're in, and Harlow, Jax, and I wouldn't have been kidnapped." Bitterness creeps into my voice, and Nana's eyes fill with sympathy, while Dad is now sporting a frown. Before he can say anything, Cole jumps in.

"So you think *you* should be allowed to vet every employee? See if they pass the Jacinta Summers standards test?" No one can miss the bite of sarcasm in his tone, and I bristle even as I shake my head, looking at Dad as I explain because I don't owe Cole a fucking explanation at all. He can kiss my ass.

"No, I'm sorry. That's not what I mean. I'm just frustrated by what we've been through. For what it's worth, I think a team is a good idea. I know how much I struggled with handling Couture on my own despite having Nana as a sounding board."

My family members are all looking at me with sympathy in their eyes, and I don't dare turn to the man next to me to see what his say. I'm sure he's looking at me with scorn and derision.

"Well, if everyone is in agreement, we'll send the five of them a job offer with the relevant details, and we can go from there." Poppy looks around the room, and my family gives him signs of acceptance. "Okay, great. Declan, is the acquisition of that theme park finalized now?"

Harlow smiles with joy at the question, and it chases away some of my negative emotions. How can I be upset when I see members of my family are so obviously and blissfully happy?

"Yes, it's officially ours. I would like to start work on a Neighpalm Amusements branding package to use in the official announcement. Cole, can you get someone on your team to work on that?" Declan looks at the man next to me.

"Of course. I'll send an announcement to the

team. If I could just grab a moment of your time after the meeting, I'd like to pick your brain about some details." His fingers fly across the keyboard of his laptop as he makes notes, and I'm embarrassed to admit that I start paying way too much attention to the man's hands. He's wearing a ring on the ring finger of his right hand. It's a funky black and silver design, and his watch is Tag Heuer. It's actually pretty cool, but I'm not admitting that to anyone.

"I need to set up an appointment with the McCallisters as well. Maybe I'll go home early and see if I can catch Miles or one of the others before they head home for the day. I'd like to see how long we have until the completion of the zoo renovations. I'd like to get them to start working on the amusement park directly after. We'll need to advertise for a management team for that too."

"Okay, I'll let human resources know to draft up an announcement for all of that," Dad says, making a note on a piece of paper next to his laptop before looking around the room. "Is there anything else you all want to talk about before we hand things over to Cole?"

When no one answers, he turns to the man in question.

"Okay, before Cole starts, I just want to fill you in on a few things. We don't normally run our business around public appearances. For the most part, we are a fairly quiet family, as you know, but we attract press wherever we go. Unfortunately, at the moment, some of that has been speculation about everything that has happened in the past few months. Some of our shareholders are not happy about the speculative publicity, and they most certainly weren't happy when Harlow and the boys' relationship was made public."

My family bursts into shouts, but Dad holds up a firm hand. "Now, they have no right to tell the seven of you how to live. I have already informed them that your relationship has absolutely no bearing on how we run this business. But we need to make sure, going forward, that we are in such a solid position that none of it should matter anyway. Nothing should make them question how we run the business. If that means making a few appearances at more events than we normally attend, I don't want to hear any arguments. Please bear that in mind with what Cole is about to say. Okay, Cole, the floor's all yours."

Cole stands up. "Thanks, Brad. I'd just like to say it's great to all be meeting you, and I want to thank you for giving me this opportunity. I'm excited to work for one of the biggest companies in the US, and I think we'll make a great team. I hope you'll excuse me, but I like to move when I'm planning." He steps away from his chair and pulls his phone out of his pocket. "The press release went out this morning announcing the news that Jaxon and Jacinta are the heirs to the Bucătaru fortune. We did tell them the truth about everything, from your mother giving you to Brad, to the discovery of the count's body below the house, the subsequent kidnapping, and Jaxon being shot. We didn't hold any of it back, and so far we've had offers from three major talk show hosts for one-on-one interviews with the twins and Harlow and a major motion picture studio trying to buy the rights to the story." He breaks off and looks up as Declan chuckles.

"Did they seriously think they would sell the story to anyone but me? Fucking vultures!"

"No, absolutely not. No to all of that." Jaxon's lips are set in a straight line, and I can see his jaw clenched with annoyance.

"Are you sure you don't want to look at the offer?" I don't know if he's trying to play devil's advocate or if he's the sort of person who actually thinks we should entertain these offers, but I can't let this slide.

"We are *very* sure. We have more money than we will ever be able to spend in our lifetimes, so none of us need the cash, nor do any of us want to relive any of it. Have people no respect? That's our lives, and the lives of our family members, even the horrible biological ones," I snap at him.

Cole nods and makes a few notes. "That's what I thought you were going to say, but I would be remiss not to let you know your options. I drafted two letters this morning before I came up to the meeting, so I'd be prepared for either response.

Moving on, we *do* have a press conference scheduled for today at lunchtime."

Harlow scrunches up her nose, and Thomas grabs her hand. "The last press conference I did wasn't any fun," she grumbles.

"They never are. They're just a downside to everything else we are lucky to have," Kai says, leaning back in his chair.

"Well, shit, now you make me feel guilty." She sticks her tongue out at him, and we all laugh.

"Forrest and I will be with you the whole time. I'll make sure that you aren't harassed, and both of us will guide you on what to answer and not to. As horrible as this all is, we need to capitalize on the press. So far, you're all looking like victims, but it won't take long for the press to put a slant on it, so we need to keep up the momentum that has the public looking at you with a more positive, sympathetic eye. In order to do that, we have a few engagements where attendance will be compulsory. We need the Summers family out and about, looking like nothing is going to hold them down. You will all be expected to attend the launch of Jaxon's new hotel in Hawaii next week. A week after that is the launch of Jace's new line in New Orleans. Then, a week after that, Shane Silvers has his photography show, and I'd like some of you to attend that." He takes a breath, looking around the room as if he's trying to assess how we're dealing with all of this information. Around the table, my brothers are maintaining their poker faces. Kai looks as cheerfully unfazed as he always is. Harlow doesn't quite look happy, but it's clear that she's going to hear him out before making any final opinions.

After his eyes come back around to his end of the table, he resumes his list. "That takes us through November. You'll have your Thanksgiving soup kitchen like you usually do. Then, in December, we have the premiere of *In the Stars*. Even if you don't stay to watch it, I'd like you to walk the red carpet. We will take a break over the Christmas period and get back into everything for a New Year's Eve party at the Neighpalm Club in New York. Invites have gone out for that, and the who's who of Neighpalm clients and celebrities have been invited. After that, I'll let you all return to your lives and melt back into the shadows."

With every event Cole rattles off, I feel my stomach sink lower and lower. That just sounds like pure hell to me. Of course I want to support our family and friends, but I know the press is going to be everywhere, and they are relentless. They'll mercilessly hound us until they find something new to latch onto. I need to pray someone else fucks up, but with all of the pending announcements—the pregnancies and Dad's relationship—the focus will be back on us.

Cole's gaze swings to me. "Jacinta, I have a few more engagements for you and Hope to attend. You two are now the single faces of Neighpalm, so we want to see you out and about, drumming up *positive* media attention." When he emphasizes the positive, I just know he's referring to catching me snorting coke the other day and his last parting shot. I squeeze my hands into fists in my lap but keep a benign smile on my face. "If you wouldn't mind making some time for me today, I'd like to chat with each of you individually."

"Of course they don't!" Nana has a gleam in her eye and a smirk on her face that suddenly gives me the urge to smack her. She better not be playing her damn matchmaking games.

"Okay, I'll send the schedule to your calendars, your PAs, and anyone else that needs to know. I need to know if you want to stay at Jaxon's hotel for the opening or if you will stay at the Neighpalm on the Beach." He looks around the room, waiting for our answer.

"I've booked the penthouse suite for us and Harlow." Jaxon smiles cheekily at his girlfriend. "I promised her we would last time we were there. I've also booked suites for Jacinta and Hope, as well as one for you, Cole. And now that Shane is going to do our media and photos, I'll book one for him and the guys if they choose to come." He turns to Dad and our grandparents. "I didn't book you guys any." They all go to argue, but he stops them with one look. "No, you will stay at the Neighpalm on the Beach. I'm sorry. You are always welcome at

Neighpalm Luxure, but not while we're there. Parents or grandparents and sex do not go hand in hand."

The three of them chuckle, and Dad rolls his eyes. "Don't you think we feel much the same way? We don't want to think about you all having sex either. Those arrangements are fine, but I will be taking Emma and Molly with me. Actually, while we're all here, and I hope you don't mind if I change the subject to something personal for a moment, Cole, I have something I want to talk about with my family."

"Do you want me to leave?" Cole asks, but Dad shakes his head.

"No, that's fine. You need to know about it anyway. I would like to ask Emma and Molly to move in with me, and although I am not asking your permission, it would be nice if you all gave us your blessing. I know it's quick, but those two women have made me happier in the last few months than I have been in years."

The room bursts into noise, everyone assuring Dad how happy we are for him and that we would love for them to move in with him.

"Molly and Emma are both pregnant," Dad eventually tells Cole. To his credit, our new PR manager doesn't even flinch at the news. He smiles and holds out his hand, a perfect professional.

"Well, I guess congratulations are in order. That's great, Brad. Let me know when the three of you want to sit down and discuss a strategy for dealing with the press."

"I guess we need to be in that meeting too." Harlow raises her hand, and Cole swings around to look at her.

"You too?" he asks, surprised.

"Ah, yeah, I'm not sure if you were briefed on the exact things that happened to Jax and me during our kidnapping…"

Cole's surprise turns to anger, and he nods. "Yes, I was."

"Well, Peter's big plan was to create an heir to the fortune." Harlow shakes her head in disbelief. "Somehow, and I have no clue how, he succeeded."

"And how do you feel about this?" Cole asks carefully, and I'm kind of surprised by the gentleness in his voice—no judgment, only sympathy. Harlow exchanges looks with my six brothers before smiling.

"Surprised but happy," she replies, reflexively putting her hand on her belly.

"Good, well, let me know how you want to proceed. Do we want people to speculate, or do you want to control it and make the announcement yourselves? I'll work with whatever you want to do."

Shortly after that, the meeting wraps up, and instead of hanging around and chatting like everyone else is, I tell Nana I'll meet her in the conference room on the Couture level. I make my escape before Cole can pin me down. As I close the door, I feel his eyes on me, and even though I get the urge to hunch, I straighten my back and stride out, looking calm and collected.

There's no way he knows I'm faking it for all I'm worth.

Chapter Twelve

Jacinta

When the elevator opens on Couture level, I wave at our front office girl who stands up and passes me a cup of coffee.

"Thanks, Susie, this is just what I needed." I take it from her, and she beams.

"Emma and Molly are in the conference room, and the first interviewee is downstairs in the foyer, waiting to be called up," she informs me.

"Okay, I just need to pop into my office, then I'll head in. Give me ten minutes before you call down to the front desk to send them up."

"Will do." She sits back down as I head off. I gave up my original office to Molly and Emma since I'm very rarely here. I took one of the small designer offices next to Rowena and Jace. Both of their doors are open, but neither of them are in, so I make it past without being delayed. Slamming open the door to my office, I quickly enter and shut it, flipping the lock behind me. My body is shaking and my heart is racing as I lean against the door. It took everything I had to hold my shit together until I got into my room.

"Fuck!" I drop all my bags on the floor, place the coffee cup on the table, and sink down into the small sofa I have for guests. Grabbing a throw pillow, I shove it over my head and scream and scream, letting out everything that threatened to bubble up and out at the meeting. I can't believe Cole was the masked man who rocked my world on Halloween night! How am I ever going to be able to work with him now? Then there's all the publicity he wants us to do. The thought of all those eyes on me makes me sick. Literally.

I jump off the couch and sprint to my little attached bathroom, dropping to my knees. The back split in my pencil skirt tears in my haste, but I'm too busy expelling the contents of my stomach to care. Over and over, I heave up all the tea I had this morning until there's nothing left to come up.

Breathing hard, I sit back on my ankles, the points of my heels poking into my ass and the stench of vomit filling the bathroom. I take a moment to breathe, then I can't stand the acrid taste in my mouth any longer. A minute later, I've rinsed my mouth out and am examining myself in the mirror. I look like shit. There are no other words for it, which means I'm going to have to duck into the Wardrobe to fix myself because I don't have any makeup here. Luckily, the split in my skirt hasn't traveled far enough for it to be indecent.

I have no idea how I'm going to get through all those media events. Thankfully, I'll attend most of them with the others as a buffer, but I'm dreading what Cole has Hope and me attending on our own. Of course, I don't have time to continue my melt-down. I have a press conference and the interviews I need to get through, and I'm not going to be able to do that on my own. Without a second thought, I grab the coke out of my bag and line it up on my desk. Subconsciously, I know what I'm doing is wrong, but I can't bring myself to care. At the moment, it's the only thing getting me through my days. I'll worry about any aftermath later.

Leaning over, I quickly inhale the two small lines before cleaning up, storing the baggie in my top desk drawer in case I need another hit before the press conference. For the second time today, luck is on my side, so I make it to the Wardrobe, my laptop and portfolio in hand, unseen.

Going to the makeup section, I fix my tear-ravaged face and redo my hair before stripping off my skirt. Considering I'm in just my thong, top, and heels, I cross my fingers, hoping that nobody comes in while I'm doing this. Once the rip is repaired, I stand up, and that's when my luck ends. I knock a box of thread to the ground and start to scramble around, picking them all up. I freeze, ass up, of course, when I hear the door to the Wardrobe open.

Why does this shit fucking happen to me?

"Jacinta, I'm pretty sure I already warned you about locking doors." Cole's voice is a lot less friendly than it was in the board meeting, and when I turn around, he's leaning against the closed door, arms crossed and a frown set into his brow. I feel my cheeks flush pink at the fact that he came in while my thong-clad ass was sticking up in the air, but that's not the only reason. There's just something about this man that sets flames of fire rushing through my body.

"There's also a thing called knocking, Cole," I snarl back and slowly get to my feet. It's not like he hasn't seen everything already, so why should I rush?

"So you don't care if anyone else walks in?" he asks as I place the box of thread back on the table and pick up my skirt.

"Hardly the first time anyone has seen me in a thong," I reply. "I wear one to the beach, and I'm sure plenty of sleazy paps have taken a photo of it. Shit, Cole, you may have been one of the last to see my ass."

I step into my skirt and tug up the zipper, not looking away from the intense stare of the man in front of me. He's watching me like he's a predator and I'm his prey, but I have news for him. I don't back down so easily.

He shakes his head like he's trying to clear it before stepping away from the door, moving closer into my space. "What is it you want? I have some interviews to attend. Can this wait until later?" I ask him, grabbing my two bags so that there's something between us.

"I was hoping to catch you so we can go over the other engagements I have you booked for." His tone is flat, not betraying any emotions, and it puts me on edge. Without that little clue as to who he is, what he's feeling, I'm a little off-kilter. I use those little clues people give me to help me figure out how to approach them—whether I should go hard, take it easy, or turn on the charm. It's disconcerting when he gives me nothing to work with.

"Well, it's going to have to wait. I don't have time now. Maybe after the press conference," I suggest. Without waiting for an answer, I slip past him and pull open the door, leaving the Wardrobe. I can feel him on my heels as I walk down the corridor. To get to the big conference room, I have to walk back past the Couture reception desk, and when I get out there, a tall, gorgeous black woman is at the desk talking to Susie. Hayden Christie is the new model we just signed to our label. I've worked with her a few times, and she's always been friendly and kind.

"Hayden, hi. Did we have an appointment? I

swear there was nothing in my planner." I look from Susie to the beautiful model who smiles and shakes her head before looking over my shoulder.

"No, I'm here for a fitting with Jace for his show, but that's not until later. We were actually looking for Cole, and they told us he was here," she replies, and I frown. *We?*

"Hi, Daddy." The little voice draws my attention to the seats in the waiting area. Seated in a chair that looks way too big for him is an adorable little boy. His hair is a curly little afro, and his eyes are the mirror image of his dad's. He's dressed in jeans and a shirt, topped with suspenders, and is swinging his sneaker-clad feet back and forth.

Cole pushes past me to pick him up, kissing him all over his face as I watch on in horror.

"Hey, my best bud."

Oh my fucking god, did I sleep with a married man? Now *that* is an all-time fucking low.

"We thought Cole might like to have an early lunch with us." He turns around, holding his son.

"Who's the pretty lady, Daddy?" the little boy asks, sticking his thumb in his mouth.

Cole walks his son back over to us. "Jacinta, you know my ex-wife Hayden, but this is my son, Spencer." The little boy snuggles into his dad's shoulder, his bright blue eyes studying me closely. I slowly release the breath I'd been holding, my body relaxing. Phew, not a homewrecker.

"Spence, this is Ms. Summers. She's my boss."

I hold my hand out for the little boy, and he reaches out to take it. "It's lovely to meet you, Spencer."

A slow grin crosses his face as we shake. "You're pretty, Ms. Summers," he says before hiding his face again in his dad's neck.

"Why don't you call me Jazzy? All my friends do." He won't look at me again, and I chuckle at his cuteness.

"Ah, Ms. Summers, they're waiting for you in the conference room," Susie interrupts.

"Crap! Okay, have fun at lunch," I tell them, and Cole frowns.

"But…" He starts to argue, and I shake my head.

"Just have lunch with your family, Cole. If there's one thing I've learned, it's that family matters more than anything, and taking the time to appreciate them needs to be done now, not later. The Summers feel very strongly about family, so you won't get arguments from anyone. Why don't you take them to the atrium and have food sent up from the café? I'm sure Spencer would love to see the fish in the pond."

The little boy's eyes widen. "Please, Daddy?" he asks, and Cole melts. Wow, gone is the hard-ass I've come to know, replaced with a man that looks like he would be loving and caring and would do anything for his son. It thaws my heart toward him the tiniest bit, though I don't want that to happen.

"Okay, champ, we'll do that."

"Spencer, there's a bench seat next to the pond, and if you lift the lid, you'll find some fish food inside. Can you make sure they get their lunch for me?" I ask him, and his eyebrows jump.

He nods his head vigorously, causing his curls to bob wildly.

"Great, so I'll see you at the press conference later, yes?" I ask Cole. Although this man rubs me the wrong way, I very much want him there. He has this presence that tells me he won't take any shit from the press.

"Yes, absolutely," he reassures me, and I feel some of the tension drain away.

"Okay, great. Nice to see you, Hayden. I can't wait to see you in Jace's designs. Bye, Spencer."

He waves as I take my leave and power walk in the direction of the conference room. I slip inside and look around. Emma, Molly, and Nana are all seated at the head of the table with a spare chair for me, and there's a woman sitting opposite them.

"I am so sorry. Hayden Christie was in reception, and I couldn't brush her off," I explain to everyone as I take a seat at the table. Pulling out my laptop, I get my shit together before looking up. There's a reflexive frown that takes over when I see that the first woman we're interviewing is Lindy.

"What's going on here?" I ask, slightly confused. Lindy applied, but she didn't even make the short list. Never mind the fact I don't like her, she doesn't have any suitable qualifications.

"Lindy here decided to take it upon herself to schedule herself an interview." Nana sounds pissed. When I walked in, I hadn't noticed that all three women were upset, but I can't miss it now.

"Why would you do this, Lindy? Molly and I explained to you why you hadn't made the short list," Emma asks, sounding bewildered.

When I see the stubborn glint in Lindy's eye, I pull out my phone, sending Riku a request to join us in the conference room.

Lindy crosses her arms and looks defiant. "Well, if you don't give me the position, I'll announce to the world that the two of you are in a relationship with Brad Summers."

"Did she just say what I thought she said?" Nana asks incredulously.

I start to chuckle, while the other two ladies are silenced by shock.

"What's so funny?" Lindy demands, but I shake my head.

"You do know what happened to the last woman who blackmailed us into giving her a position?" I ask her, and she looks confused. "Cecelia is dead," I gleefully share, and she blanches. Of course I'm letting her assume the worst even though her death had nothing to do with the blackmail. What Lindy doesn't know won't hurt us.

Nana gets over her shock and picks up the

phone on the conference table. "Yes, could you please call the police? Have them come pick up Lindy for extortion."

Lindy looks panicked after Nana puts the phone down, but then she gets that smug smirk again. "You can't prove anything."

I chuckle even louder this time. "Lindy, I swear I have no idea how I put up with you for so long. You're as dumb as a box of rocks. We record all of our interviews because we go back over them afterward. See the little red dot in the corner over there?" I point out the camera. "Smile." She pales considerably with that news.

The door to the room opens, and Riku sticks his head in. "You wanted me, Ms. Summers?"

"Yes, thanks, Riku. Could you and Franklin escort Lindy down to the security offices and wait with her until the police arrive? Oh, and Lindy, consider this your notice of termination."

She jumps to her feet, hands clenched at her sides. "You'll pay for this!" she shouts, and I roll my eyes at her cliché parting remark.

Riku grabs her by the arm and escorts her out while she screams profanities at both him and poor Franklin who I can see waiting in the hallway. Thankfully, the door quickly closes behind them, blocking out the sound.

"Holy fuck, that woman is batshit crazy," Molly murmurs into the suddenly silent room. The four of us exchange a look and start to laugh.

"She wasn't always like that," I tell them, and Nana shakes her head.

"No, she was such a sweet girl when we first hired her, and she did a great job. It's only in the last year that she started to change. I think a little bit of the notoriety went to her head. She was Jacinta Summers' personal assistant, and we allowed her access to the Wardrobe and tickets to movie premieres and concerts and things. I think she got a little too big for her boots and over-imagined her own importance." Nana sounds sad about that, but she's always been one of the nicest of us all. Do I recognize that Lindy is in a bad position? Yes. However, I don't see any way that it's not entirely her fault. Plenty of people have spent a lot of time around our family without losing their minds.

"I don't know what happened, but I'm not sorry to see her go. How she thought she was qualified to run a business like Neighpalm Couture, I have no idea. And blackmail? I wonder who put that idea into her head!" I'm still slightly flabbergasted by the whole situation.

"Shall we get on with interviewing the real candidates?" Emma asks, and we all agree. She picks up the phone. "Susie, please have the next applicant come up."

Chapter Thirteen

Jacinta

It takes us a good two hours to interview three applicants, then I need to leave for the press conference Cole arranged.

"Do you want us to wait?" Nana asks as I pack my laptop away, but I shake my head.

"No, don't make them wait any longer. Interview them, send me the recordings with all your recommendations, and I'll have a look over them tonight after I've had dinner with the guys."

"Oh? Who are you having dinner with?" Molly asks, leaning forward to rest her chin on her hands.

"Jace, Alex, and Shane. They invited me when I walked them out last night. I'm going to stay in the hotel tonight, but I'll be driving back out to our place tomorrow so I can keep working on Willow Castle."

The three women exchange conspiratorial glances. "That sounds lovely, dear. They're such good boys." I roll my eyes at Nana's approval. Deep down, something in me almost preens at the fact that she's happy with my potential choice because it means that I can probably trust it, trust *them*, but I'm not ready to think about that too seriously at the moment. "But make sure you take Riku with you."

"I will. I promise." I lean down and give her a kiss on the cheek before giving Molly and Emma the same. I'm smirking as I walk away because that surprise kiss was enough to get them all to shut up about my dinner date. Sometimes I even amaze myself.

As quickly as I can, I go back to my office so I can have another hit before the press conference. I've been doing okay, but I could feel the nerves and anxiety building the closer the clock hands ticked toward twelve-thirty. I only make it a few steps before I hear someone call out my name. Fuck, I don't have the time or energy to deal with Rowena, but I don't want to invite her into my room, so I pivot and go back to her door.

"What is it, Rowena? I'm kind of in a hurry. I have to be downstairs for a press conference in about ten minutes." I'm leaning on her doorframe, not wanting to step in in case she delays me too long.

"I saw Lindy dragged out of here before. What

happened?" she asks. She's likely just fishing for information since there's this look on her face that almost seems like she already knows, but I answer anyway.

"Lindy tried to blackmail us into giving her the traineeship CEO position. That's extortion, so Nana called the police." She blanches, hunching in on herself like she's afraid some kind of hit is going to come at her next. Unfortunately, I can't really fire someone for being a pain in the ass, so she's safe for now. If she tries to pull any shit like Lindy did, I will gladly have her escorted out too.

"Oh okay, wow. She said she was going to do that. I tried to talk her out of it, but she was determined." For the first time, she sounds unsure of herself. I guess that's what happens when her only support gets taken away. I sigh before throwing her an olive branch.

"Look, Rowena, I think Lindy might have set you on a little bit of a rocky course. She never had as much influence around here as she implied, and it kind of seemed like she may have steered you in the wrong direction. You wouldn't be working for us if Nana and Harlow hadn't seen talent in your designs, but so far you've presented nothing to Molly, Emma, or me for consideration, and you've been downright combative. Why don't you take the next week to assess if this is what you want or not? If it is, you have to prove to us you have the drive and the ambition. If you're able to get some things together, I will make sure that Emma and Molly take the time to sit down and have a look at what you've got."

Her eyebrows jump in surprise. "You'd do that for me? I haven't exactly been the nicest person."

"Trust me, I haven't always been a nice person either, and it took Harlow coming into our lives and my family giving me an ultimatum to realize I need to do better. This is my chance to do that, and for you to do that too."

"I'd like that, thank you. Is there anything in particular you'd like to see?" she asks, and that gets me thinking about the cute little boy I met this morning and the idea I had over the weekend.

"How do you feel about children?" I ask her. She looks startled at first, then a smile spreads across her face, turning her from an uptight snob to a friendly, approachable woman.

"I love them. I have five brothers and sisters, and they all have children. I have lots of nieces and nephews."

"Well, with all the pregnancies yesterday, it got me thinking about how we may be shortsighted in not hitting the childrenswear and maternity markets. Would you like to have a go at designing a line of both of those?"

Her eyes widen in excitement, and she moves from her desk to her drafting table. "I would love to. I actually draw things for my nieces and nephews in my spare time, and I'm sure my sisters and sisters-in-law would love to give me input on what they found comfortable during pregnancy." She opens her sketchbook, and her pencil flies across the paper.

"Great, I can't wait to see what you come up with. I'll set an appointment for next Thursday. That gives you ten days to get something organized, and if you want to make a mock-up of some of the designs, feel free to head out to the workshop and play around."

She stops and looks up. "Thank you, Jacinta, really. Lindy told me I needed to be catty and nasty to get anywhere, but that's really not me. I feel sick that I played along with her games. I appreciate you giving me a second chance, and I'm sorry for yesterday's comment. Can we chalk that up to too much champagne and a devil on my shoulder telling me I wouldn't be good enough unless I was mean?"

"Seems like getting rid of Lindy is benefitting both of us. I'll see you later."

I leave Rowena happily sketching and race to my room. Riku will be up to get me any moment, and I need to be ready. I can't have another employee catching me with drugs.

Chapter Fourteen

Jacinta

The press conference was horrible. So many invasive questions and sly remarks from paps looking for an even juicier story than the one we gave them. Come on, how much juicier can you get than murder, kidnapping, and inheritance drama? I'm absolutely exhausted once it rolls to a close.

"Are you coming home now?" Jaxon asks as we leave the media room, his hand firmly in Harlow's.

"No, I've got a few more things I need to get done here, then I'm having dinner with Alex, Shane, and Jace." I push the button for the elevator as Riku and Harlow's security quietly step up behind us. They're so good at being unobtrusive that I would forget they're there, except Riku puts off this calm strength that I'm really drawn to.

I see them exchange a smirk in the elevator mirror as we step in. "Well, that sounds lovely," Harlow says, but as we start to move, I see the color drain from her face.

"Are you okay?" I ask when she puts a hand to her mouth and groans.

"No, morning sickness isn't strictly on time for me." Thankfully, we slow to a stop, and as the doors burst open on the Records floor, Harlow blasts past a startled Holden. She only makes it as far as a potted plant in the corner before we hear the sound of violent retching.

My brothers exchange a look as I hold open the door.

"Not it," they say in unison, and Hope huffs and rolls her eyes.

"You two fucking suck. If you're adult enough to put a baby in her belly, you're adult enough to hold back her hair while she pukes. I know neither of you actually mean that. Get over there and help her," she says, pointing in Harlow's direction. She's now slumped down against the wall, and I can see the receptionist looking at her in shock before her eyes narrow in suspicion. My brothers hurry over, with Holden grabbing a bottle of water out of the mini fridge we keep for our clients. Harlow's security guard steps out too.

"She ate something funny at lunch," I call over to the woman, which gets me a totally unconvinced raised eyebrow. "You better deal with that," I tell Hope, nodding at the secretary.

"Fuck, why can't people just mind their own business?" she asks. When she hurries away, leaving me on my own, I step back and let the elevator close. At least that gets my family off my back. Now it's just me and Riku in the elevator, alone. I lean back against the wall, closing my eyes.

"Are you okay, Ms. Summers?" he asks, and I crack open my eyes again.

"What did I tell you, Riku? Call me Jacinta, especially when it's just the two of us. I'm tired. Today has been a bit much," I tell him as the anxiety and nerves creep back in. We leave when we get to the Couture floor, which is quiet once more. Susie waves as we pass, but I don't stop to speak to her. That's not my job anymore, and I couldn't be happier. I just want to sit down and draw. Rowena's door is closed when we pass by, and Jace's office is empty. Where has he been all day? Do we just keep missing each other? When we get to my door, Riku stops me with his hand on my arm. He makes his way into my office first, coming back out to wave me in once he's sure it's empty.

I pause with my hand on the handle. "What do you do while I'm busy?"

He smiles and pulls his phone out of his pocket. "I have the kindle app on my phone, so I sit in reception and read until you need me."

I feel my eyebrows jump in surprise. "You like to read?"

He chuckles. "Don't sound so surprised, Jacinta. Lots of people like to read."

I feel my cheeks pinken again, and I want to slap myself. "I know, but… You just have this air of coiled violence about you. Like a spring waiting to be sprung, deadly when need be. I guess I don't imagine you sitting still long enough to read." I know I'm not very elegant about it, but he seems to understand what I mean.

"So much of being security is sitting around and waiting, same with surveillance jobs. Stakeouts are all about patience. Reading is one of those things that's easy to do while we wait. Simon does crossword puzzles or plays games on his phone, but I enjoy delving into a good story. Some of the other guys will clean their weapons or play cards."

"Awesome, maybe we need to compare kindles one day." I can't believe I just offered to share my kindle with him. Fuck, talk about putting my foot in my mouth. If I follow through on that, he'll see all of my books are mommy porn with questionable kinks.

"I'd really like that."

Without saying another word, I wave and go into my office. It's only once I close my door that I realize that while I'm with Riku, none of the anxiety or nerves or insecurities eat at me. I just feel like I can be myself. There's no need for an act, playing the part of wealthy heiress or fashion mogul or anything fake. I'm just me, and it feels glorious. But now that he's gone, the press conference slams back into me—all those shouted questions, the barely veiled innuendos, the speculation.

"Is it true that the Summers family has had a falling out?"

"Why didn't you all celebrate your birthday on the weekend at Club Neighpalm?"

"Jacinta, are you upset about your brothers being in a relationship with Harlow?"

"Harlow, aren't you afraid your promiscuous reputation is going to affect the opening of your sanctuary?"

"Does instability run in both your families?"

One of them in particular plays over and over in my head.

"Only one body was found. What do you think happened to your father?"

It's the ten-billion-dollar question, isn't it? Because, of course, if Dragos was around, our inheritance would go to him. So where is he? Are we going to find another body somewhere on the grounds of Willow Castle? Not all of the enclosures have been explored yet. As surprised as Julia was that his body wasn't in the vault, how far could he have gotten with bullet wounds?

I feel my teeth grinding together as I pace back and forth across the room. After that shit show, I have no desire to draw or create anything, but I can't go home because I promised the guys I'd have dinner with them.

Collapsing onto the chair behind my desk, I open my handbag, grabbing my phone to call Jace and cancel, but Riku's sister's business card falls out. Picking up the pretty pastel green and pink card, I flip it over so I can read what it says, and my lips lift in a smile. *Bun in the Oven.* It's cute. Maybe I just need to do some shopping. I've got four babies to shop for now, and what better way to ease my anxiety than some good ole retail therapy? Especially retail therapy escorted by tall, dark, and handsome. Getting up, I take my handbag, leaving my laptop and portfolio on my desk. I'll grab them when we come back.

Making my way back to the reception area where I know I'll find Riku, I spot Jace, finally in his office for once, so I stop for a moment. Leaning against the frame, I watch him at his drafting table, brow furrowed in concentration, lip trapped between his teeth. His pencil flies across the paper beneath it in long swooping arcs followed by short furious coloring. He stops and reaches forward to grab a sample of fabric from the other side of the table and finally notices me there. A slow smile lifts his lips, and his mismatched eyes sparkle behind his black frames.

"Well, hi there, darling, I've been wondering if you've been hiding from me." He drops his sample and pencil and stalks across the room to where I am. "I thought we might have scared you off last night when we shared how we feel." He pulls me into his arms and dips me in a big show of enthusiasm that has me giggling before he kisses me and raises me back up. It all happens so quickly that I get disoriented for a moment.

"No, not at all," I tell him breathlessly, my hands against his chest, his arms still wrapped around me. "I've had meetings all morning and a press conference."

He grimaces and gives me a quick hug. "I saw the headlines today, and when I arrived, the press had lined the streets. They were even in the parking garage. Shane had to wait for security to come and get me before I left his car."

I shrug. "That's the good thing about the helicopters, no press." I pull away and drag him over to his desk. "Show me what you've been working on."

He looks at me carefully before he decides to throw me a bone and accept the subject change. "I just got back from a fitting with Hayden Christie, and I found some inspiration while we were talking. Have you met her before?" he asks as I look over his new sketch.

"Yes, one or two times. She's really lovely, which can be rare amongst the elite models."

"Her son Spencer was there, and he is freaking adorable. I had to take in the dress in a few places, and he wanted to be my assistant, so I let him hold my pin cushion. He told me all about his goldfish and that his daddy is Batman."

"His daddy is our new PR guru Cole Chambers," I tell him as I run my finger over the gorgeous lines of the dress, not meeting his eyes, before picking up the piece of fabric.

"Oh really? What's he like? Shane was saying he's pretty cool, but I want to reserve judgment until I've met him."

"Yup, he referred to Hayden as his ex-wife, but they sure seemed cozy when they had lunch today." When I look up, Jace is staring at me, his mismatched eyes feeling like he can see all the dirty things that Cole did to me on Halloween.

"Hm, well, that's interesting," he muses.

"This is really gorgeous, Jace." I quickly go on before he can probe any more. "I can't wait to see it made up. Listen, I need to run. I have somewhere to be, but I will see you later. Five o'clock, right? That's when Shane said he'd be here?"

I back out of his room, not waiting for an answer. The downside of spending so much time with Jace on our trip to Prague is that I feel like he can see inside me. That he instinctively understands what I'm feeling, which I know is just plain ridiculous. But I might avoid that stare just in case because I'm not ready to share anything with him about Halloween. I don't want him to be disappointed in me.

I stride across the foyer, calling to Riku, who is

exactly where he said he would be, sitting on the reception sofa. "Come on, I need to get out of here."

"Jacinta!" I hit the button on the elevator just as I hear Cole call my name. When I spin around, he's leaving the conference room with Nana and his little family. Nana is holding Spencer, tickling him. "Do you have time now to go over those appearances?" he asks, but I wave my hand.

"Sorry, Cole, I've got another appointment. Just schedule something with Susie, and she'll let me know." Riku joins me as the elevator opens, and we both step in. When I turn to face the front, I see Nana frowning at me, but the doors close before she can say anything. I let out a sigh of relief and slouch against the elevator wall.

"Everything okay?" Riku asks, his quiet voice super loud in the silence of the elevator.

"No, Riku, I'm afraid it's really not, but I don't want to talk about it."

"Okay then. Want to fill me in on where we're going?" he asks, no judgment in his tone, just mild curiosity.

"I need to do some mindless shopping, so would you mind calling your sister and asking her if she would close her shop down for an hour or two? I'll make it worth her while." I'm practically begging him. I cringe at the sound of desperation in my voice, but his eyes soften, and he pulls out his phone, making the requested call. He has a quick conversation in what I'm assuming is Japanese before he hangs up.

"They're looking forward to your arrival," he tells me, and I can't stop myself from reaching out and grabbing his arm.

"Thank you."

He looks down at my hand on his arm and shakes his head. "It's no problem. I can't imagine it's easy to be you, especially in light of recent events. If you don't mind, I'd like to send out the limo in the hope that the press will follow it. You and I can take one of the other cars."

"Good thinking. In fact, how about I message Hope? She has a friend who owns a club. Maybe she can tweet something about me being there. An heiress's day drinking is bound to catch their attention and throw them off our trail." I pull out my phone and shoot Hope a message. She assures me she's on it and will get it sorted.

Thankfully, when we arrive in the parking garage, it's clear. Security must have thrown out the press Jace had mentioned, so it's an easy walk to a nearby sedan with tinted windows. Riku opens the backseat for me, and I climb in before he gets into the driver's side.

"It takes about half an hour to get there from here. Why don't you rest your eyes for a moment or two?" he suggests, looking at me in the rearview mirror.

"Could you put on some music, please? Something soothing?" I ask him. The car is filled with the sounds of something classical, and I feel the tension drain out of my body.

"Jacinta, if you don't mind me asking, are you going to be coming into the office tomorrow? It's Simon's day, and I need to tell him where to meet you."

"No, we will be heading back home in the morning. Why do you ask?" I feel my brow wrinkle, a little confused by his questions.

"Oh, you said for Cole to set something up with you tomorrow." I snort, more at my intended surprise for Cole than Riku's confusion.

"Yeah, I was blowing him off. If he can't give me the details of the appearances I need to make, I have an excuse not to go to them." I close my eyes and lean my head back as he smoothly maneuvers the car out of the building and into traffic.

"Okay, we're happy to run interference if you want," he offers, and I crack an eye open.

"Thank you for the offer. I may just take you up on it."

Chapter Fifteen

Jacinta

The peaceful ride to Bun in the Oven is just what I need to get my head on straight again. When we arrive, Riku parks near the back of the store in the staff parking so we can enter through a back door. He goes first to make sure his sister has cleared it like she promised, and it's not long before I hear him calling me.

"What are you doing, you idiot? You can't call her Jacinta. It's Ms. Summers," I hear a female voice hiss at him, and I don't bother smothering the grin that breaks out on my face. His sister speaks to him like I do my brothers. It warms my heart. God, I just get all the feels from family moments.

"It's fine. I asked him to," I reassure the petite Japanese girl as I step out from behind the curtain that blocks off the stockrooms from the front of the store. Riku is standing with her and a blonde woman. "There are three of us, so it just made more sense for him to call us by our given names. It would be confusing if my sisters were in the same room as me. Hi, I'm Jacinta." I offer a hand to the girl, who startles in surprise, but she recovers and grabs it to shake.

"Jacinta, this is my sister and her wife, Aimi and Lacy Andrews."

We exchange greetings and niceties, but my attention is torn away from the women. "Oh my god! This is amazing." I see the two women exchange a grin as I take in the riot of color and texture. "I was expecting the typical sterile baby store with whites and pastels, but this is something else."

The storefront is huge. It's separated into sections, kind of like Ikea, with full nursery setups in each themed area. From where I'm standing, I can see a circus, zoo, music, sports, and vehicle themes, but there are many more to be explored. Each one is an explosion of color with options that cover everything, from wallpaper and vinyl stickers to rugs and bedding.

"Tell me about all of this," I demand, and thankfully, they understand what I mean. I didn't mean to slip into my bossy voice, but I'm just so excited and want to learn about all of it right now.

"We only stock a small range of the major ticket items a baby would need, so cribs, strollers, changing tables, and feeding chairs. There are only a couple of options," Aimi explains before Lacy takes over.

"We personally tested everything when we were deciding on inventory and asked ourselves why we would buy things we didn't like. In our store, all of the major items come in black or white base colors. From there, you can go crazy with your theme because, let's face it, that's the fun part of having a baby. We have fifteen different themes on display and another fifteen options available to look at online." We walk over to an ocean display as Lacy tells us more.

"Everything you can see has been designed by either Lacy or Aimi," Riku adds, sounding proud as punch of his sister. It's so fucking cute and just makes him even more attractive that he wants to show off what his sister has accomplished.

I push my finger at a mobile, making it move around, watching the various fish and other sea creatures dance back and forth. "How am I ever going to decide on what to buy my family members?"

Oh shit. I spin around and look at Riku for help. I just told two complete strangers, not bound by confidentiality, about our family expecting babies.

"It's okay, Jacinta. Lacy and Aimi know how to be discreet," he reassures me, and the two women nod their heads.

"Of course we do. Nobody will be hearing from

us that you've been shopping here. We can even put an alias on your order so that none of our shop assistants know either." Aimi sounds quite fierce about it, which helps me relax again.

"Well, okay then. For now, I need to outfit two nurseries. Shit, I don't know anything about babies. Would you put two in the same nursery? Or would you have one for each of them if you're having two babies?"

"That's okay. That's why we're here to help. We've got years of experience and a child of our own. So, twins?" Lacy heads back to the checkout desk and picks up a notebook and pen.

I bite my lip, still not entirely sure I should be sharing this sensitive information with these two women. I can see security cameras throughout the room, and I'm worried about the footage.

"Look, if it would reassure you, we would be happy to sign NDAs. Would you like to get your lawyer to send them over to us?" Lacy asks, and Aimi gives her brother a little push.

"Go and turn your cameras off too, please. That might make Ms. Summ—Jacinta feel better."

"No, it's okay. I trust you, and if this goes well, I may have a proposition for you." Their business would be the perfect place to sell our maternity clothes and childrenswear. We could even help them with expanding if they decided to grow their business.

"Oh, you've got your business face on. That's

how Lacy looks when she's making plans." Aimi waves her hand between the two of us. "Like two peas in a pod," she teases.

"Not twins." I return to the previous subject. "My brother is expecting a baby with another woman. I expect you will read about it in the gossip columns eventually, but we've kept it very hush-hush for now. Basically, the woman took a used condom and artificially inseminated herself with what was in the bottom of it." The two women exchange a horrified glance.

"Are you serious? That sounds like something out of a soap opera." Lacy sounds disgusted, and I think Aimi is speechless, which are both totally appropriate ways to feel. I'm pretty sure I went through both of those stages before I accepted that this would actually be part of our family history now.

"Welcome to the life of being a Summers. It gets worse. She's been accused of attempted murder and will go to jail for a very long time, but they want to wait for her to go full term so that she doesn't do any harm to the baby. She's due in three months, and my brother Kai will get full parental rights."

"Okay, baby one." Lacy writes down. "Boy or girl or not sure?"

"A girl," I tell her, and she makes a note.

"And the second baby?" Aimi asks. I can see

she's dying to hear the rest, but not in a gossipy, want to share with the world kind of way.

"My sister Harlow."

"Who's not your blood sister and is in a relationship with all six of your brothers," Aimi continues.

"Yes, that's right." I brace myself for the judgment, but there is none. Just cool and casual acceptance, which is so refreshing.

"I don't know how she does it. One is enough work for me," Aimi says.

"Hey!" Lacy objects before the two of them start to giggle. "So your sister is pregnant. How far along?"

"Only a month, I think."

"Okay, we don't know what sex either, and there's going to be a seven-month age difference. To be honest, I would put them in separate nurseries. If they were twins, I'd put them together, but a newborn may disturb a seven-month-old's sleeping pattern, and I tell you, *never* fuck with a baby's sleeping pattern." The other two nod along with Lacy's advice.

"So I'll need two of everything then," I think aloud. "And let's give Kai's baby a Hawaiian-themed nursery. Harlow's can be all about zoo animals. Is that okay?"

"Yes, it's freaking perfect. Let's show you what we've got." Aimi tucks her arm into mine and drags me over to the furniture, Lacy following behind.

"Are you coming?" I ask Riku, and he smiles and shakes his head.

"My sister will probably skin me if I get in the way. I'll make us some coffee on her fancy machine out back."

I don't get a chance to reply before Aimi's dragging me toward a wall with cribs. "About time you made yourself useful. Grab the baby monitor, would you? Your niece is due to wake up from her nap soon. When she does, can you get her?"

Riku salutes his sister and picks up a monitor from the counter before he heads back out the way we came in.

"She's going to be so excited to see her *Oji*. You should see them together. They are *so* freaking precious," Aimi tells me, her eyes sparkling with mischief. "He's going to be such a good daddy one day. He's a good provider too, owns his own business, looks after his body, doesn't smoke, do drugs, or drink to excess."

"Jesus, Aimi, settle down. You sound like your parents trying to sell him off to the first woman who comes along. Jacinta might already have a boyfriend!" Lacy scolds her wife, but she raises an enquiring eyebrow, not at all repentant.

"Ah… well… I…" How do I get myself into these kinds of situations? You know what? Why should I feel guilty? "Actually, I have three potential boyfriends I'm having dinner with tonight."

"Three? At the same time?" Like her brother,

there's only honest curiosity in her voice. I'm finding the entire family to be very open-minded so far. There's something about both of them that makes me feel like I can be open—up to a point, anyway.

"Well, I think that's what they're hoping. They're in a three-way relationship." I can see her thinking about it, then I hear Lacy mutter something.

"Now you've done it."

"Well, good, what's one more in the grand scheme of things? You should consider adding Riku to your harem! He has to go away on business sometimes, so having brother-husbands will probably work well for him. He won't worry while he's away." Aimi stops in front of the cribs and starts rattling off specifications like what she just said is a done thing.

"Just go with it for now. She'll be distracted soon enough," Lacy whispers out of the side of her mouth. "I love my wife, but she's flighty as fuck."

And with that little piece of advice, I spend the afternoon shopping for the impending arrivals. I didn't grab anything for Molly, Emma, or Melinda yet, but I asked if they would be willing to shut the shop down again so I could bring the three of them in, and they assured me they would be delighted to.

I really felt like I had made two new friends by the time Riku and I left. His three-year-old niece, Kiko, was so put out when we announced we had to go, she clung to him like a koala. He promised to call her and wish her good night. We exchanged hugs all around, and as we walked out, Aimi extracted a promise from Riku to bring me to dinner one night. Despite Lacy's assurance Aimi would forget, she was still firmly wearing her matchmaking hat when we walked out the door.

T he drive back is quiet once more. I think Riku can tell I'm a little overwhelmed with everything we achieved, but I'm so freaking happy with my purchases. I can't wait for everything to be delivered to Willow Castle.

Riku breaks the silence first. "I'm really sorry about my sister. She's just so happy, and she wants me to have the same thing." Aimi wasn't shy about talking up her big brother, but what she didn't realize is that she didn't need to. I already see his appeal. I just don't know how that's going to fit in with what I'm starting with the other guys. Or if he's even interested. He didn't shoot her down, but maybe he was just being polite.

"Don't be. I loved her and Lacy, and Kiko is adorable. Your family is lovely."

We fall into silence again until we pull into the underground parking, and my phone beeps. It's a message from Hope, assuring me the decoy plan went perfectly. The press is currently surrounding her friend's club, hoping to get a shot of me day drinking. It's such a relief to be out without needing to constantly look over my shoulder.

"Jacinta, you know I have to escort you to your dinner tonight, right?" Riku asks, and I sigh.

"Yes, I do. It's okay. I know everyone is just trying to keep me safe. Hopefully, some new scandal will crop up so we can fade into the background."

Riku is silent for a little longer, but then he continues. "Jacinta, you're a very wealthy woman now, even more so than before, and your father feels like you need to have a full-time security team permanently. If you're not happy with my company, I can make a couple of recommendations to him, giving you the chance to try out someone else."

I sit there for a moment, absorbing what Riku just told me. "Why didn't Dad tell me this?" I ask, feeling off balance.

"I think he did, but like you didn't remember meeting Simon and me directly after your kidnapping, I think it might have been one of the other details you missed."

I try to think back to the few days after I escaped. Rushing to the hospital, waiting while Jaxon was in surgery, sitting by his bed, waiting for him to wake up. They were the longest moments of my life, and I really don't remember much of anything. All the voices were like a humming background sound, so I guess it's no surprise that I did miss it.

"Are you okay?" Riku asks as he pulls the car into a space and turns it off. He turns around to look at me, his brow creased with worry.

I examine how I feel, but there's no annoyance or anger, just a sense of relief and acceptance that I'm going to have a buffer against the world everywhere I go.

"Riku, I am better than okay. You have no idea." I lean forward and grab his hand, squeezing it.

"And you're okay with me and Simon? If you want someone else, you can meet any of the others on my payroll," he offers, but I shake my head.

"No, that's okay. You two are fine. If that changes, I'll be sure to let you know."

He nods, relief in his eyes.

"Okay, how about we get out of here? I have a dinner date, and they aren't going to want to wait for my late ass." I drop his hand and hop out of the car, but I swear I hear him say something about waiting forever for an ass like that. He puts his hands on my back, escorting me to the elevator like a gentleman, and we make our way upstairs.

RIKU

L eaving Jacinta with my sister and her wife, I grab the baby monitor off the counter and head out back to make coffees for everyone. Thankfully, my sister's machine is one of those where you put a pod in and press a button. Even the milk frother is automatic, so I fill it up and turn it on. While I'm waiting, I look around the staff room. My sister has half a dozen people working for her, but she sent the ones that were here home for the day.

The sound of her squeal when I announced we were coming was still ringing in my ears after I hung up.

Aimi is a little bit of a gossip hound—nothing malicious, she just likes to read about who's doing who as she puts it. She'd never gossip about a client.

Speaking of clients, I've become increasingly worried about Jacinta over the month I've been working for the Summers. She was fine as long as she was at home or at Willow Castle, but the minute she was expected to appear in public, I could tell something was wrong. Simon and I had to physically help her from the awards ceremony she attended. The woman was halfway drunk before we even arrived. How she managed to walk in those heels and present an award without stumbling or giving away the amount of alcohol she had consumed is beyond me.

By the end of the night, she was a mess. Luckily, there was no press around to see the Summers' princess completely hammered. Then there was her birthday. She and Hope stumbled out of their club early on in the evening. We had been briefed that they would be staying late, but without eyes inside, I have no idea what happened. To me, it looked like she was coming down from something other than alcohol, but I can't know for sure.

At her birthday, she seemed perfectly happy surrounded by family and friends, so maybe I was imagining things. I was curious at the end of the night, so I discreetly followed her outside with her friends. Although it isn't technically part of my job like I told her it was, I guess I wanted to see a little more of what their dynamic is. There had been plenty of flirty touches between the four of them, but I was also under the impression that the three men were a throuple.

To say I was a little surprised when I overheard their conversation is an understatement, but as I watched each man embrace and kiss her, I felt my cock harden. Instead of being disgusted, I was turned on and intrigued when I heard them tell her that they wanted her to turn their throuple into a quadruple.

After they left, I had scared her, and she automatically went on the offensive, accusing me of being judgy. I defended myself, but it made me think about what her life must be like, always worrying what other people think or how they perceive her. Not actually allowed to live her life as she wants without having to carefully weigh everything she does. I can understand why their family is so close. Never knowing if you can trust a person is your friend for the right reasons must be exhausting.

I can't deny that Jacinta Summers intrigues me. She's certainly wrapped up in a gorgeous package, all long, slender limbs with a womanly body. That long straight hair that I imagine draping across my thighs as she runs her tongue up my cock. Fuck! I can't think like that even though I've seen the mutual interest in her eyes. I want to wrap her up in bubble wrap and keep her safe from the world. I see the insecurity that hides behind her bravado. The utter relief when I told her my sister was waiting with an empty store was like a weight had been lifted off her shoulders. Knowing I could do that for her, I felt like the king of the world. I think I might be in trouble.

A noise on the baby monitor jolts me out of my thoughts. "Mama! Mama!" I leave the machine and rush into my sister's office where she has a pack n' play set up. My niece is leaning against the side, and when she sees me, her eyes light up.

"*Ojisan!*" she squeals in a high-pitched voice while holding her hands out for me. I reach in and pick her up. She's a chubby little thing but still weighs next to nothing. I bring her against me and blow raspberries into her neck.

"Yo, chibi chan." Hello, little one, I say to her in Japanese. She giggles and wiggles.

"Down! I need to go potty," she tells me, so I walk toward the attached bathroom. Placing her down, I watch as she pushes a little plastic turtle step next to the toilet. She wriggles her underwear down and climbs up. "See? I a big girl now." She grins at me while she pees, then I watch as she struggles to grab toilet paper and stay on the seat. She wobbles, so I go over and hold her in place as she wipes. "Thanks, *Ojisan*," she says, giggling. She jumps down, flushes, then pushes the turtle over to the sink where she climbs up and washes her hands. She can't turn the faucet, so she asks me to do it.

"Wow, you're such a big girl now! You've grown so much since I saw you," I tell her after I wash my hands too.

She claps her hands and jumps down from the turtle.

"I miss you, *Ojisan*." She wraps her arms around my leg, and I just about melt. This little girl has my heart. I bend down and pick her up. "Come on. I'm making your mommies and my friend coffee. How about we read a story when I'm done with that?"

"Yes, yes, yes!" she cheers, so we head back out to the staff room. While I finish making coffee, she picks a book. She's occupied, so I quickly run it out to the three of them before returning to my niece. I manage to keep her distracted for about an hour until she demands to meet my friend. I was a little unsure how she would get along with Jacinta, but to my surprise, they're drawn to each other. Not only did the heiress pick my niece up, she carried her around and let her "help" pick things out.

I watched on with amusement as Jacinta carried her around, taking all of her suggestions very seriously.

When Aimi tried to stop her, Jacinta insisted, "What better way to get the right things for a baby's nursery than having an expert pick?"

Although Kiko didn't really understand, she beamed with pride.

When we left, my sister was in full matchmaking mode, but I'm afraid I'm going to have to let her down gently. I can't be seen fraternizing with the client, much to my and probably her disappointment.

Our conversation in the limo as we headed back to Neighpalm Industries was good progress for our relationship. Jacinta actually understands the importance of security. I can't deny I was relieved when she insisted that Simon and I stay her guards... Maybe a little too relieved. Only time will tell if I'm making a mistake. I just hope that it's not something that's going to bite me in the ass.

Chapter Sixteen

Jacinta

We take the elevator directly up to Couture, and when we step out into the lobby, I stop suddenly. So suddenly that poor Riku isn't able to keep up. He plows into me, causing both of us to stumble. His hands come up to grab me so I don't fall over, but my heels make me unsteady. Instead of my waist, where I think he was aiming, he ends up with his hands cupping my tits. Once we're stable again, I need to process that fact before looking up at what made me stop in the first place. Jace, Shane, and Cole are just standing there together. Jace is hiding a smirk, that asshole, but Cole and Shane look just as surprised as Riku and I probably do.

"Good catch," Jace says, not hiding the laughter

in his voice, and Riku springs away from me like I'm a bomb about to explode.

"I'm so sorry," he quietly mutters. "It was *not* my intention to grope you." When he steps up next to me, I can see how flustered he is, and both Shane and Cole start grinning too.

"It's okay, best bit of action I've had in months, so I should be thanking you," I say breezily, which makes Cole's smirk drop into a frown. *Yes, she shoots and scores!* "I'm sorry. Were you waiting for me? I'm afraid my appointment ran over."

Cole crosses his arms. "Would that appointment be drinks at Club Chaos surrounded by your sycophants? Seriously, Jacinta, do you crave attention so much that you need to be drinking during the day?"

"Hey, man, that's uncalled for." Riku steps forward, holding his hand up at Cole, but I stop him before he can go any further.

I sneer at him. "Well, Cole, if you really were good at your job, you would have checked your sources and the legitimacy of the claims."

"My sources are impeccable. I use them all the time."

"Your sources are ripping you off if you're paying them for their services. Where's the proof? Do you ever ask for it?"

"I trust them." With a scowl, he steps toward me, the movement aggressive, but I'm not going to let him intimidate me. I step up to him so that we're chest to chest. Both of us are breathing heavily, the rest of the world fading away as my anger for this man blocks out everything else.

"Well, you shouldn't, because I wasn't anywhere near Club Chaos, and I most definitely haven't been day drinking unless you count the coffee Riku made me."

"Where were you then? We have to go over these appearances I've booked."

He's seriously not going to apologize for his assholeness? Alright, let's do this. "You mean the appearances you booked without checking with me first? And I don't see how it's any of your business where I went." We're practically yelling at each other now, and I give him a little shove, but he quickly gets right back in my face again, his own voice rising.

"It's my business because I'm the one who is going to have to clean up after your messes."

An arm pushes between us, and Riku maneuvers me backward when Cole doesn't seem to take the hint.

"How about you back off Ms. Summers," Riku growls at Cole.

"Whoa, whoa, hey now, let's all settle down a little bit and take a moment." Shane pulls Cole to the side, furiously whispering in his ear as Jace joins me and Riku.

"Are you okay?" Riku asks, his concern clear.

"That man just makes me fucking furious! He's as bad as everyone else, assuming the worst of me."

"Yeah, that wasn't cool, but you didn't have to

go all Xena warrior princess on him either. He's just doing his job," Jace says. His tone says he's scolding me, but he says the words lightly enough that I can't find it in me to hold it against him.

"Not very well," I mutter.

"Okay, now that we're all calmed a little, how about we get moving? We can finish this discussion over dinner. Alex decided to try his hand at cooking, and he'll kill me if I don't get you back in time." Shane looks between me and Cole pleadingly.

"He's coming to dinner too?" I can't hide the surprise in my voice, and Cole smirks. I just want to smack that smug ass smirk off his fucking face, and I feel my hand curl into a fist.

"Yep, Shane and Jace invited me just before you arrived. We haven't caught up in ages, and I told him I was looking for you, so he said we might as well kill two birds with one stone."

I can't help the feeling of hurt that slams into my chest. I thought it was just going to be the four of us, and Riku, of course, but that can't be helped. Now, they've invited the man who knows things about me I really don't want to share.

I look at the two men in question. Shane's face is annoyingly blank, but Jace winks at me. Okay, another person I want to smack. Riku grabs hold of the hand that's curled into a fist and pulls me toward my office.

"That sounds fine. Jacinta just needs to grab a few things from her office. Maybe the three of you should go ahead, and I'll drive Jacinta over. That way we don't need to catch a cab to the hotel later."

My bodyguard needs a fucking raise. He read the room perfectly and diffused the situation in one go.

Jace's face falls in disappointment, but I'm annoyed at him right now. How dare he make assumptions? Sometimes dislike is just dislike.

"So we'll see you soon?" Shane calls after me. "Please, Alex will kill me."

"Yes, Shane, I will be ten minutes behind you. I promise," I call back, not turning around.

When we step into my office, Riku closes the door. I throw my arms around him and hug him tight.

"Thank you." I exhale into his chest as his arms slowly come up to hug me back.

"Is something going on with you and Cole?" he asks into my hair, and I sigh before pulling away. "Because that seemed overly emotional compared to what you're like with the rest of the employees."

I step away from him and walk over to my desk. "Can't I just dislike the guy?"

"You can, but I think there's something more. Both of you seem particularly volatile when you're around one another. Do you two know each other from a previous encounter?"

"I slept with him on Halloween, not knowing who he was. He also caught me snorting coke." The words rush out of me like a dam has broken open.

Fuck, did I really just admit to the coke usage? I can't even look at Riku.

"Oh." His voice rises in surprise, so I'm definitely not looking at him now. Then the unexpected feel of his hands on my waist has me turning around to face him. He has this wrinkle of worry in between his dark eyebrows, and his lips are slightly pursed. I kind of want to kiss them, but I hold myself back.

"Well, okay, let's break this down. Did you enjoy sex with Cole?"

Huh? Not what I thought he was going to say. "Yeah, it was mind blowing, but he's a fucking douche canoe, and now I'm his boss."

"But you're Jace's boss too, and you're considering sleeping with him."

"Damn you and your logic, Riku," I growl, pushing away from him and going around to the other side of my desk, needing a little bit of space between us. I can't think with him just there. "And technically, I'm occasionally Shane and Alex's boss too. But I don't know. I was friends with the three of them first. Cole and I went from zero to a hundred in point two seconds. Not to mention he's not a very nice person."

"Let's table that for a moment. What about the coke? Is that a party thing or something else?"

I refuse to look at him because I don't want him to see the truth in my eyes, though that's probably going to give it away within itself. "It was a one-time thing, a small rebellion on my part. It was nothing," I lie through my teeth as I gather up the couple of sketches I was looking at earlier in the day and shove them into my portfolio. "Come on. I don't want to be late and get Shane into trouble with Alex. Somehow, I don't think this evening is going to go quite how I thought it would. We may need a secret signal to leave."

"Okay, well, as long as that's all it was. You don't want to go down that slippery slope. It's a hard one to come back from, trust me. Why don't you just breathe, Jacinta? You're wound so tight. Try to enjoy your evening and think before you jump down Cole's throat," Riku suggests. I hand him my laptop bag and portfolio while I grab my little pink handbag.

"Fine, but he better as well." I hear him sigh like he's dealing with two wayward children. I mean, he's not far off, but there's something that just makes the two of us act like that. Is it mutual attraction, or is it just disdain?

The guys' penthouse apartment is warm, bright, and inviting when we arrive. "Something smells delicious," I call out as the elevator arrives on the top floor.

"I'll wait down in the car for you. Message me

when you want to leave," Riku murmurs, stepping back into the elevator as Alex hurries across the entry.

"Nonsense, I made enough for everyone, Riku. I was expecting you to join us." Alex comes to a halt, and he runs a lazy eye up and down my figure, a smirk on his lips. "I don't know about everyone else, but I'd rather be eating this one up. You look delicious." He swoops in and kisses me, paying no mind to the fact that Riku is right there. It's quick and intense and leaves me wanting more, but before I can respond, he has me by the hand and is dragging me across the room. "What would you like to drink? I've got wine, beer, and liquor. There's also some juice or soda if you don't want anything hard."

When we step into their living area, I get a chance to look around. It's this wide-open space with plenty of windows, a comfy-looking seating area, and a kitchen/dining area.

"There you are!" Jace exclaims, waving excitedly from the couch as Shane and Cole watch on. All of a sudden, the attention of five different men is on me, and I feel a little bit flustered.

"I hope we didn't keep you waiting." The apology is automatic, even though I know we didn't.

"Not at all." Shane stands up and comes over to me. "Alex was just about to put everything on the table. Why don't I show you where you can wash up?" He leads me down a corridor. "You had a deer in the headlights look going on. Are you okay?" he whispers.

"Yeah, I'm fine. I guess I'm not used to being the center of attention."

He opens a door and flicks a light switch on. We step in, then he makes sure I'm looking at him. "Jacinta Summers, you are the center of attention wherever you go. Surely having the attention of five men is no different," he jokes, but when he sees my frown, his smile slips.

"That never means anything. This is different, very different, and I don't know where I stand. With the paparazzi, it's easy. I know what they want and how to act. Here, I'm at a loss."

I can't believe how easily I bared my soul to this man. The words just flowed out, and I see when he finally comprehends.

"I'm sorry about inviting Cole. It didn't occur to me that you two might not be friends. Cole's a great guy, and I thought it would be nice for us to catch up. But I also messed up because this was supposed to be about us convincing you to consider taking our friendship further. Him being here messes with that. So let's put that aside and have a meal between friends—no pressure. I'll give you five minutes, and if you don't come back out, I'll send Alex to get you," he threatens with a smile, and I quickly agree. I like the way he takes control of the situation. Having even one less decision to make feels like so much more has been removed from my shoulders.

He comes closer and kisses me gently, like they're trying to get me used to the affection, and I'm not going to complain. "My bathroom is just through there. Help yourself to anything you need, then come back out and join us."

When he pulls the door closed, I look around the room. It's a large bedroom done in gray, black, and white with a huge bed in the middle. On the wall are photographs in black frames, and it smells just like Shane. It's neat and tidy and exactly what I thought his bedroom would look like, but the mirror on the ceiling has me pausing. I can just imagine what it looks like to see the three of them rolling around on this bed and what it might look like with me included.

Shaking off that thought, I push through a door, hoping it's the bathroom and not a closet. Thankfully, I got it right. Much like the bedroom, this is decorated in silver, black, and white. A large shower dominates one corner with a separate toilet and a large vanity. I study myself in the mirror. I'm still not thrilled with what I see, which seems to be happening a lot these days. Guarded, tired eyes stare back at me. Just one day at the office, dealing with all the press, is enough to exhaust me. I'm so glad I'm back home again tomorrow.

"Come on, Jacinta, get your game face on. You can do this. A little flirting and conversation with some sexy men, no pressure. Just be yourself. They're your friends first and foremost, and that is the most important thing. Real friends who want nothing from you."

My gaze slides to my handbag with the knowledge that the little baggie of coke is in the bottom if I need it, but I don't reach for it. Instead, I grab a face cloth out of the cabinet and run the hot water. Running it underneath, I proceed to take all of the makeup off my face. Next, I pull out my sleek pony and finger comb my long dark hair before sticking it up in a messy bun, sighing as the pressure on my skull is relieved. Bending down, I tackle the straps of my shoes, removing both of those. There's nothing I can do about the rest of my clothes, but maybe I can find a pair of sweats in Shane's drawers. So I leave the bathroom, my shoes hanging off a finger. Dumping them on the floor, I try the other door and step into the closet soaked in Shane's signature fragrance. I'm not sure what it is, but it's sexy and heady, and I sway at the smell of it, breathing deeply. I rustle around in a few drawers before I dig out a T-shirt and a pair of sweats with a tie in the front. Going back into the bedroom, I strip off my pencil skirt and top, as well as my bra, leaving me in just my panties. I quickly replace my clothes with his before adding socks as well. It's all way too big, but I feel more comfortable than I have in weeks.

I can't put it off anymore. I have to head back

out there, so I place all of my things neatly on Shane's bed, not wanting to forget them later. Smiling to myself, I head back out, wondering how they're going to react. The rumbling voices of the five men roll down the corridor as I walk back to them. The sound of their laughter is actually comforting, and it brings back some of my confidence.

"Sorry I took so long. I decided to take you up on the offer of getting comfortable. Those clothes are pretty and all, but not good for relaxing," I announce as I step back into the large living area. All sound stops as the five men turn their attention to me, and I can see some degree of heat in their eyes.

"Well, I've got to say Shane's clothes look better on you than on him." Alex breaks the silent tension and gestures to a spare seat at the table. "Come sit down and tell me what you think of my cooking. I wasn't sure what you'd like, so I made a couple of dishes. I called Mrs. Heyton to get the recipe for your favorite mac and cheese, and I made my special lasagna."

It's only then that I take in the smells of the room and how delicious everything looks. "You did that for me?" I ask, incredibly touched at the effort he's gone to.

"Of course I did," he whispers in my ear as I take a seat on the chair he's holding out. "I'm trying to woo you."

A shiver runs down my back, and goosebumps erupt over my skin as the noise at the table picks up again, with drinks being shared and food being passed around. I moan when the first taste of Alex's food hits my tongue, bringing the table to silence once more, but Jace laughs and breaks the tension.

"Wow, that sounds pretty good. I can't wait to taste it." The words are laden with sexual innuendo, but I don't care. I'm starving, so I dig in as the conversation flows around me.

Chapter Seventeen

Jacinta

Dinner was amazing. It was like the six of us had been friends for years instead of some of us only having known each other for hours. The conversation and wine flowed, and everything was easy. Even Cole put his asshole behavior on the back burner.

"Oh my god, that feels so good." I groan as Jace's thumb digs into the arch of my foot. After dinner, we adjourned to the living room, where the drinks had continued, and we talked about all sorts of things—Shane's upcoming exhibition and Jace's debut show as well as the renovations I've been assisting with at Willow Castle.

"I, for one, have no idea why you shove your feet into torture devices like that every day." Riku has his arms stretched out on either side of him, looking relaxed. He hasn't touched a drop of alcohol, but he reminds me of Harlow's panther Nyx when she's lying in the sun. Watchful and alert but enjoying his surroundings.

"Because they make her ass look amazing… Not that it's not amazing without them," Alex tells him, grinning.

"I certainly don't miss them when I'm at home, that's for sure. I can't wait to get back into my chucks. Declan arranged for all the old Romanian books to be collected from their library, and they're coming to get them tomorrow. I need to be there to supervise. Harlow will be working in the zoo, and the guys will be in the office, so we better get moving. I need to get some sleep if I want to be a fully functioning adult tomorrow."

I tug my foot out of Jace's hand, and he reluctantly lets me go, his fingertips trailing along my foot. "Why don't you just stay here tonight?"

"Thank you, but we should get going. It's late, and Riku still needs to drive us back to the hotel and then home in the morning."

"I thought you and I were going to get together and talk about the appearances I have you scheduled for." Cole leans forward in his seat, frowning, and I feel a little guilty about it now that we've been civil to each other all evening.

"Sorry, I must have mixed up my days when I looked at my calendar. Can we do it over the phone? I'll call you after the book people leave." I give the peace offering, hoping he'll take it.

He gives me a quick nod, but he stays where he is on the sofa as the other four get up.

"I just need to grab my things from Shane's room," I tell Riku, who makes a move to help Alex and Jace tidy up.

I'm just gathering up my clothes, procrastinating on changing, when the door opens behind me. Alex and Shane slip in.

"Oh, look. That was good timing. She's still wearing your clothes." Alex stalks across the room and grabs me by the arms, spinning me so my back is to his front, his mouth at my ear. "I think it's the best I've ever seen your sweats look, Shane, except when they're on my floor." His words tickle me, and my nipples pebble as I feel his hard body press against my backside. Shane studies me, running his thumb across his lip like he hasn't just eaten a huge meal, and I'm his dessert.

"You know, there's something about a woman wearing your clothes that makes a man downright primal. I want to beat my chest and roar about the fact that you're covered in something that's mine." He steps up close so I'm sandwiched between two hard bodies. "Now, I know tonight didn't quite go as we planned," he starts, and Alex snorts.

"You think? I could have killed him when he dragged Cole in, but I guess it turned out for the best. We now see we have a little competition, and, well, none of us like to lose." Alex drags his nose over my ear.

"Competition? Lose?" I'm breathless and distracted when Shane wraps one hand around my waist before circling the other around Alex's. He drags us all together so there's no space between us now.

"Oh yes, that man has his eye on you, and it is *not* strictly in a professional capacity," Shane assures me as he places a kiss on my lips before turning his head and doing the same to Alex.

"And the bodyguard. He's very happy to be guarding your body, but that's okay. I like both men, and goodness knows you're woman enough for all of us." Alex slides his hand up and grabs my chin, tilting my head so he can kiss me too. For a few moments, we exchange kisses, and my heart beats so fast I swear Shane can feel it through his clothes. My knees get weak, and I'm just about to suggest we take this horizontal when, with seemingly choreographed movements, they both step away.

"Leave the clothes on, darling. I like the idea that you'll be sleeping in them tonight if you can't be in my bed," Shane tells me, kissing me on the forehead and quietly leaving.

Dazed and confused, I sink down so I'm sitting on the side of his bed, blinking up at Alex. "What was all that?" I ask, a little annoyed that they got me all worked up. He sinks down next to me and takes my hand.

"Babe, I know you're used to calling the shots, but this time, you're doing things our way. And by the time we're finished, you're not going to be able to form one reasonable explanation as to why this is not going to work. We're going to wear you down, and you won't ever be on your own again. We'll give you a little time to adjust to it all before we dive into the big stuff. We're in this for the long haul, and sex just complicates things, especially if you're having sex with more than one man. So we'll take it slow and ease into this. We want to make a solid foundation because the three of us aren't going anywhere."

"I'm just a little confused about why you think Cole and Riku are interested."

"Babe, you're lying to yourself if you can't see that they are," Alex low-key scolds, but I shake my head adamantly.

"Okay, Riku, yes, maybe, and I feel the same way. There's something about him that draws me in, but Cole? No, I've just met the guy. I know absolutely nothing about him, and he's been antagonistic and aggressive in every interaction we've had!" There's no way I'm owning up to our fiery first interlude.

"So… sparks from the moment you met? Isn't that telling you something? That's pure animal attraction, pheromones and all the rest." He's grinning now, and I want to smack him.

"No, absolutely not."

"The lady does protest too much, I do believe, but that's between you and them. The three of us would be hypocrites to say you can't see where things go with them considering we're all in a relationship as well."

"But—"

He places a finger over my lips. "Come on, let's get your things. Riku is waiting to take you to the hotel."

I nip his finger, but he just grins, so I get up and gather my clothes and handbag. He takes my shoes out of my hands and carries them as we head back out.

Cole gives us a small wave goodbye from the sofa as Shane, Alex, and Jace walk us to the elevator.

"Thank you so much for having us. The meal was delicious, and the company wasn't half bad," I tease the three of them.

"It was our pleasure," Jace says as Riku pushes the button to call the elevator. "We can't wait to do it again."

"Yes, what about next week in Hawaii? There's this amazing restaurant overlooking Waikiki beach that I've been dying to try, and we're all going to be there for the hotel opening," I suggest, already missing these men.

"That sounds great, but I was also wondering if you would attend the Hawaiian Tourism luau with me. They're throwing the luau for all the press that are there to cover their new tourism campaign. Alex and Jace hate those kinds of things, and I was kind of hoping to get you alone for the evening." Shane bites his lip, giving away his nerves. It's kind of exhilarating knowing I can make this man nervous. Right now, the decision and the power are in my hands, but this isn't a decision I mind making.

"I would love to," I tell him, reaching for his hand. "I love a good luau."

"So do I," Riku pipes up, and I roll my eyes.

"Yes, we know you'll be coming too. Is that okay? I don't like to go anywhere without him at the moment," I ask Shane, who nods emphatically.

"Of course, I completely understand."

Alex weaves his arm with his boyfriend's and gives him a little pinch in the side. "What fun! You get two gorgeous escorts for the evening." He winks, trying to lighten the atmosphere, but I'm not upset. Riku is going to be a part of everything I do for the foreseeable future, and I really am okay with it. I just hope they truly understand and won't eventually get annoyed by the permanent third wheel. Fourth wheel? Fifth wheel? I guess it depends how many of us are out at once.

"That's settled then. I'll touch base with you during the week, and I'll let you know the details for dinner. When you get to Hawaii, make sure you ask the front desk to let me know. I'll come find you." I'm a little excited about next week. Maybe getting away and relaxing is exactly what I need to get back to normal.

"I'll go down and start the car," Riku tells me, stepping into the elevator to give us a moment alone. The door closes behind him, and the sexual tension ratchets up.

"We already said our goodbyes before, so we'll let Jace see you out." Alex and Shane both give me pecks on the lips before the two of them go back into their living area, leaving me and Jace alone. As soon as they disappear from view, he pushes me against the wall next to the elevator doors and kisses me hard. I groan before wrapping my arms around him and kissing him back. Our tongues wrestle with each other, his familiar taste bringing a fire to my belly that I'd been missing. I hitch a knee over his hip and let him grind against me.

"God, I've missed you. I can't get enough of you," he mumbles, placing kisses across my cheek and nuzzling my neck.

I run my hands through his hair and yank his head back to my mouth. "More," I demand, then we're kissing and grinding again before we both pull back, breathing heavily. His eyes are hooded, and I can feel his chest heaving.

"I won't be backing down this time, Jacinta. Whatever is going on in your life, we'll work through it together. No more excuses. I've been patient." His voice is low and husky and dominant, and I shiver with his half threat, half promise.

"No, you're right. No more excuses. I want this. I want it all," I tell him. "But let's not rush it. I want to do all the coupley things with you, all of you—dates and phone calls and text messages. Let's not skip all the fun things too."

He runs a hand through his hair and steps back, his sweats tenting with his hard dick. "And making out! Don't forget the making out. Maybe you and I can grab a movie this week?"

I frown and think about being out in public. "What about if we do it in Dad's theater room?" I suggest, and he nods, his eyes shining with understanding.

"Yeah, that sounds awesome. I can't wait. I'll bring all the snacks. This is awesome!" He does a little shimmy. "Once I tell the guys, you better watch out, because we are about to woo the shit out of you." He grins and places a kiss on my hand before I step inside the waiting elevator.

Him dancing across the foyer is the last thing I see before the doors close. A huge grin is on my face, and I do a little shimmy myself.

Bring on the wooing.

Chapter Eighteen

Alex

We leave Jace to get his sugar, heading back to where we left Cole. While Shane takes a seat, I go over to the fridge where I pull out another round of beer for us all. Popping the lids, I dance over to the guys, handing one to Cole first, then to my boyfriend, followed by a kiss, before I flop down on the end of the long sectional and put my feet up next to me.

Shane chuckles at me. "You're in a good mood," Shane says before taking a sip of his beer.

Jace returns with a goofy smile on his face, and I can't say I don't blame him. Jacinta Summers really packs a punch.

"Of course I am! A beautiful woman is agreeing to spend time with us and see where this relationship goes."

Cole's quiet in his seat, but the scowl on his face speaks louder than any words could. He leans forward. "So you're telling me you're asking her to be in a relationship with all three of you?"

"Yeah, do you have a problem with that?" Jace asks defensively, and the answer doesn't make Cole any more relaxed. He stiffens up, and I turn my head a little to the side, trying to hide my smirk. I knew he was interested in her. We just need him to wrap his head around being in an unconventional relationship.

"No, I guess not. I honestly thought she was trying to come between the three of you," he admits, leaning back again and running his free hand through his hair.

"I can see how you might think that." Shane really is the most levelheaded of us, so it's a good thing he's jumping into this conversation. "And I can't deny that women haven't tried that in the past, but Jacinta is well aware that this is an 'as well as' situation and not an 'instead of' situation. A lot of people don't understand that."

"Yeah, I can see how that might happen."

"And you don't have a problem with the three of us in a relationship, do you?" I gesture to my two partners, and he immediately shakes his head.

"Not at all."

"Well, what's one more?" I shrug, and I can see all this new information running through his head. "You know her brothers are in a relationship with one woman. So why shouldn't she be allowed to have the same thing?"

"No, I guess I'm just surprised you'd choose her. She seems so flighty and superficial. I never would have thought she would go for something where she's not the center of attention."

"Bullshit," Jace snaps and stands up. "You've been reading tabloids and made your opinions of Jacinta on what you've read instead of taking the time to get to know her on a personal level."

My eyes widen as our laid-back country boy pokes his fingers in Cole's direction. "Shame on you. You should know all of that is biased. Shit, it's your job to do that kind of thing. Jacinta Summers is the most kind, loving, and genuine woman I know. She generally cares what you have to say. Yeah, she's made mistakes, but she owns up to the fact that what she did to Harlow was horrible. She's only human, and she has her own insecurities like the rest of us."

"Whoa, okay." Cole puts down his bottle and holds his hands up. "I'm sorry, man. You're right. I did let my judgment get clouded. I apologize."

"Hmm, I think maybe Jacinta has caught your interest. I think you can see that all is not as you thought it was, and I think you're intrigued." I rest my chin on my fist and watch as the guy squirms ever so slightly.

"She certainly is one hell of a woman. I

wouldn't blame you for being interested," Shane tells him, smiling.

"Just be aware that if you decide to go there, we're not stepping away. You're welcome to turn the quadruple into a…" I break off and look at my boyfriends. "What's a five-way called?"

Shane chuckles, and Jace shrugs.

"A quintuple?" Cole says helpfully.

"Yes, that." I point my beer at him. "But don't even think of trying to get between us, or I will knock you the fuck out," I finish on a growl, which is totally not my norm. I can't help it though. I want this woman, and I don't want anything threatening that. "And don't be surprised if that quintuple becomes a sextuple. Now, that is something to aim for."

He frowns. "She has more boyfriends?"

"Didn't you notice the way Riku looks at her? I don't even think he's realized it yet, but I can't wait to see what happens there." Jace's quick burst of temper is over, and just like that, he's back to being relaxed. I pull him into my lap and nuzzle into him. I love how he squirms.

Cole and Shane ignore us. "But he works for her," Cole says, and Shane snorts with laughter.

"So do you."

Cole sputters and tries to insist he's not interested, but I do believe the man is trying a little too hard. Next week's trip to Hawaii is going to be so much fun.

Later, after Cole has left and the three of us have climbed into Shane's bed, Jace is pinned between the two of us. He and Shane are kissing while I run my hands over his delicious body.

"We're going to need a bigger bed," he pants out, pulling away from Shane.

"If you can think about those kinds of things, we aren't doing a good enough job," Shane rasps, grabbing his jaw as I reach around and start stroking his cock.

"No, I was just thinking of what it will be like with Jacinta in here too." Jace groans as Shane shifts down and nibbles on his nipples before moving farther down the bed, removing my hand, and replacing it with his mouth.

I reach up and turn him so his neck is strained back, letting me kiss him while Shane sucks his cock. "Think later," I tell him before taking his mouth with mine.

Jacinta

Riku and I are up early this morning, arriving back at Dad's in time for breakfast. He heads to the staff quarters now that I'm safe inside, while I sit and eat with everyone. Nana, Molly, Emma, and Hope pepper me with questions regarding my date while Dad and Poppy quietly discuss something at the other end of the table. I watch them out of the corner of my eye, and whatever they are talking about doesn't look good. Both are frowning and whispering like they don't want the rest of us to hear.

"We're going to follow you over to Willow Castle today," Emma tells me, drawing my attention back to them.

"Oh, you are? You're not going to work?" I can't say I'm not a little surprised since they both take their temporary position so seriously.

They exchange a loving glance. "No, your dad has asked us to move in here, and we've accepted it. There's no point in waiting, so we're going over to our cottage to start moving things."

"That's awesome!" I jump up and give them both hugs. I think they're both a little surprised, but they return them. "I was going to give him a week before I started nagging him. Now, do we need to arrange a remodel to the master suite of his wing?" I think about what Dad's side of the house looks like.

"He's way ahead of you. He's going to have a wall knocked down and turn the bedroom next to his into a closet for the two of us and the bedroom next to that into a nursery. Since the babies should be close in age, they can share one." Emma still looks a little shell shocked when she says the word *babies*, and there's a hint of worry in her voice too.

"Is everything okay?" I ask them, reaching for her hand. "I guess this is all so sudden. It must be a shock to you both." Emma sighs and shrugs, looking at Nana who instantly clues into the situation.

"Speak freely, my dear. Brad might be my son, but he's still a man, and we know what idiots they can be."

"Emma is worried that Brad wouldn't have asked us to move in if it wasn't for the babies. She feels like we're doing much the same as Veronica is to Kai, albeit unintentionally." Molly grabs Emma's other hand and gives it a squeeze.

Nana and I exchange a glance before bursting into laughter. The two women look a little pissed, so I hurry to get myself back under control. "Sorry, I'm sorry. I know this is no laughing matter, and you guys have a right to your feelings, but let me tell you something about Dad. He is happier than I have ever seen him before." The look of disbelief isn't hard to see on their faces. "No, I promise I'm not lying. Dad puts on a good show, but I swear there has always been this air of sadness to him. I really think he loved Harlow's mother, and she broke his heart. I didn't ever think he was going to get over her, but the two of you have managed the impossible. His smiles are full and real, and he is over the moon thrilled with the fact that both of you are pregnant."

"Brad always wanted a big family. It's why he

adopted all the kids when he was told he wouldn't have any biological ones. He is capable of so much love, and despite how the pregnancy happened, there is no way he thinks you trapped him. If he thought getting you pregnant was possible, he might have insisted on using protection for your sakes, but if he wasn't happy, he wouldn't have asked you to move in." Nana takes a sip of her coffee, giving them a chance to breathe and hopefully .absorb what she said. I, however, jump back in. I made my brothers' journey to happiness that much harder, and I'll be damned if I don't atone for some of that by helping my dad find that too.

"You two are the best thing that's ever happened to him, and I hope you feel the same way about him."

"God yes." Emma's sigh is wistful and relieved. "I love that man like crazy."

Molly nods enthusiastically. "Yeah, neither of us thought we'd ever be in a relationship with a man again, but all it took was the right one. And now we're having babies! I tell you it was a bit of a shock to go from knowing there was no chance of either of us naturally getting pregnant to both of us peeing on a stick and it showing up as positive. But despite it all, I'm thrilled."

"Well, that's settled then. You're thrilled, Dad's thrilled, and all of us are thrilled." The four of us laugh. "Do you two need help moving?"

They shake their heads. "No, Brad is going to

come with us. Most of the furniture will stay in the house, so we're just going to bring a few personal items," Emma explains, and Nana leans in.

"You two will be the ladies of this house now, which means if you want to change anything, don't be afraid to speak up."

"But what about—"

Nana doesn't even let Molly finish her sentence. "I only decorated this house for Brad. I am quite happy in our suite in our wing, so you need to make this house your home. Living here will probably take some adjustments on all your parts. It has always worked for us as a family, but if we find it is not working, then Howard and I can move out. Jacinta and Hope can do the same thing. There is plenty of land on this property and enough places for us all to build large houses."

I feel a small pang of disappointment. I love my house and had always dreamed of raising a family in it, but of course things change, and I need to learn to adapt. My therapist would be so proud of me, knowing that I'm not throwing a tantrum or plotting to ruin someone's life.

"Oh god no. This house is way too big for us. We love that everyone lives here. We want all of you to stay. There's more than enough room for all of us."

"Are you okay with the McCallister brothers taking up one of the floors in our wing?" Hope's been quiet this whole time, but I guess that's on her mind now. "Because it will be no problem to tell them they have to live somewhere else."

My mouth drops open in shock at her vehemence while Nana, Molly, and Emma exchange a conspiratorial look. I know that one, and I'm glad the focus is all on Hope at the moment.

"Oh no, we wouldn't dream of putting the poor boys out! They're working so hard to get Harlow's zoo up and running as fast as possible, and they need somewhere comfortable to relax at the end of the day."

Emma nods, supporting Molly's adamant words. "Yes, and what better place than here? It's practically a resort with the theater and the indoor pool and the hot tub."

Hope grumbles quietly enough that I can't make out what she's saying.

"Now, dear, I know that you've had your problems in the past, but why not give them a chance?" Nana pats Hope on the hand, and Hope grimaces.

"What, just like they gave me a chance when I was kicked out years ago? No, I don't think so. Harlow's zoo can't be finished quickly enough."

"But then they're working on the amusement park, *and* they're going to do the changes to our wing," Emma points out helpfully, and Hope growls again before standing up.

"Maybe I should have kept my apartment in town. It looks like I'll be staying in the city more than I'll be coming home." She storms off in the direction of the kitchen, taking her empty coffee cup and plate with her.

"Oh dear." Nana watches her go with a sad look on her face.

"Don't worry about her. She'll be fine. They just need to get it all out. Hopefully it will come to a head soon so the five of them can hash it out. I would say just leave them be and work through it in their own time, but I know you better. Just be a little more subtle than you usually are. Hope won't thank you if you force them down her throat. They hurt her big time." How I'm the voice of reason in this situation, I have no idea, but I hope the women listen to me. I want my new sister to be happy too, but I think she's going to need some time to want that for herself—as far as those brothers are concerned at least.

Chapter Nineteen

Jacinta

Apart from the four people packing up all the boxes in the library, Willow Castle is quite quiet today. The movers all seem to be happy doing their thing, sticking to the "public" parts of the house, so I'm not really needed.

Simon is watching me today since Riku is having a day off. I was a bit disappointed about that, but Riku deserves time off. It's unrealistic to expect him to spend all of his time with me. I *am* just a job, after all. I leave Simon to keep an eye on the movers, not wanting them to wander the house, and take off to do my own thing after I assure him I won't leave without letting him know.

There are so many rooms in this house that it's easy to lose track of them, so today I'm going to do a walk-through with my phone and notebook and make notes of everything's status. I need to know what's done, what still needs work, and what we might have forgotten in all the craziness.

I'm on the second floor in one of the mistress rooms, mid-morning, when I hear a helicopter outside. I can't see the front of the house from this room, but I'm assuming it's landing on the property since they cleared a space for it. One of the guys must have come home early today. I'm sure whoever it is will find me if they need me, but they'll probably go looking for Harlow first.

The mistress room needs to be completely gutted since we concentrated on the bedrooms for the guys first. I need to have the furniture trashed, the carpets and curtains removed, and the room repainted. I'm hoping there are hardwood floors under these carpets. Most of them have been, but you never know with old houses. I'll have them polished and get some throw rugs to go in here. Stepping out of the room, I walk down the corridor to the next door and push it open. It's a room I haven't been in before. I was expecting another bedroom, but it's a cozy sitting area. It has fancy chaise lounges and uncomfortable-looking chairs, but there is a huge picture window over-looking the lake at the back of the house and a fire-place that would make the room super warm in winter.

"Well, this is nice. I think I just found the perfect playroom for my niece." I run my finger along the chaise before taking a seat in one of the little armchairs. "But this furniture has to go."

"Did you know talking to yourself is the first sign of being crazy?" The voice at the door has me screaming and throwing my phone at the intruder.

Cole ducks, so my phone hits the wall and lands at his feet. He chuckles as he bends down to pick it up, but my heart is racing and my breathing is labored as I try to get myself under control.

"Fuck, Cole! You scared the shit out of me." My voice is trembling in an obnoxiously obvious way, and his chuckle dies off.

"Shit, I'm sorry. The people downstairs told me you were up here. I thought you might have heard me coming."

"No, I was lost in ideas. I didn't hear a thing. What are you doing here? I thought it was one of the guys coming home." Now that I have some semblance of calm, I'm curious as to why he's here.

He comes over, holding out my phone for me. "I'm here to go over those appearances with you," he says, and I feel a wave of fury wash over me. I thought maybe, just maybe, he was here to see me, but of course he's all business.

"What the fuck do you want from me, Cole? Can't you take a hint? I don't fucking want to do any appearances." I stand up and start to storm out of the room, but before I can get past him, he grabs me by the arm and shoves me up against the wall. He pushes his body in close, much too close, and leans down until his mouth is beside my ear.

"Damn it, Jacinta, stop being so fucking selfish. Your family is under fire, so for once in your life, it's time for you to step up and help them. Draw the attention away from your dad and his new relationships and your brothers and theirs. It's time to put on a pretty dress and a vacant smile and draw everyone's attention to you. Get drunk, get caught blowing someone in a closet, have a cat fight, but make sure everyone is looking at *you*."

I struggle in his grip, but he just pushes tighter against me. "Because you're no longer CEO of one of the companies, it won't look as bad as all of the past press. They will see a rich, bored socialite and lose interest in what the rest of the family has going on. Hopefully, this will help Neighpalm Industries weather the storm that's coming."

"Storm? What storm?" I sneer at him. "We've had some bad shit happen to us. Anyone else would have crumbled under the pressure my family has been under, but we've come out the other side stronger than ever."

"Don't be stupid, Jacinta. Brad and Howard weren't as honest as they probably should have been during that board meeting. You're in a *very* vulnerable position at the moment. A source has told me that Urie Sokolov is gunning for you. He is not happy about being beaten out for NW European Airlines, and he's not happy about the fact that he can no longer return to the States because Thomas exposed him for stealing military secrets. He has combined forces with Diamant Unlimited, and they want to see your company torn down around you. All this bad publicity is just one of the tools in their arsenal."

"Diamant Unlimited? Aren't they that diamond company with rumors of blood diamond trading and ties to the Angolan government? Why on Earth would they be trying to bring Neighpalm down?"

"Having a legitimate tie to America will help them smuggle their diamonds in despite regulations making blood diamond trading illegal. I'm sure Urie made a case for why Neighpalm would be the perfect choice for their Trojan horse."

"How is me appearing in the press going to fix any of that? Surely it will just make it worse." I'm not ready to give up my argument yet, because what he's suggesting makes me feel ill. Contrary to his belief, it's not because I'm selfish. It's because when I think about going out in public, I'm crippled by fear, not that I'll ever tell this asshole that.

"It would be even better if you took on the count's family name too. Then we can have the focus all on you and not on Neighpalm Industries as a whole."

I feel like he just stabbed me in the gut with a knife. *Give up being a Summers?* But he doesn't seem to notice as he keeps talking. "We need a scapegoat, Jacinta, and you're it. While the others get to smile and save puppies and try to generate positive attention to make the public forgive their so-called sins, we need less eyes on them. They can only do so much to help themselves, and everyone loves a new trainwreck to make them forget the last."

"And my family is okay with this? This is what Dad and Poppy want?" I ask quietly, losing all of my fight. Cole must realize this because he eases off me a bit, shaking his head.

"No, Jacinta, they have no clue I'm asking this of you. They wanted to ride it all out. They're confident that this company is strong enough, and with the impending launches of the Sanctuary and Cruise Lines and the new hockey team, they think Neighpalm will generate enough income and positive publicity for the shareholders to be happy. But all of that is still months away, and Urie is buying up as many shares as he can in the meantime."

Time for a last-ditch argument. "Our family owns the majority. He will never own enough to take over."

"But he can make life very uncomfortable for you all," Cole points out. "I just don't understand what the problem is. You've never been shy about being in the spotlight before. I would see you at things all the time, looking pretty and having a blast with California's wealthy and influential."

There's no way I'm telling him the truth, so I roll my eyes. "They grow so tiresome and boring.

But fine, if this is what it's going to take to save our company, you can count on me."

I'm feeling a little less annoyed about all of this now that he's explained everything, especially the fact that this is all his idea. Dad had never used me like this before, and it hurt to think he ordered all of this without talking to me about it.

I push him away, aware we've been pressed against each other for far too long, but despite the uncomfortable conversation, my body isn't uncomfortable at all. It remembers all too clearly what it feels like to be manhandled by this annoyingly sexy man, and it desperately wants more.

He steps away, and I wave a hand. "Come on then. Let's go to my office. We can go over everything you've set me up for, but I'm not promising anything about how long I stay at any of them, and of course my security goes where I do."

I lead him out of the little sitting room and down the hallway. "Sure, of course, I don't want to compromise your safety."

"No, just my sanity," I mumble under my breath.

"This house is really something." I smile at the awe in his voice, glad to let the subject change. "Did you really inherit properties all over the world?" he asks, and I frown a little, but when I look back, there's no hint of greed or envy in his eyes.

"Yeah. Jax and I haven't quite worked out what we're going to do with them yet. I guess one of us should visit and check it out. It will probably be me because he has the new hotel, and he'll want to work closely with the Cruise Line team since it was his idea. Not to mention Harlow, the zoo, and this house."

"I wonder if the other places are as interesting as this one." He stops directly in front of the painting of the count that's covering the elevator that goes down to the vault. "Is this him? I can see the family resemblance with Jax."

"Yeah, they aren't entirely sure if they want to keep the painting of him up or not," I lie to him. The reality is we can't move it until we find someone to paint us something new to cover the secret elevator. Kai had a look at the mechanism and assured me I just needed to find something big enough, then he could swap them out. I'm just not sure what. I was thinking about asking Shane to take a photo of them to put there, but I think we'll wait until the babies arrive. That would be cool. "Everything we're learning about him points to him not being a very nice man. But then it *is* part of our history."

We keep walking until we get to my office. I take a seat behind my desk, thankful there's some space between me and this frustrating man. He takes out his phone and starts to tell me about the various events he's got me booked for.

Most of them are just appearances at parties or being seen at hot spots around town, but I still feel my body getting more and more tense with each thing that I add to my calendar. There's no less than three things a week leading up to Thanksgiving.

"What are all these? Where are you finding them all?" I burst out suddenly.

"What do you mean?" He frowns, looking up from his phone. "These are all just invites that came in through the Neighpalm PR office. They're the same events that you've always been invited to."

I shake my head. "Fuck no, Hope never passed any of this kind of thing on. It was always a blanket no. If we attended anything, it was through personal invitation only—something that was sent directly to me or to my dad. We've never attended any of these publicity generating things. Because you know that's why any of us get invited. The place or people want publicity with their new venture, and they think being able to throw one of our names around will guarantee them press."

"Those kinds of events are perfect for our needs. But if you do decide to do something scandalous, can you please let me know so we can spin our own press on it?" He's not even looking at me, he's swiping across his phone. I snort in disgust.

"Scandalous? Do you have someone picked out for me to be caught on my knees with, or can I pick my own partner?"

He smirks, but it's not friendly. "Come on, Jacinta, don't act all high and mighty. It's just you and me now, and we both know you have no problem with getting fucked by a stranger."

I stand up, slamming my hands down on the desk. "Fuck you, Cole. I've never done anything like that before. Ever."

"You know you're quite the little tease. I bet Shane, Alex, and Jace have no clue what we did, do they? It was all I could do to keep my mouth closed the other night. I bet they wouldn't be so interested in you if they knew that I had fucked you like I owned you."

I grit my teeth to stop the scream from escaping. "You wish. It was all I could do to fake a response," I snap, and that finally gets a reaction other than snarky amusement.

"Like fuck you did." He's on his feet now, stalking toward me. I back away as he rounds my desk, but when I hit the bookcase behind me, I have nowhere else to go.

"There was no faking it when your pussy gripped my cock so tightly I thought it was going to strangle it. There was no faking the way it gushed all over me." Once again, he pushes me up against the wall, and my body shudders with excitement, the traitor. "I haven't been able to get you out of my mind. You were so fucking responsive, and now I find out you're just a fucking cock tease. Playing three other men against each other as well." He slams a hand beside my head, and his fist opens and closes like he's trying to stop himself from grabbing my hair.

"I'm not pitting them against each other! They want to add me to their relationship. We would all be together," I tell him, my anger fading with the building sexual tension.

"Yes, they set me straight after you and Riku left. I asked why they were willing to ruin their own relationship for a piece of pretty ass. Jace just about decked me, but Alex and Shane laughed in my face. Taunted me with the fact that I was just a little too interested in what they were doing with you and how there was room for one or two more in your harem."

I scoff. "My harem, what the fuck?" Before I can argue any more, he swoops down and takes my mouth with his. And just like the other night, I melt against him as he ravishes me. His tongue tangles with mine, his teeth biting my lip. It's an explosion of passion, and it's all I can do to hang on to the bookshelf behind me and enjoy the ride.

Suddenly, he pulls away. "Fuck! What am I doing? Goddamn it." He stalks across the room as I try to get my breathing back under control and picks up his phone from my desk. "Make sure you go to these things, Jacinta, I mean it," he growls before leaving the room.

I'm frozen in shock, but that only lasts a minute before I grab a book off the shelf and hurl it in the direction he went. "You fucking asshole!" I scream, then I hear the sound of feet and the slamming of a door just before Simon appears through my office door, gun in hand.

He surveys the room before he relaxes. "Are you okay?"

"Yes, yes." I wave my hand at him and push off the bookcase. "Just angry at that asshole."

"Mr. Chambers? I'm sorry. He said he had an appointment, which is why I let him in."

"Not exactly, but that's okay. He just makes me mad, Simon. There is nothing to worry about," I assure my bodyguard who shoves his gun back into the holster.

"Okay, just let me know if you need me." He goes back to watching the movers as I hear the sound of the helicopter winding up. I peer out my window, and I can see him sitting in the pilot's seat. He flicks a couple of switches, completely engrossed with doing whatever it is pilots do when readying a craft for takeoff. Of course he has to be a control freak like my brothers. Why else would you want to pilot an aircraft when you could be perfectly happy in the back being the passenger? I flip him off as the helicopter lifts into the air, but he doesn't see it.

"Fuck you, Cole Chambers. You want an out of control party princess? Well, I'm going to give you exactly what you asked for."

Chapter Twenty

Jacinta

Unfortunately, I never get to have my movie night with Jace as the next week passes in a blur of public appearances, cocaine, and alcohol. My anger is steadily growing in a slow burn, but every time I get ready to attend something, my anxiety and nerves take over, and I need to rely on the stimulants to get through the night. I attend a club opening, a movie premiere, and a birthday party for a minor member of British royalty, which is three events too many for my loosening grip on my sanity.

I socialize with the hottest stars of Hollywood, the modeling world, and Hollywood as well as socialites like the Kardashians. Simon and Riku stay close enough to protect me when needed but far enough away that they can't monitor the amount of alcohol I'm consuming.

It's at Lord Lavington's birthday party that I find myself at a table with Selena Cross and Evangeline Masters. Both actresses are represented by Neighpalm Productions. Evangeline is a good friend, but Selena has only been friends with me in the hope of getting in Declan's pants. Even now, although she's aware he's off the market, she's digging for dirt.

"But how can a virile man like Declan be satisfied by a woman who has to split her attention six ways?" She shakes her head as she pulls a bottle of pills out of her bag. I'm just about to snap at her and tell her to fuck off, but the sight of the pills stops me. I guess Evangeline can feel how tense I am because she jumps in to defuse the situation.

"For fuck's sake, Selena. Get over Declan Summers! He's never going to be yours. You should be grateful you still have a fucking job after lying and telling them you could ride. You could have been blacklisted completely."

"Fine, maybe you're right. Maybe I need to set my eyes on someone else like actual royalty." She's looking into the crowd, and I turn to see who she's watching. Lord Ashton Lavington is a fucking sexy man, all aristocratic bone structure and plump lips with artfully styled black hair and dark brown eyes you can sink into.

Again, Evie snorts. "Good luck with that one.

He's a notorious playboy, and the rumor is he prefers peen to pussy."

I drag my eyes away from the man who's surrounded by women and men vying for his attention. Selena shrugs, opening the bottle and tapping out a pill into her hand before popping it into her mouth and tossing back the rest of her cocktail.

She sees me eyeing it, and she blanches. "Just a little X to make this fun. You won't tell your brother, will you?" she asks, and I shake my head.

"No, not if you share," I tell her, holding out my hand. Her eyes widen before she smirks and hands it over.

"Deal."

I start to shake out my own pill, and before I can pop it into my hand, Evie stops me.

"Are you sure? You hate being out of control."

I shrug off her hand and pop the pill into my mouth. "I've got security. They'll look after me." She's still frowning when I toss back the rest of my drink. "Come on, Evie, don't be a party pooper. It's a celebration." Evangeline takes a pill for herself and tosses it back, dry swallowing.

A couple of guys slide into the vacant chairs at our tables. One of them nods at the pill bottle just passed back to Selena.

"Are you in charge of party favors tonight, Lena?" Matthew Shaw, a TV actor who's in one of the hottest teen shows at the moment, wiggles his eyebrows at Selena. He's known for his goofy sidekick characters, but in reality, he's nothing like that. I think he has a bit of a complex about never being the lead man. He tends to overcompensate in his private life. He's regularly in the gossip columns for drug and alcohol fueled benders.

I see Selena sigh with annoyance before handing them over. "Fine, but you need to supply at the next party." He takes one before handing it to his friend. Chase Anderson is another TV actor, but he earned a lead role in a young adult movie, and his star is quickly on the rise. I hope that his best friend doesn't drag him down.

"Where's Anna?" I ask Chase as he pops a pill into his mouth and chases it with a sip of beer.

"She had a night shoot. She's going to come over when she's done." His girlfriend Anna Sinclair is the lead actress on the same show as Matthew.

"Anyway, it's bros before hoes tonight, am I right?" Matthew slings an arm around his friend, lifting his hand for a high five. Chase returns it, albeit reluctantly.

It takes about ten minutes for the ecstasy to work its way into my system, then I'm ready to hit the dance floor with everyone. Selena, Evangeline, and I push our way through some people until we hit the middle of the dance floor. Lord Lavington is surrounded by people, but Selena pushes her way through and starts to dance with him. He looks a little startled, but he grabs her hips and starts to move in time with her. Another of his friends moves in front of her, and the three of them get lost in the music.

"Woo-hoo!" I throw my hands in the air and join in with Evangeline swaying next to me, her eyes closed, a look of rapture on her face. A woman slides up to her, which isn't a surprise since it's well known that Evie is gay. The woman runs her hands over her hips, and Evie's eyes open. She gives the woman a lazy smile before pulling her close. They grind on each other, leaving me with Matthew and Chase.

I don't know how long we've been dancing, but Chase's girlfriend Anna eventually finds us on the dance floor.

"Jacinta," she squeals, "I haven't seen you in ages." She gives me a hug before her boyfriend drags her out of my arms and into his. He nuzzles into her ear, and she giggles. "Did you pregame without me, baby?" she asks, and he whispers in her ear again. She continues to giggle as they make their way over to Selena. Selena passes the pill bottle to Anna, who takes one, and I see Lord Ashton and the other man dancing with them help themselves too.

"The whole gang's rolling now. Maybe it will be an orgy later." The voice in my ear has me jumping and twirling around. Matthew is way too close to me now, and I feel uncomfortable with the way he's leering at me. Chase and Anna return, and she slides in between us.

"Come on. I need a drink. Let's grab one." She drags me off the dance floor and over to the bar before I can respond. The feel of her hand in mine has me moaning, and she shoots me a look.

"Ha-ha, you're rolling really good. I need to catch up." She waves down a bartender and orders us a couple of drinks.

"Thanks for the save. Matthew was just a little too close." I see her grimace before she plasters on a smile.

"Yeah, he can get pretty handsy when he's partying. He also doesn't like to take no for an answer." She mutters the last bit, but it's still loud enough to hear. "Come on. Let's get back to the dance floor. I hate it when Chase goes out with Matthew and indulges when I'm not with him. Matt always gets him into shit. Chase is in a good place in his career, and one scandal could destroy it."

We finish our drinks and make our way back to the dance floor. My body tingles as it brushes across everyone, and I feel light and floaty and amazing. I'm not sure how long I dance for, but when I look around a little while later, I realize I'm all alone. Everyone I was partying with has disappeared. Feeling a little annoyed, I decide to take a trip to the bathroom. The X is still making me feel pretty damn good, so I'm not worried about the come-down yet. Riku and Simon have been invisible tonight, but I know they'll have their eyes on me.

I push through the crowd, enjoying the way skin against skin feels. I kind of wish one of my guys were here so I could grind against them. It's only as I move off the dance floor and toward the bathrooms that I realize I'm being followed. I stop to check my lipstick in a mirror, and behind me, I recognize a familiar face. Camilla Carlos is a renowned blogger, and she never has anything nice to say about anyone. Before I can tell her to leave me alone, a raised voice farther down the corridor catches my ear.

"Get your fucking hands off!" I move toward the sound, all thoughts of Camilla gone. Around a corner, I find Matt pushing Anna against a wall.

"Come on, you know you're a dirty little slut. I see the way you look at me on set. You want a bad boy, not someone like Chase. You want someone who can really give you a good fuck."

He must not see me behind him, because he continues to try to force his hand up Anna's skirt. I consider tackling him myself, but he's a lot bigger than me, so I look around. I find my security not far from me and wave them over. They can't see what's happening from where they are, but the minute they get closer, they spring into action. They tear Matt off Anna and drag him away. I hurry over to wrap my arms around her just as Chase exits the men's bathrooms. "What happened?" he asks, dragging his girlfriend out of my arms and into his.

"Your asshole best friend just tried to cop a feel.

My security is taking him outside now," I tell him, and his eyes widen.

"Oh, babe, I'm so sorry."

She pulls back, still sobbing. "I've told you time and time again, I don't like him! He's gone too far, and now you need to choose. Me or him." She wipes her eyes and storms away while he looks at me helplessly.

"Dude, it's a no-brainer. Even if you and Anna don't last, Matt is bad news. You need to make a decision. Do you want a career and a girlfriend, or do you want to stick with your boy who is just going to drag you down? Be smart." He nods before running after his girlfriend.

Phew, that was some drama. I look around, relieved that Camilla hasn't followed them out. She's perched off to the side, pretending to drink and watch the crowd, but I know she's waiting for me.

Rolling my eyes, I move farther down the corridor until a door pops open in front of me. Turning to the side, I'm surprised to see Lord Lavington in a closet with the other guy that was on the dance floor. Selena is nowhere to be seen, and Ashton is having his fairly impressive dick sucked.

"For fuck's sake, Ash, Camilla Carlos is out there. She can't see you from where we are, but she's moving this way."

Panic appears on his face, and he hauls the guy up off the ground. The other guy is rolling pretty fucking hard and has this dreamy look on his face. "Fuck, I can't get caught in here with him. Help me, please," he hisses to me, and I look around. It's too late for him to leave without Camilla seeing.

Shit. Well, Cole wanted me to cause a scandal. I push into the closet and pull the door closed behind me. It wasn't subtle at all, and I know we only have a few moments before she sticks her head in to investigate. I push the other guy behind some hanging coats, hissing, "Stay here."

He's so far gone he just giggles and rubs against a fur coat. Turning back around, I glare at Ashton. "You fucking owe me," I tell him and get down on my knees. His dick is still hard and glistening with the other guy's saliva as well as precum. Fuck, I hope my guys can forgive me. I lean forward and grab hold of it, making it look like I'm about to take him into the back of my throat. It's hard and thick in my hand, and I feel my pussy spasm with want. Ashton grunts with surprise and looks down at me.

"You don't have to," he whispers. Little does he know how untrue that is.

"Shut up and grab my hair." He follows my orders just as the door opens. Camilla pokes her head around, phone flashing as she takes a picture.

"Hey!" Ashton yells, but it's too late. She's gone, already having slammed the door behind her. Ashton lets go of my hair and grabs for the handle.

"Fuck, she locked it from the outside," he curses as I let go of his cock and scramble to my feet. I'm so fucking horny from the ecstasy that I was actually tempted to wrap my lips around it, and now I'm stuck in this closet with the sexy lord and his giggling friend.

"I'll message my security, and they'll let us out. It might be a while though. They were just taking out the trash." I pull out my phone and text Riku, who responds that he'll be a moment. Matthew caused more problems outside, so he's waiting with Anna and Chase until they get a cab. While I'm texting, Ashton pushes past me to check on his partner. When he opens the jackets, we discover he's fast asleep against the wall. He turns back to me.

"Fuck, that was close. Getting caught having my dick sucked in a closet is bad enough, but a male partner would have sent the tabloids into a frenzy. Thank you for that." He runs a hand through his dark hair.

I shrug. "It was my fault she was there. She was following me, looking for dirt. I guess I gave it to her. How did the door pop open anyway? You would have been perfectly safe if it hadn't."

"That idiot lost his balance and grabbed hold of the handle to steady himself. He wasn't even doing a good job." He sighs, his hand tucking his still hard dick back into his pants. "I'll get him to finish it off once you're let out." He grins wickedly at me in the dim lighting. "But I must say you looked mighty pretty at my feet with my dick in your hand."

I roll my eyes at the playboy prince. "Next time,

find a better spot if you're worried about being caught." I feel a little sorry for the guy. It's got to suck having to keep yourself in the closet for the sake of your family.

The door to the closet slams open, and Riku is standing there. "Are you okay?" he asks, looking between me and Ash.

Ash grins lazily and leans against the wall, pulling out a packet of cigarettes from his pocket. "I'd say she's alright. Had her princess fantasy for a moment," he quips before flicking his lighter to ignite the smoke in his mouth.

"You're an idiot, Ash, and you're going to set fire to the coats." I grab the cigarette from his mouth and step out of the closet. "Are you coming?"

He winks at me and shakes his head. "Nope, I've got unfinished business. Stay safe, Princess Jacinta. Thanks for the save."

I flip him off and slam the door shut, making sure not to hit the latch, though I *am* tempted.

"What was that about?" Riku asks as we head back across the dance floor, his arm on my wrist. I'm slowly starting to come down from my high, and I think now would be a good time to leave before it all becomes too much for me.

"Nothing but me saving an idiot from himself." I grab Riku and pull us into a corner. "Promise me you won't believe anything you see in the tabloids tomorrow. I swear there's more to the story than it looks."

"You mean the fact that there was another set of legs in the closet?" he asks, raising one eyebrow in question.

"Yeah, something like that." He silently nods as we continue across the club and down the stairs to the exit where Simon is waiting next to my car. He opens the door, and I climb in. They both go around to the front, Riku getting into the driver's seat and Simon the passenger. I lean my head back against the seat as we pull out into traffic.

"Everything okay, Jacinta?" Simon asks, and I open an eye and smile at him.

"Everything is peachy, but shit is going to hit the fan tomorrow."

"So we'll need to dodge press on the way to the airport?" Riku asks, and I shrug.

"Probably." I close my eyes again, and before I know it, Simon is shaking me awake as we pull into the valet parking at our hotel.

We get out, and Riku tosses the keys to the valet as we head inside. There is no press out in front of the hotel, but it's three in the morning. I'm not delusional enough to think it'll be the same case when we wake up.

The guys escort me up to my room, searching it before leaving me be for the night. I almost ask Riku to stay, but I don't want to risk him saying no. I'm still wound up from having my hand wrapped around Ashton's dick, so I strip off my clothes and climb into the fresh sheets, moaning at how they feel draped across my body. Sliding my hand down, I make quick work of getting myself off to the memory of Ash's glistening cock.

It's not until I'm done that reality hits me again. Hopefully, the guys will give me a chance to hear my side of the story.

RIKU

Simon and I escorted that scumbag out to the front of the club. He fought all the way, and when we finally let him go, he tried to start something with us.

"Who the fuck are you? Don't you know who I am? How dare you put your hands on me! I'll have you charged with assault," he spits out as we release him onto the sidewalk.

Simon and I exchange a glance, and he chuckles. "You're welcome to try. We were just following our boss's instructions, but if you'd like to take on the Summers in court, you're welcome to." The dumbass pales after hearing that name.

He sneers. "It's none of her fucking business what I was doing." Luckily, the line to get into the club is nonexistent, but out of the corner of my eye,

I notice when someone recognizes him and raises their phone, probably recording what's happening.

My phone signals a message, and my eyes widen when I see that Jacinta is locked in a closet.

"No, but thank goodness for her, you fucking cocksucker." Out of nowhere, Chase slams his fist into the side of Matthew's face, and he stumbles backward with a grunt.

"What the fuck, man? She was practically begging for it. Your little slut is always giving me those 'fuck me' eyes on set. We could have tag teamed her."

"Don't come near me or her again," Chase growls, wrapping an arm around his teary-eyed girlfriend.

"Here, let me grab you a cab," I offer. Simon watches Matthew so he doesn't come at us when our backs are turned, and I wave down a ride for the couple that is happily accepted when it pulls up to the curb. It drives away, its passengers settled in, and I turn back to the drunk and certainly high Matthew.

"Go home and sleep it off. Pray you haven't ruined your career. Doesn't Declan Summers produce that TV show you're on?"

"Fuck him! I can find a job anywhere. I have plenty of offers." Matthew spits at Simon's feet and stumbles away down the street.

"What a fucking douche." Simon shakes his head.

"Hey, can you grab the car? I'll wrangle Jacinta."

He quickly agrees, and I head back into the club. On the way up the entrance stairs, I pass a woman who's rushing in the opposite direction. I could have sworn I saw her following Jacinta before. I'm tempted to stop her and ask questions, but before I can make up my mind, she hails a cab and disappears into the darkness.

I make my way through the busy club and find the locked door exactly where I left Jacinta. Opening it up, I feel my eyebrows jump in surprise when I see her in there with the birthday boy. I don't know much about Lord Lavington, but this seems like a stupid idea. Well, at least he's not my problem—back to Jacinta. Scanning her to make sure she's okay, I notice a pair of legs farther into the closet.

"Are you okay?" I ask, looking between her and the British royal.

Ash grins lazily and leans against the wall, pulling out a packet of cigarettes from his pocket. A flippant comment flies out of his mouth, which Jacinta shoots down, before we leave him to his unfinished business.

She steps out and slams the door behind her, muttering about idiot playboys in the closet.

I grab hold of her arm as we cross the dance floor, noting the way her pulse is racing under my fingertips. That's extremely fast for someone who had just been standing around. I'm pretty sure half the crowd was on some kind of recreational drug tonight, and now I suspect that Jacinta may have been too.

My worry increases, and I decide that I need to keep a closer eye on her because I know how hard it is to come back from addiction.

Chapter Twenty-One

Jacinta

The door to my room bangs open, and I jolt upright in my bed. Disoriented, I grab the first thing I can reach from my bedside table and pitch it at the intruder. Unfortunately, that means my phone goes flying across the room. Again.

"Ow! Fuck." Cole's annoyed voice reaches my ears as I finally shake off the queasy, shaky feeling and rub my eyes to help them focus. When I pull my hands away, Cole is standing in my doorway, rubbing his hand over his chest. I must have nailed him this time. I feel a small sense of satisfaction before my annoyance takes over.

"For fuck's sake, Cole, what are you doing in my room and so fucking early?" His hand has stilled on his chest, and his eyes are locked on me, but lower down. I look down, and a small screech escapes my lips as I haul my blankets up and over my naked tits. I just gave Cole a good eyeful this morning.

Before he can answer, he gets shoved out of the way. Hope comes into the room, waving her phone. "Oh my god! What did you do? You're fucking royalty now?"

I groan and sink back into my bed, pulling the blankets over my head. "It's not what it looks like," I mumble, my head throbbing with my hangover.

"So you're not giving Lord Ashton Lavington a blow job in the closet of Club Quake?"

"God no. Ash is gay. He was in there with a dude, and fucking Camilla Carlos was stalking me when the door to the closet popped open. He begged me to help him, so we shoved the guy out of the way, and I got down on my knees so that it looked like he was there with me. His family would disinherit him. I thought you would be happy, Cole. This is exactly what you wanted," I tell them both from under my blanket.

"Ash is most certainly not gay. He's bi, everyone knows that," Hope argues, and I pop back up, making sure to keep my tits covered.

"Really?"

"Yes, he and Alex used to have a thing. It was one of the worst-kept secrets, but they were discreet enough that there was never any photographic proof. Apparently, it blew up big time at some point." I feel my stomach lurch. That definitely impacts the odds of the guys letting me explain.

"Fuck!" I groan, and Cole is finally able to get a word in over Hope.

"Well, you certainly made a splash. The headlines are huge. There's speculation as to whether or not you're going to be the next Lady Lavington, especially with your fortune. It would be completely acceptable for him to marry you considering I think their family home is basically falling down around them because they're so busy keeping up appearances. Or that's what Camilla Carlos speculates. Fuck, Jacinta, I wasn't actually serious when I said get caught blowing a celebrity!" Cole is practically yelling toward the end, and Hope is staring at him with surprise.

"Ah, dude, you need to calm down. She explained what happened. We'll send out a 'no comment' statement and let people draw their own conclusions. It will blow over soon. Now, how about you get out so Jacinta can get dressed? We've all got a plane to catch."

Hope pushes Cole out of my room and closes the door before throwing herself on my bed. "Wow, that dude is seriously high strung. I've never seen him act like that before."

I groan and throw myself backward again, pulling the blankets up. "Batman," I mumble, and she stops her bouncing.

"I'm sorry. What did you say?" she asks quietly.

"I said Batman."

Hope shrieks and pulls my blanket back. "Just so that I've got everything straight… Cole was Batman? *The* Batman who fucked you so good you were still feeling it the next day?"

I put my hand over my face since she's still got my blanket. "Yes. I had no clue until I met him at the board meeting."

"But he would have known who you were. Your costume wasn't hiding anything."

"Yup, used my name and everything. I don't know how these things keep happening to me."

"Was what you said about Ashton the truth? Because that blur on the photo didn't leave much to the imagination. It looks like his royal scepter is quite impressive."

I push her out of the way and climb out of my bed, going into the bathroom. "Yes, I really thought he was gay, and yes, his dick is huge. I was a little drunk, and I seriously had to stop myself from having a taste. I mean, there was the other guy, and I thought Ash was only into guys, and, well, there's Alex and Shane and Jace." I'm babbling now, and I need to stop before I say anything stupid.

"Didn't the fact that he was still hard with your hand on it tell you anything?" I hear her call out with laughter in her voice.

"He was rolling on X! I figured it was because of that," I tell her as I pee, clean my teeth, and brush my hair. Hope throws some sweats into the room, and I grab them and pull them on.

When I go back out, she's perched on the bed, a small frown on her face as she looks at her phone screen.

"Hand it over. I need to see it. Fuck, I hope Dad hasn't seen it." I look at the picture and curse the advent of decent camera phones. There, in living technicolor, is me at Ashton's feet looking like I'm giving him the blow job of his life even though my hand on his dick is blurred out. In the next photo, both of us look startled. The headline reads "Is the Lord's Lady Actually a Tramp?"

"Fuck." I hand Hope back her phone and pack all my shit into my suitcase.

"What did Cole mean when he said he wasn't serious about you getting down on your knees?"

"Come on, let's go. I'll fill you in on the way to the airport. Or Cole can if he's coming with us since it's his idea. But you have to swear not to tell everyone else."

Hope looks skeptical but agrees. She grabs her suitcase from her room, and we head downstairs, Riku and Simon joining us at the elevator with Charles and Franklin, Hope's security.

"Good morning, ladies." Riku greets us pleasantly enough, but he won't look me in the eye. "There is a fair amount of press in the lobby, so we're going down to the parking garage and getting in the car there. It's parked just outside the elevator doors. Please hand your luggage to the guys. They will take care of it as you two get directly in the car. We've scanned for press, and there don't seem to be any down there, but that might change in the time it takes us to get down there. I'll ride with you in the limo, and the guys will go ahead to make sure we have a clean run to the jet. The rest of your family should be on board or boarding as we arrive."

The elevator doors open to reveal Cole standing there with his own luggage. He nods good morning to the security and moves to the side so we can all get in.

The ride down is quiet, and I chew on my lip, worrying over Riku's less than enthusiastic greeting. Maybe I'm worrying about nothing. I mean, he *is* on the clock. Hopefully, when he hears the full story, he'll understand.

C ole and I explain what we're doing on the ride over. Hope's shocked to hear about the hostile takeover plan, but by the end, she agrees—albeit extremely reluctantly—with Cole's plan.

"I think we should make an announcement in the business pages introducing the new trainee

CEO you selected to intern with Emma and Molly. That'll show that you're distanced from the company. I think it probably wouldn't hurt if we started another rumor where you've had a falling out with the family because they don't approve of your behavior. I can whisper in a few ears and get that started." She taps the side of her head, thinking. "Or we could actually use this to our advantage. We could make it seem like you're in the running to be the next Lady Lavington. Ash would probably go along with it so he can stay in his family's good graces. Then we're dragging the attention off of Neighpalm, but it's not necessarily bad attention. In fact, this could be the best thing that ever happened to us." She reaches for my hand and gives it a squeeze. "I still can't believe you agreed to do this. You *loathe* public attention."

Cole's eyes widen slightly, and I sigh deeply. "But she was always in the gossip columns." He's shaking his head.

"Hardly. Maybe once or twice a month. And you should know better than to believe anything you read, Cole Chambers," Hope scolds. "You know just how the press can be manipulated. We've been doing it for years because she hates going out and being seen as vapid and superficial."

Cole stutters a little bit before frowning. "So why did you agree to this plan?"

"Because, Cole, I would do anything for my family. They have all been through enough recently.

I can't help feeling like it was my fault. All of that happened because my grandfather was a giant dick. If I can make it better, even at the expense of my own reputation, so be it."

He narrows his eyes contemplatively as Hope continues to hold my hand. Riku seems to believe my story, but he's still holding back a little bit. I'm hoping it's just because the other two are around, but he was a lot more relaxed when we had dinner with Cole and the guys, so I'll worry until I get a chance to ask him.

"We're going to have to fill the family in. Otherwise, they're going to think that you're having a mental breakdown after the kidnapping and Jax's shooting. They're not going to like it one bit," Hope warns.

"Please no. Let's just leave it be. We'll explain about the photo, saying I was just doing Ashton a favor, and leave it at that. Please."

"Well, I'd like to go on the record as not liking this at all, but I will keep my mouth shut as long as it works. If it makes no difference, then I will be telling everyone about your horrible plan. You better hope it doesn't cost you your job, Cole. You should reach out to Ashton and see if he is interested in generating some decent publicity. He can be your escort to all the other things Cole has us attending." Hope finishes speaking just as the limo pulls alongside the big plane.

We hop out of the limo, and James is there to

greet us. "Good morning, Jacinta and Hope. How are you this morning?" Even our damn pilot is looking at me with concern, so I just pat him on the hand.

"Made a stupid mistake last night, James. I'm going to blame it on the alcohol. Have you met Cole Chambers? He's our new head of PR." I introduce him as our security gets our luggage out of the back of the car and passes it off to the baggage handlers. Now that the stalker has been caught, we can start trusting all of the staff again.

They exchange a greeting before James claps his hands. "Okay, you are the last to board. If you make your way up the stairs, Jilly will show you to your seats, and we can get this show on the road."

At the top of the stairs is Jilly, my favorite flight attendant and friend. "Hey, girl." She greets Hope and me with a hug before I introduce her to Cole and security. Once greetings have been exchanged, Jilly shows the others to their seats, but I don't have the energy to face anyone at the moment.

"Hope." I stop her before she can follow the others. "Can you tell everyone I'm hungover and sleeping it off? I just can't face everyone right now. Maybe a little later. Give me a couple hours to sleep, then I'll come out and face the music. I promise."

"Fine, but you owe me." She sighs and heads farther down the plane while I move to the master bedroom closer to the cockpit. I just hope Harlow and one of my brothers aren't in it, or worse, Dad, Molly, and Emma.

But when I pull the door open, it's free, so I heave a sigh of relief. Closing the door behind me, I strip off my sweats, leaving on just my panties, and climb into the fresh sheets. The sound and the vibrations of the engines quickly send me to sleep. I probably shouldn't be lying down for takeoff, but I'm truly shattered, and I need a few more decent hours of sleep before I have to face reality.

COLE

I'm completely distracted on the ride to the airport. The memory of Jacinta's tits is all I can see in my mind. If Hope hadn't been there, I would have closed the door and pounced on her. I haven't been able to get out of my mind how responsive she was, and I'm starting to realize that maybe my preconceived notions of who Jacinta Summers is were wrong, which somehow makes her even more alluring.

I can't believe she hates publicity. When Hope said that, I thought she was joking, but no, despite hating being seen in public, she readily agreed to go along with my plan because her family means everything to her. The picture I had of a spoiled, stuck-up, cold princess is nothing like the woman I've seen. She's full of fire and determination, and I love seeing her eyes fill with ire when I walk into the room. I love that I can cause that kind of reaction.

My conversation after dinner with the other three guys really was eye opening. I can't believe that they would be willing to not only share a woman between themselves but also welcome me to have a relationship with her too. I'm not sure how I feel about that yet. Although I'd very much like to get my hands on her again, I'm not entirely sure I could share her. I like my things to be mine. Unexpectedly, there's a little part of me that quite enjoyed watching her with the others. They have such an easy going, tight-knit friendship that I can't help but want to be a part of that.

I don't have a lot of my own friends. Sure, Hayden and I have remained friendly since our divorce, but that was specifically because of Spencer. If he hadn't happened, we probably would have drifted apart, only seeing one another if we accidentally ran into each other. I've been so focused on my career that not only did my marriage fail, but I've lost track of everyone I called a friend. As for family, they're all back home in Wyoming on the farm. My sister is the only one who left, apart from me, and she's still at college. Maybe I need to start working on my personal life so I don't end up growing into a lonely old man. I never thought I'd say it, but I want what Jacinta has—the family, the support, people who love me and actually *want* me around.

The Summers family welcomes me with open arms as the flight attendant shows us to some seating for takeoff. I cannot believe this family. They are so friendly and accepting, and I had expected something completely different—much like I'd made assumptions about Jacinta too. Like Hope said they would, they've made the transition to my new job a piece of cake. I appreciate that they let me do my job without micromanaging me.

"Where's Jacinta?" her twin brother Jaxon asks, looking behind us to see if she's still coming. "What the fuck happened last night? Do you know what's going on, Cole? Those photos looked incriminating."

"Surely they have to be photoshopped," Holden says, drawing my eyes to where he's sitting, next to Oliver of course. It's still a bit jarring to me that they're in a relationship, but Hope gave me the background story. I guess it's taking me a little time to wrap my head around the fact that they were a couple prior to being adopted by Brad.

"Nope." Hope appears, but there's no sign of Jacinta. "Jazzy is taking a nap. She is extremely hungover, and she's promised to explain everything when she gets down here. Go easy on her. There's a good explanation, and she doesn't need you all jumping down her throat."

"Of course we will. We always give the children

enough rope to strangle themselves with," Grace says wryly, and Howard and Brad chuckle.

Harlow stands up. "Should I go check on her?"

"Nope, no time. Please take your seats and strap in." Jilly reappears from the back of the plane. She showed the security guards to another section, leaving me back here with the rest of the family. Hope takes a seat in an empty row, so I grab one next to her as the plane starts to move across the tarmac, taxing out to the end of the runway.

"I'll bring refreshments down once we hit cruising altitude, and I have some muffins and snacks ready for when you get hungry. I'm going to move back and give security a rundown of emergency procedures since you all know what to do. Hope, if you could fill Cole in, that would be great."

The engines start to rev up, and we move down the runway, gaining speed with every yard.

After she's done explaining the safety procedures, Hope leans closer, her voice dropping to a whisper. "Hey, just while everyone is distracted, I want to give you a heads-up. The Summers are a welcoming family and fantastic to work with, but if you fuck Jacinta over, expect to never work in this business again. So, before you do anything else, make sure you're doing it for the right reasons. If you just wanted to say you nailed the heiress, well, congrats, you've done that. Walk away. But if you're genuinely interested, tread lightly, because Jacinta has more issues than you will ever know. Get her to open up to you and learn everything about her if you want to stand a real chance."

"Are you giving me your blessing?" I ask sarcastically, and she shrugs. We feel the plane launch itself into the air, and my stomach lurches slightly before settling back down.

"I think Jacinta needs you. Shane, Alex, and Jace are besotted. They will give her whatever she wants and treat her like she's made of spun glass. I believe you will challenge her at every turn, and you're obviously sexually compatible," she replies matter-of-factly, and I can feel a tinge of a blush heat my cheeks.

Fuck, of course they talked about that.

"I'm not saying you have to marry the girl, and it's complicated because she won't give up the other three to be with you, so you need to be open-minded enough to willingly accept a multi-partner relationship. I figure if the Summers guys can do it, maybe you can too. But be aware this only goes one way. Don't think just because she has multiple partners, you can. That's something the two of you need to talk about, but I can't see Jacinta being the sharing type. That girl loves too fiercely."

I shake my head at the crazy redhead as my ears do funny things thanks to the altitude. "Even if I was interested in something like that, and despite what the other guys insist, Jacinta hasn't shown any interest in me in that way."

Hope chuckles. "Dude, you are fucking blind. You just have to walk into the room, and the sexual tension between the two of you ratchets up."

"Fine, but it's not just me I have to think about. I have Spencer and Hayden to consider as well."

She raises an eyebrow. "So Hayden vetoes all your dates?"

"No, of course not."

"Well, this is none of her business either. You're not endangering your child, and he doesn't even need to know anything unless your relationship starts to go anywhere. And if it does, Jacinta loves kids. I have it on good authority that her guys do too. All it will mean is he has some extra people in the house as he grows up. What's the saying... It takes a village to raise a child. Well, you'd be giving him that."

I'm quiet while I try to equalize my ears. "I'm just not sure about anything."

"You're spending the weekend with us. Take some time to think about it, but be sure. If not, step back. I can run interference between the two of you while this crazy plan plays out. After that, you won't have to deal with her regularly since she's decided to stick to designing—maybe only when it's time for a new line or launch." Hope clicks off her seatbelt and stands up.

"I don't know about you, but I need coffee. I'm going to give Jilly a hand. She's got a lot of people to serve, and she's down a flight attendant because we're a little bit gun shy on that at the moment."

She squeezes past me and disappears toward the front of the plane, leaving me with a lot of things to think about.

Chapter Twenty-Two

Jacinta

A knock on the door has me groaning and throwing the blankets over my head once more. Can't a girl catch a break?

But when the door opens, it's my sister, the nice one, not the annoying pain in the ass that Hope has become. "Jazzy, are you awake?"

"I am now," I mumble back, and within moments, I feel her sit down on the bed beside me. She gently pulls the covers out of my hands and peels them back so I can see her. She's wearing a gentle smile, but I can see the worry in her eyes.

"Hi, I just wanted to check on you. Here, I brought coffee." She passes me the mug of caffeinated goodness. I carefully sit up, not flashing Harlow my tits unlike Cole this morning, and take it. Blowing over the top, I take a large sip and shudder as the coffee and caramel taste bursts on my tastebuds.

"You are a fucking goddess, and my brothers aren't good enough for you," I tell her, taking another large sip, and she chuckles, settling herself in the space next to me. She leaves me alone for a moment, but I know she's just waiting for me to get a little more with it. At least she's giving me that. I would have dived right in.

"How much longer do we have to go?" I ask her, stalling a little longer.

"About an hour. I thought you'd want to get it all out of the way so we can enjoy the rest of the trip."

"How upset is everyone?" I quietly ask, and she turns her body and pats her hand on my arm.

"Nobody is, babe. What you do with your life is your business. If anything, they're furious at that fucking Camilla." She pauses for a moment. "I think they're more confused than anything. We thought you were starting something with Jace, Alex, and Shane."

"So I can only have three men while you get six?" I snap, and she snatches her hand back, the hurt on her face instantly making me feel guilty. I reach for her hand again, giving it a squeeze. "Oh, fuck, I'm sorry. I'm so hungover my head is throbbing. Did Cole and Hope not explain the situation?"

She shakes her head, biting her lip before she

answers, "No, they said you needed to explain to everyone. But don't fucking think that I haven't noticed a change in you." My hand involuntarily tightens around hers. "You've gone out more in the last week since I've known you. In fact, the only events you attended before that were the movie premiere—" I grimace at the reminder— "and the Neighpalm Gala. What the fuck is going on?"

I go to reply, but she doesn't let me. "And you should know better! I don't care if you have three dicks or thirty-three dicks. It's just not like you to risk being caught in public."

She's not wrong. Prior to the kidnapping, I never would have risked something like that. It just shows how much I've changed. Whether it's me or the drugs, I'm not entirely sure, but there was something about getting fucked by Cole in public that made it that much hotter. Even while faking it in the closet with Ash, there was a small part of me that wished it wasn't fake.

"If you give me a moment, I'll get dressed and come explain it to all of you. Then I don't have to tell the story more than once."

She looks at me carefully, and I almost flinch. It's like she's looking into my soul, like she can see how freaking messed up I am inside. But it's only then that I realize she's looking a little pale. "Hey, are you okay? How is our baby? She treating you well?" A rueful smile twists her lips as she stands up, rubbing her flat tummy.

"Baby Jax is definitely making themself known at random times of the day. Thankfully, it's over quite quickly. I've been reading that some women are queasy and constantly sick through their whole pregnancy. I hope I'm not one of them, because I don't have time for it at the moment. At least there are lots of plants that I can emergency puke into at the zoo."

I look at her stomach with awe. Leaning over, I place a little kiss on it and whisper, "Hey you, this is Aunty Jazzy. How about we give your mama a break? Wait until you get out and you can have fun with all your daddies." God, all of these pregnancies are making me feel my own biological clock ticking. Little snippets of golden blonde girls with green eyes or icy blond boys with mismatched eyes pop into my thoughts. Shane taking those children to the park or the zoo. Fuck, I am hungover if I'm having those kinds of delusions.

I sit back and grin up at my sister. "Okay, things are good now. We've come to an understanding." She giggles and leans down to give me a kiss on the cheek.

"Get dressed and get moving. Stop trying to distract me."

"Yes, ma'am." I salute her with my spare hand and quickly drain the rest of my coffee. Putting the cup on the bedside table, I throw back the covers and stretch. Everything aches, so first things first, I need something from my handbag.

I hop up and go over to where I left my basic black bag that goes with everything and search around for some Tylenol. Tucked into a zippered pocket are the few little baggies of cocaine I brought with me. The good thing about a private jet is that we don't have to go through a security checkpoint.

I pop out a couple of pills and grab some water from the attached bathroom. Once the Tylenol has been swallowed, my hair is in a messy bun, and I'm back in my sweats, I can't dawdle anymore, so I take myself out to the lounge area. When I open the door to the bedroom, Jilly must hear because she pokes her head out of the galley.

"Hey, there you are! Are you feeling any better?" she asks me. Jilly is gorgeous, and if I swung that way, I might have made the same kind of mistakes as my brother and slept with one of the flight attendants. But as it is, we've become good friends over the years. I love to hear tales of her various partners and her adventures in other countries.

"Yeah, a little. Another cup of caramel coffee wouldn't go astray though." I lean against the galley as she makes easy work of the small cappuccino machine that's there. "Did we put you and the guys up at the new hotel?" I ask her, and Jilly grins cheekily.

"You sure did, and I *cannot* wait. I haven't spent

any time with the guys recently, and I miss them. So, if you don't see us at the grand opening dinner, don't come looking for us."

"Just stick a Do Not Disturb sign on the door. No one will bother you." I chuckle. "I'm so freaking envious."

She gives me the side-eye. "Oh, from the look of the tabloids, you've been having your fair share of excitement."

"Despite how it appeared, I really wasn't," I mumble as she passes over the cup of coffee.

"Oh, so you just tripped and ended up in a closet with the gorgeous Lord Ashton Lavington?" She wiggles her eyebrows, and we both laugh.

"Yeah, something like that. Thanks for this. I better go face the music."

"They love you, babe. They will forgive any mistakes." She gives me a squeeze on the arm and starts to clean up the mess.

As I walk down the passage to the lounge area, I hear the low-key hum of voices over the engines. But when I step out into view, everyone stops dead.

"Wow, way to make a girl feel comfortable." I flop down on the sofa next to Hope, who's shifted over so there's room between her and Harlow. When I look around, I realize that Cole and my brothers are missing.

"Where are the boys?" I ask.

"They're watching a movie. How are you feeling?" Dad asks. He has Molly and Emma on either side of him, and they look like they might have been doing a crossword puzzle together if the book in Dad's hand is any indication.

"That must have been a mighty hangover." Poppy has a novel in his hand, and Nana, who is next to him, has her knitting out. It looks like she's working on the quilt she's making for Kai's baby. She's the one who passed on her love of knitting to me, but I haven't had a lot of time for it lately.

I groan and slide down a little more, taking a larger sip of my coffee. "I may have made a few mistakes last night."

Hope snorts. "A few?" Harlow smacks her on the back of the head.

"Can you message the guys and get them down here? I've already explained what happened to Hope and Cole, so I only want to explain one more time."

Harlow does as I asked, and within a few quiet moments, the guys all make their way into the lounge area, finding places to sit or stand. Oliver leans in, giving me a kiss on the cheek.

"You dirty lucky wench. Ashton is delicious." Of course, he has no indoor voice, so Harlow hears, delivering him a smack to the back of the head. "Aw, babe. I'm allowed to look! I mean, we probably should vet who our sister is having sex with. You know that my heart lies with you and Den."

Holden and Harlow both roll their eyes, but neither are upset.

"So, you want to explain what the fuck happened?" Declan, my control freak big brother demands, his arms crossed as he leans against a wall, frowning at me.

"Dude, calm down. I'm sure she has a perfectly acceptable excuse." Kai, the peacemaker, waves his hand at Dec.

"She fucking better," Jax growls, and I wince. I love all of my siblings equally, but there's a part of me that is programmed to care most about what my twin thinks. When he looks at me with anything like he is now—disgust, anger, or disappointment—my heart just hurts. There's no other way to describe it.

"Guys, she's an adult, and what she chooses to do in her private life is her own." Thomas sits at Harlow's feet and leans back against her legs. Her hands drift down to his hair, running her fingers through it.

"Yes, but *private* is the key word in that statement. Not splashed all over page one." I flip Declan off, so not in the mood to deal with one of his tantrums.

"Like I fucking meant for that to happen!" Before I can say anything else, Cole jumps in.

"Look, why don't you let her explain before you all jump down her throat?"

Holy shit. Did he just stick up for me?

"Cole's right. Tell us what happened, Jazzy," Emma quietly coaxes.

I explain exactly what happened, leaving out the reason I was partying in the first place since Cole and I agreed we wouldn't tell them what we were doing. By the end of the story, they're all laughing except Dec.

"Fucking Camilla is a pain in the ass. Always trying to paint us in a bad light." He's got his growly voice on. "Can't we sue her for something?"

"Well, with evidence such as that photo, I don't think we have a leg to stand on," Hope points out dryly.

"I'm so sorry. I know we're trying to look better for the shareholders. I really was just helping out a friend."

"Of course you were. Poor Ashton, having to hide his sexuality. His grandmother is a real dragon. She's all that's left of his family since his mother died just after he was born, and his father drank himself to death. Poor dear was raised by nannies and that monster." Nana sighs. "That estate of theirs is falling down around their shoulders. She's been trying to marry him off to a wealthy family for years. Although she threatens to disinherit him, he already has the title, and the estate goes with the title, I'm sure she's guilted him enough over the years that he may believe what she says is true. But she's actually living there on his good nature."

"Bullshit. He doesn't hide his sexuality at all.

He's just usually very careful. There's no photographic proof of anything with any male partners. There's plenty of him with women."

"I don't know. I recognized that look of panic on his face when he thought he was going to get caught. He wasn't faking it," I say, arguing with Jaxon. I'm not sure why, but I feel protective of Ash. I can kind of relate to the whole pretending to be someone I'm not thing.

He shrugs. "Well, he owes you after that. It doesn't hurt to have him owe you a favor."

"Indeed, but be careful. That grandmother will probably set her sights on you now. You are wealthy in your own right and have a title yourself. You're exactly the kind of woman she wants him to marry," Nana warns as the guys take their leave and return to their movie for the rest of the flight.

"Yeah, well, I hope this doesn't ruin what chance I had with Alex, Shane, and Jace." I look around, not wanting to admit to my family that we're going to ask Ashton if he'll pretend with me for a while. "Where are the security guys?" I'm a little sad that Riku isn't here, though I don't regret him missing another explanation of the blow job closet fiasco.

"They were watching the movie too. They must have decided to let us have a family chat," Hope explains as Poppy goes back to his book and Dad, Emma, and Molly return to their puzzle.

"Family plus Cole," I grumble, and Hope leans forward to look at Harlow.

"Ask Jazzy how Batman became her favorite superhero."

"You bitch," I hiss out of the side of my mouth before proceeding to tell my other sister about my wild birthday adventure. Minus the coke, of course. I think I'll still keep that one to myself for now.

Chapter Twenty-Three

Jacinta

The manager of the hotel comes bustling out to greet the family on arrival. He and Jaxon put their heads together to arrange our room allocation. Dad, Molly, and Emma, as well as Nana and Poppy, are all here because we're meeting Aunt Merideth for a late lunch. They'll check in at the other hotel after, so their luggage was sent separately.

The foyer is teeming with familiar faces as everyone checks in prior to the opening party the following night. I'm standing off to the side with Hope and Harlow, waiting to be issued my key, when a voice sounds out from the other side of the room.

"Yoo-hoo! Summers family." The slightly British accented voice has me spinning around, a genuine smile breaking out across my face. "Aunt Mer!" I call as we watch the tall, statuesque older woman sashay from the elevators. Her chestnut-colored hair is artfully styled, and the pantsuit she's wearing fits her svelte figure to perfection. My aunt's heels can be heard clicking on the marble floors from the other side of the room.

"Brace yourselves! Incoming," I announce to my family. Poor Harlow and Cole look clueless, but the rest of us are ready for Hurricane Merideth.

"Darlings, you're finally here! I've been waiting so long for you. Oh my goodness, look at you all." She brushes past everyone, her sight laser focused on Harlow, who's standing with Declan.

"Look at you! Aren't you absolutely gorgeous? I am so happy to finally meet you." A wave of her perfume tickles my nose as she gathers Harlow up into her arms, squeezing her tight.

Hope and I can't control our giggles at the startled look on Harlow's face before she returns our aunt's hug.

"Now, did you get my gift? I mean, I'm sure you are perfectly capable of keeping six strapping young men like my nephews interested, but it doesn't hurt to have a few toys to play with too." Aunt Mer's voice carries across the lobby, and Harlow turns as pink as a dragon fruit.

"Oh hush, Merideth, we don't need to share our private lives with the whole hotel. And I'll have you know that our Harlow can indeed keep up with our boys, so much so that she's already carrying their first baby!"

Harlow groans as Nana steps up and gives Merideth a hug. "You're pregnant? That's wonderful." She starts to hug all the boys but stops when she gets to Cole.

"Oh, hello there, you're not one of my nephews." She looks him up and down. "But you are a very handsome man. Who do you belong to?" She bats her eyelids at him, and Cole looks to Dad for help.

"Oh, for god's sake, woman. Keep it in your pants for five minutes. Don't you dare go scaring off our new head of public relations." Poppy drags his sister away from poor Cole. Aunt Mer had been running her hand up and down his arm, and he was starting to look a little nervous. I giggle again, unable to stop myself, and of course she hears it. She spins, and now Hope and I are in her sights.

"Fuck, now you've done it," Hope mutters under her breath.

"Ah, there are my pretty girls! Hope, it's about time they adopted you. I'm so happy I can officially call you my niece now." Merideth gives her a hug before turning to face me. "Oh, Jazzy. You have been naughty, darling. Your technique looked a little lacking. While you're here, you should take a blow job lesson from one of our experts. Maybe that's why you haven't snared yourself a harem like Harlow has." She turns to look at Hope, her eyes narrowing. "I should book you both in with one of our experts."

Before I can reply, Jaxon finally joins us and starts handing out keys.

"Jaxon, dear, there you are. Is everything all organized for our grand opening?" Thank God Merideth gets distracted and bustles off again.

"Thank fuck that woman has the attention span of a goldfish." Hope sighs in relief, and I snort.

"Please don't let that act fool you. She's as sharp as a knife and acts like that so people will underestimate her."

Jaxon hands us all our cards. Hope and I have rooms below the penthouse where Harlow and the guys are staying after the big party. They're doing tours during the opening gala tomorrow night, so they have a suite on our floor tonight. Then they'll move to the penthouse, where they plan on spending the week relaxing and taking a break before returning home.

"Okay, let's all meet in the dining room in half an hour. That gives you time to change into something more appropriate for dining in." Merideth turns her nose up at all of us. Every one of us wore something casual and comfortable on the plane— clothes that are not up to her particular standard. Though Dad and the girls and Nana and Poppy changed before we landed.

We escape to the elevators, and I watch Aunt Merideth zero in on Molly and Emma. Of course they're not going to escape her interrogation. I bet they'll be wishing they could drink by the end of it. I can't wait to see what her reaction is to the both of them being pregnant. She'll probably take all the credit somehow.

Luckily for them, Aunt Merideth hasn't noticed our security following us yet. I pity them when she does, because Riku isn't the only handsome one among them. I'm sure she'll make it her mission to seduce one or two of them before the weekend is over. She does like a younger man.

I've barely been in my room for ten minutes, still trying to decide what to wear to lunch, when there's a knock at my door. I'm only in my underwear, so I grab one of the silk robes and pull it over me before peering through the peephole. My stomach sinks when I see a rather annoyed-looking Alex, with Jace and Shane behind him. They seem to be trying to calm him down, but Alex looks determined. I heave out a sigh and open the door, prepared to face the music now that I know he and Ashton had been intimately involved.

Alex dramatically brushes past me, followed by the other two. "Come right in, won't you?" I mutter sarcastically as I close the door behind them.

Before I can say anything, Alex starts ranting.

"What is this? Are we not good enough for you? Are you playing us for fools? Let me tell you, that man will *never* commit to you. He will never be happy pretending to be straight for anyone, but he won't ever be honest because he's scared to death of that vile grandmother of his."

"Hey, hey, calm down." Shane gathers Alex in his arms and squeezes him tight. "Why don't you give Jacinta a chance to explain? I'm sure she has a perfectly good reason for what happened. Plus, we haven't really established boundaries within our relationship. We never asked her to be exclusive."

Alex sneers. "I kind of thought it went without saying." I can hear the hurt in his words, but I still feel a wave of annoyance.

"Sure, yet here you are encouraging me to spend time with Riku and Cole. So is it only people you're interested in that are allowed in this relationship?"

Alex flinches like I've slapped him. "Those men are completely hetero. There's no interest on my behalf at all!"

"Oh, so it's only men that you approve of then? My wants and needs don't come into this?" He pulls out of Shane's arms, and he and I are chest to chest much like Cole and I were the other day.

"No, but it would be nice to be consulted if you're going to bring anyone else into this relationship."

"And it would be nice to be trusted," I growl back at him.

"Well, short of having your mouth actually wrapped around his cock, you've got to admit the photo is pretty… damaging," Jace points out as he lowers himself onto the sofa in my room.

"How about we all take a moment to breathe?" Shane pushes between me and Alex and has to forcibly move us. I can't deny I'm pissed and breathing heavily, but I let him do it because he's probably the most rational of us all right now.

Whirling, I throw myself on the sofa next to Jace, who smiles and puts an arm around me, pulling me in next to him. I snuggle closer and breathe in his masculine scent, taking a moment to calm down.

Out of the corner of my eye, I see Shane quietly whispering to Alex who relaxes as we watch, losing the stiff frame and the balled up hands. I decide to put him out of his misery.

"If you really must know, I am one hundred percent acting as his beard." I roll my eyes and explain exactly what happened. By the end, Jace and Shane are looking less stressed, but Alex still looks upset. "To be honest, I had no clue he was bi. I thought he was gay this whole time."

Shane sits down and pulls Alex down with him. Alex runs a frustrated hand through his hair and blows out a breath of air.

"Ash and I were a thing. I was completely and

utterly in love with him. I thought he was the one, but we were young and stupid, and I assumed he would happily come out of the closet so we would live happily ever after. I failed to realize how important it was for him to carry on the family title. His horrid grandmother told him that they will have no *fruits* in their family and even sent him away to 'gay camp' to have it beaten out of him. He learned how to pretend, and he keeps all his male dalliances private and secret. I got sick of coming second to a title, so I gave him an ultimatum and was fucking devastated when he chose the title."

Shane takes over talking. "Alex and I had worked together before, but we had always kept it platonic even though I was extremely attracted to him. I knew how much he loved Ashton. I could tell every time they were together. We ran into each other about three months after they had broken up. Alex had gone a little bit crazy, fucking anything he could get his hands on, and he tried to seduce me after a shoot one day."

Alex chuckles and looks affectionately at his partner. "Yeah, that completely backfired on me. I found myself bent over a hard surface with Shane spanking me for all my bad behavior. I fell for him right there and have never looked back."

"Alex just wanted to come first in someone's life, and I gave him that. We've regularly shared partners, I know Alex isn't made for monogamy, but you two are the first people we've ever wanted to permanently add to our dynamic," Shane shares, and I feel a warm tingling rush run over me.

"Are you going to keep sleeping with others?" Jace asks, and I can hear the worry in his voice. "Are you like Jilly, wanting an open thing with us, because I kind of thought it would be closed eventually." Shane and Alex exchange a glance, then Alex gets down on the floor, crawls over to where we are, and lays his head in Jace's lap.

"No, sweetie. I'm perfectly happy with you two and Shane. It's everything I've always wanted," he assures him, stretching up to kiss him. He turns to kiss me, but I hold up a hand.

"You might want to wait until you've heard what the plan is."

I tell them everything. Well, everything except for the fact that I need to use drugs to be able to go anywhere without crippling anxiety, but that's none of their business. Or that's what I'm going to tell myself. There's a part of me, the mature adult part, that says they'll need to know that eventually if I want a real relationship with them, but I'm ignoring that part for now. "Hope thinks it would be good for me to be seen dating Ashton. Even if we're partying all over the town, it might settle the shareholders," I finish up, and none of them look happy.

Shane rubs a hand over his chin, pulling at his short beard. "I don't like it, but I understand. Your family is everything to you, and I don't blame you for wanting to help out in this situation."

"I think it's a crap plan, but what do I know about public relations? I trust Hope and Cole aren't leading you astray," Jace says, placing a kiss on my head.

"Alex?" He's awfully quiet. It's not like him to have an opinion and not share it. He reaches out and grabs my hand.

"I just want you to be careful. Ashton is very easy to fall for, and I don't want you to get hurt when you're inevitably done with the charade. Though who knows? Maybe he's the one who needs the warning. He might fall just as hard for you. I know I did." I lean down and place a kiss on his lips. He tries to deepen it, but a knock at my door has me groaning into his mouth.

"Fuck, lunch. I'm not even dressed yet." I push him out of the way and hurry back over to the bed, grabbing the outfit I planned to wear. I move into the bathroom while Shane gets up to open the door. As I shimmy into the dress I picked, I hear Riku's sexy voice enthusiastically greet my guys, and they return it equally. I smile at the thought that at least these four get along.

"Hey, why don't you guys come to lunch with us? I can introduce you to my aunt," I suggest as I grab my handbag and slip on a pair of heels.

"Is this the aunt who owns Sugar and Spice?" Alex asks, sounding more enthusiastic than he's been since he walked into the room.

"Yeah, but I warn you, she is somewhat of an *acquired* taste."

"I'm pretty sure my ass is bruised from where she pinched it," Riku confesses to the three guys.

"Oh, I would not miss it for the world!" Alex says as we leave my room and make our way downstairs.

"I was looking at the in-room special menu," Jace says, using his fingers for quotation marks. "You can hire an expert to give you all kinds of sex lessons." He sounds slightly bemused.

The elevator is empty as we step in, and the doors close behind us. "Yeah, and they're hands-on too, if you want them to be. It's how we're getting around Hawaii's prostitution laws. By offering it as a class, whatever happens behind those closed doors is up to our 'expert' and their 'student.'"

"So… if I hired someone to give me a blow job class, I could get a blow job?" Shane asks, sounding slightly surprised.

"Well, yes, but on paper, you're hiring them for a demonstration and some tips. The women and men are all highly trained escorts from one of Aunt Merideth's establishments. They are all here because they want to be. None are being coerced or have to do it for money or anything. All of her people enjoy their jobs."

The elevator opens, and we step out. I don't continue to talk about it because you never know who's listening, and prostitution is illegal in Hawaii.

We make our way to the dining room where everyone is already seated. The noise coming from our table sounds joyful but loud. I feel a little sorry for other diners, but as I gaze around the room, there don't seem to be many others around.

"Ah, there you are!" Aunt Merideth can't wait for us to approach. She stands up and waves, her eyes widening then zeroing in on the fact that Shane has his hand on my back. Riku melts into the background with the other security while I ask the hostess to place three more chairs at the table.

Before Aunt Merideth can fuss, Molly gets up to greet us. She gives each of the boys a kiss and hug then comes over to me. "Thank you," I whisper to her, and she giggles.

"That woman is a hoot, but whoa, she's a lot. Tell the boys to keep their backs to the wall. Our poor security and Cole have been molested and are a little shell shocked."

Chuckling, I introduce them all to Aunt Merideth, and thankfully, she stays where she is. They all give Hope and Harlow a kiss on the cheek before sitting down. I try to join them down on their end, but Aunt Merideth stops me, pointing to the free seat next to her. "Come and tell me about everything, or everyone, you've been doing," she says, and I know that it's not actually a request. So I smile and take a seat and brace myself for an inter-rogation worthy of an army general.

Chapter Twenty-Four

Jacinta

The opening party the following night was a huge success, and Jaxon's new hotel made a splash on all the right websites and news channels. There was even a feature writer from *Indulgence* magazine practically gushing about the resort. We nearly reached capacity for advance booking for two years, so he can step back and concentrate on becoming a dad and building a family and home with Harlow. He might even have time to check out some of our inheritance together when he's not trying to sneakily micromanage Cruise Lines.

I waved goodbye to them at the end of the night, all of their belongings having been moved into the penthouse. I'm pretty sure I do not want to go anywhere near their room for a few days.

My date with Shane is the evening after the gala. I'm giddy with excitement as I get ready. I have this pretty strapless body-con dress that goes down to just above my knees. It's covered in red hibiscus flowers. I've put my hair up in a sleek pony-tail, and I've got a simple gold chain around my neck. My makeup is only a touch of mascara and eyeliner and some tinted lip gloss. I'm all ready to go with about ten minutes until he comes to get me.

Pacing across the room, I'm wearing a path in the carpet, my hands opening and closing as the anxiety and nerves creep back in. Damn it. I was fine last night, but I was surrounded by family and friends. I managed to keep the quiet, insidious voice under control, but now it's whispering to me once more, telling me I'm useless and worthless, and I don't deserve to be happy. I stop as I suddenly realize it sounds very much like my mother on a meth binge. Fuck, I really need to stop rescheduling me therapist appointments. Putting it off isn't doing me any favors.

Shaking it off, I hurry to my bag and get out my drugs. A hit of coke is what I need, so I prepare and snort it before Shane can arrive. I clean everything up, and it's just kicking in when he knocks on my door.

"Perfect timing. I just finished getting ready." I beam at him when he pulls a bouquet of orchids and baby's breath out from behind his back.

"Wow. You look amazing." His eyes heat as he scans my body, and my heart races. He looks incredible in a pair of dress pants, with a black shirt and brocade-patterned waistcoat over the top. I am so glad this luau is semi-formal. Smiling, I take the flowers from him and go back into my room, placing them on the bed.

"They're gorgeous. Thank you so much. I can't remember the last time someone brought me flowers. On the way out, I'll ask housekeeping to come up and put them in a vase."

I step out of the room and close the door, but before I can walk away, he stops us. "Hi," he says before leaning in to kiss me. The slow, sensual slide of his lips against mine makes my breath hitch and my body melt into his.

He pulls back, and my eyelids flutter open. I hadn't even realized I closed them. He's got a slight smirk, but I'll forgive him because that was one hell of a kiss.

"Hi," I murmur back, getting lost in his deep ocean blue eyes.

A chuckle behind me has me stiffening and turning around. Standing there in a sexy ass suit that fits his incredible body perfectly is Riku. "Come on, love birds. If we don't get moving, you're going to be late."

Shane takes my hand, and Riku leads us to the elevator and down into the foyer. I stop at the front desk to make my request about the flowers, but we make it out of the hotel without running into anyone we know. Specifically Aunt Merideth. I love that woman, but she is a dreadful cougar, and I want to claw her eyes out every time she looks at any of my men, including Riku.

The cool evening breeze feels amazing on my coke-heated skin, and I turn my head up to feel it. The limo pulls up, and Riku opens the door, but before I can get in, Shane stops me. In his hand, I see a big beautiful red hibiscus bloom. He tucks it into my hair behind my ear. We stare at each other again until Riku clears his throat. Both of us laugh a little sheepishly before we climb in, with Riku following after us.

The luau is fun, and Shane introduces me to lots of his colleagues. Riku hangs in the background, a comforting presence at my back. We're there for a few hours before I start to feel a little restless, or maybe it's just the coke wearing off. In any case, I start to fidget. I don't want to make Shane leave early, but if we're going to stay longer, I need another hit. Before I can ask him, he smiles at someone over my shoulder, his eyes lighting up with joy.

"Hey, gorgeous. How are you?" Shane hugs and kisses a beautiful sun-kissed blonde who approaches from behind me. When she turns, giving me a good look, I do a double take.

"Maddy? Wow, it's been a long time." Madeline Owens is the sister of my brother's friend Justin.

He's a Red Bull sponsored surfer, and he's dating Kai's distant cousin Erica.

"Holy shit! Jacinta Summers. You were not a face I was expecting to see here at all." She gives me a quick hug. "Erica told me she and Justin attended the opening last night. Kai hooked her up with a couple of nights in the hotel. She was over the moon, bragging about it to anyone who would listen. Are you two here together? Where's Alex?"

She looks around the crowd, but Shane shakes his head and slides his arm around my waist, dragging me closer to him. "We left Alex at home and came out for a night alone." The way he makes it clear that I'm important to him makes me feel all warm and tingly inside.

Her eyes widen a little, but she smiles. "Oh cool, that's awesome. You're a lucky bitch to have two men at your beck and call!"

"Actually, it's three. We have another boyfriend who works with Jacinta at Neighpalm Couture. He's a designer and is just about to launch his first line." Shane is so super cute talking up his—our?—boyfriend.

"Oh hey, yeah, I'm shooting that down in New Orleans next week for Harpers. Then I've got an invite to your showing, and I'm so excited to see some of your new work before I jet off to Africa for Nat Geo." Like Shane, Maddy is an amazing photographer, but where his focus is mainly fashion and some dabbling in scenic photography, she's the opposite. She works a lot for *National Geographic* and a variety of sports magazines, specializing in action shots.

"Holy crap, woman, do you ever stop?" I ask, shaking my head.

"No way! I'll sleep when I'm dead."

We shoot the breeze a little longer, but I start to shiver. Although there are lit torches all around, the temperature has really dropped since the sun went down, and the breeze has steadily picked up.

"It was amazing seeing you, Maddy, and we'll see you next week in NOLA. I'm going to get Jacinta out of the cold." We wish her goodbye and make our way to the car where Simon is waiting.

"Are you okay?" Riku puts his hand on me when he sees me shudder.

"Cold," I stutter, but I'm starting to think the comedown from the coke is affecting my temperature regulation, because I've never been this cold before. He quickly shrugs out of his jacket and wraps it around my shoulders.

"Thanks, man, I didn't think to bring one, which was stupid of me." Shane sounds annoyed at himself but grateful to Riku.

I squeeze his arm. "I was just as stupid. I should have brought at least a wrap or something. I mean, it's not the middle of summer."

The car is on, toasty warm, when we slide into it, and I send Simon a grateful smile as Shane slides the dividing screen up between us.

"Let's see if we can warm you up some more." Shane pulls me in tight against him and starts to kiss me. Our tongues tangle as he plunders my mouth, making me squirm, trying to ease the ache he's causing in my center. I pull back before I get too carried away.

"Riku's here," I whisper to him, panting slightly, but he just grins.

"I'm sure he won't mind." There's a wicked light in his eyes, and when I get brave enough to look at Riku, there's not even a shadow of disgust. In fact, I would say he was totally into watching me make out with my handsome, growly man. "Maybe he could help me out? What do you say?"

I'm no longer cold. My body feels like it's going to overheat with the anticipation of his response.

Riku silently nods, and Shane's grin grows even more wicked. "Good. Could you hold Ms. Summers' hands for me, please?" Shane gestures for Riku to move onto our side of the bench seat. When he does, he pulls my hands over my head and lays me down along the seat, passing my hands to Riku. "Please make sure that Ms. Summers stays restrained until I tell you otherwise," he instructs, his deep gravelly voice making me shiver with excitement. As he drags his hands back down my body, he hooks his finger into the top of my stretchy body-con dress and drags it down, exposing my tits to his eyes.

"Your breasts are spectacular, Jacinta," he

rumbles as he caresses them, cupping and squeezing. "Don't you think so, Riku?"

My eyes fly up to my bodyguard above me. His hands tighten on mine as he grunts his agreement, but he doesn't say anything else. I watch his tongue flick out to wet his lips, but Shane grabs my attention by flicking his own tongue across one nipple.

My eyes drift closed as he nips and sucks at one, then the other. My panties grow even wetter with my desire, and I start to squirm. "Eyes on me," Shane orders before he nips one of my nipples harder.

My eyes fly open, and he smiles. "Good girl."

His hands slide past my waist to the hem of my dress, and this time he drags it upward. My dress is now reduced to a scrap of material at my waist, so when he pulls down my panties, I'm naked to their eyes.

"My mouth is fucking watering at the thought of tasting you." Shane sticks my panties in a pocket as he rolls up the long sleeves on his shirt, exposing his sexy forearms. He has a tattoo on the right one, but before I can make out what it is, he's sliding his hands under my ass and lifting my pussy up to his mouth. I'm stretched out like a feast for him, and he wastes no time devouring me.

He slides his tongue from my ass to my clit, moaning as he does. "You should taste her, man. She's delicious." His beard scratches against my core, which feels incredible combined with what he's doing with his tongue. He licks and sucks and slurps, paying special attention to my clit. I can't control the sounds escaping my mouth as he licks me with strong, sure strokes, burying his tongue deep in my center before moving back to flick at my clit.

I start to writhe in his hands, only my head thrashing back and forth since Riku's still holding my hands, as Shane slowly builds my impending orgasm higher. Riku's nostrils flare, and I know it's because the scent of my desire is filling the back of the limo.

"Please." The word tumbles out, and Shane looks up at me, his beard glistening with my desire.

"Oh, I do love to hear you beg. Did you want something, Jacinta?" he teases, his eyes sparkling as I groan my frustration.

"I need more," I pant out, and he slides a finger back and forth before slipping it into my aching channel.

"Is this what you want?" he asks, pumping it in and out a little, but it's not enough. I don't feel full enough.

"More." My throat aches as I sob out the word.

He slides another finger in next to it and flutters his tongue across my clit. I feel my core start to tighten once more, my whole body curling in anticipation, but Shane stops, removing his fingers and denying me my release.

"No!" I cry out as he removes his hands from

my ass and lowers me back down on the seat. "Please," I beg, and he chuckles.

"Patience, baby, I've got what you need." I'm jelly as he rolls me off the seat and positions me so I'm on my knees in front of Riku. He still has my hands, and now my face is in his lap as Shane slides his hands down my back, and I hear him unbuckle his pants. He slaps me once on the ass, causing me to squeal, then groan, as he rubs the sting away.

"Good girl," he murmurs again as I hear a foil wrapper rip. He slides his dick back and forth through the wet mess that is my pussy, lubing himself up before lowering himself over my back. "Hold tight to Riku, love, because I'm about to destroy your pussy."

The erotic words in my ear have me moaning into Riku's lap. His steel hard cock is under my face, and I wrap my lips around it through the material. Riku gasps in shock, but that's the only sound I manage to entice from him.

Just as I'm about to suggest he get it out, Shane slams home, ripping any words from my mouth. He's thick and long, and it takes a moment or two to adjust to his invasion. I breathe through it as he mutters, "God, you're so tight. Feel so fucking good, your pussy gripping my cock like it's made for it." He slaps me on the ass again, and I'm so close to orgasming.

"Please move," I beg him, and he slowly withdraws before sliding back in. Over and over, he does this, getting faster with each slide. His hands cup my breasts as he curls over me, our bodies as one, plucking and pinching my nipples, sending intense pleasure rippling through my body.

"So close," I gasp into Riku's lap, and Shane chuckles wickedly when Riku's groan slips from his mouth.

One of his hands slides from my nipples, his hand rough against my skin as he aims for my clit. All it takes is for him to flick it, and I soar off the edge of the cliff I had been precariously balancing on. Pleasure like nothing I've felt before explodes outward, sending a wave of skin-tingling sensation washing over my body, my toes curling as I silently scream into Riku's lap.

"Oh yeah, baby, oh, that feels fucking amazing. You're strangling my dick." Shane thrusts a couple more times before he stills and finds his release too, groaning loudly as my channel continues to milk his cock.

Riku's pants grow damp beneath my cheek, and my eyes jolt to his face as he silently finds his own release. Whoa, he looks so sexy, his eyes closed and a serene look on his face, but when they open again and meet mine, there's no sign of what just happened.

Shane caresses my back, running his hands up and down my arms. "You can let go now," he tells Riku, who releases me like I'm a snake about to bite him and quickly moves over to the other seat again.

I flinch slightly at his reaction, but then Shane whispers in my ear. "Easy, baby. He's having a crisis of conscience. We'll get him sorted." He cups my chin and turns my head so he can kiss me deeply, his cock still buried inside me as the aftershocks of our orgasms wreak havoc on our bodies. He slowly slides the top of my dress back up before withdrawing, then opens one of the little cupboards to find some napkins. He cleans us both up before pulling my dress back down over my ass and helping me onto the seat. We exchange kisses and quiet words until we get back to the hotel. I'm excited and relieved that things are finally starting to move in the right direction with these men.

For once in my life, something is going how I want it to go.

Chapter Twenty-Five

Jacinta

With Shane's body deliciously wrapped around mine, it was not easy getting out of bed the next morning, and showering might have taken extra long as we made sure the other was super clean. But we have a breakfast date with our boyfriends, and I can't deny I'm missing them like crazy.

"I can't believe I miss them so much already," I tell Shane as we step onto the elevator, shadowed by Simon and Riku.

He chuckles. "Both of them worm their way under your skin until there's no way out for them." He pulls me in so we're hugging.

It's like he can't keep his hands off of me, and I have no complaints. I've never felt so truly *wanted* before. This isn't some superficial thing between the two of us. It's almost magnetic.

"It's weird because I was sure I was going to be a bachelor all my life. I was twenty-nine, and he was only twenty-two when Alex and I got together. I'd always found him sexy, and when he was finally single, I decided to take a chance. I thought it would be a quick affair, a rebound relationship for him, but we both fell hard and fast, and six years later, we're still together. Jace was just the same. We felt an instant spark when Harlow introduced us, and he was like this little lost chick in the big wide world, so Alex and I took him under our wing. We weren't expecting to fall for him like we did, but it's been amazing, and now it's happening again with you."

I stare at him with surprise. "I think that's the most I've ever heard you say," I tell him, and he pinches my side.

"Sassy bitch." He kisses me hard and fast as the elevator opens, then we make our way into the outdoor dining area. It's a bright and beautiful morning, warm enough to enjoy dining alfresco.

"Well, well, well, don't you two look all loved up?" Alex claps his hands enthusiastically and stands up to greet us, kissing one after the other before dropping back in his chair. Shane leans in and kisses Jace too, though the younger man seems a bit preoccupied. "Go on, Jacinta, kiss your other boyfriend while he's having a moment of insecurity about whether there's a place left for him." Alex waves his hand flippantly, but he's basically ensuring that Jace doesn't get left out, not that I ever would forget him. I fell for him first, heart and soul, in Prague. I sit down on his lap and wrap my arms around his neck as the other two look over the menu.

"Hi. I missed you," I whisper, and he releases what I think is a sigh of relief. The worry leaves his eyes, replaced with something much warmer.

"I missed you too. Did our man look after you?" he asks quietly as his cock starts to thicken underneath me.

"Oh my goodness, did he. And he even used Riku as a prop." Jace is all ears as I tell him what we had done in the limo last night, and by the time I'm finished, his dick is rock hard.

He groans as I shift.

"I can't wait to get my mouth on that." I don't know if I'd normally say this at a brunch date, but I'm embracing my inner vixen who really wants to be an outer one.

He stands up and pulls me in front of him. "We'll be right back," he says to the other two, then he tugs me in the direction of the elevator. I can hear Alex and Shane chuckle behind us, but I'm so freaking turned on I don't care.

He stabs the button, calling it down to us, and thankfully it's empty. He pulls me in, and just before the door closes, Riku slips in next to us. He blinks once or twice at Riku, but I guess he makes a decision because he hits the emergency stop button, and we come to a shuddering halt. "I hope your brother can wipe the security tapes," he mutters, and I grin, dropping to my knees just like I did the other night for Ashton. Feeling Riku's eyes on me makes it that much sexier. I need to talk to him about all of this, but I'll worry about that later.

"There aren't any in here for this exact reason," I assure him, and he throws his head back as I make quick work of his shorts and underwear until his cock is sitting in front of me, dripping with precum. It's exactly like I thought it would be, long and thick and perfect. I slide my tongue around the rim of the head, and his knees buckle before he grips the elevator rail.

"Fuck, you're going to kill me," he mutters, looking down at me. I feel so fucking powerful looking up at him, seeing the worship in his eyes. I slide my hand along the length, caressing his balls when I get to them, before sliding my hand back up. I pump it a couple of times, wanting to see more precum dribble out, before licking it all up. It's hot and salty, but I don't care. I just want more.

Finally, I put him out of his torment and take his thick length into my mouth. Working it back and forth, hollowing my cheeks, I use both my hand and mouth to give him pleasure. It takes me a couple of goes, and I've covered him in spit, but I eventually get to the base. Breathing through my nose, I hold there a moment before pulling back with a gasp. I have a gag reflex, but I've learned to control it for small amounts of time, long enough to be able to deep throat him, and when I do it again, his moan echoes in the elevator.

I'm so turned on my nipples are rock hard and aching, and I can feel my panties getting wet with desire. I reach down with my other hand to touch myself, but Jace has his own plans. He pulls me off of him, and in one quick movement, he has my ass resting on the rail and my dress pulled up around my waist.

"Help me here, will you, buddy? Peel her underwear off for me?" he asks Riku, and I jolt. I'd been so caught up in what we were doing that I'd forgotten he was in the elevator.

When my eyes meet his, I think he's going to refuse, but he pushes off the wall he'd been leaning against and adjusts himself before stepping up. Jace holds me in place as Riku's hands slide up my thighs, and he hooks a finger over my panty line and pulls. They slide down, and I can feel his finger slide over my clit as he drags the underwear away. I shudder and moan loudly at his participation. Fuck me, I'm in so much trouble. I desperately want that man, and Shane and Jace are doing everything in their power to make me admit it.

Riku steps back, reaching his other hand into a pocket to pull out a condom that he tosses to Jace, who grins up at him.

"Thanks, man. Hold her for me?" Riku's hands replace Jace's as he rips open the packet and slides it onto his hard length. I'm breathing heavily, and Riku's dark gaze is locked on mine. Even as he releases me, Jace replacing him, we don't break our stare down.

Jace leans in to kiss me and whispers, "I won't be upset if you continue to stare at him like that because I know I'm the one who has his cock buried deep in your cunt, pulling all those noises from you."

And with that, he drives himself deep into my pussy. My back arches, and I gasp, my legs hooking around his waist and my heels digging into his ass. "Fuck yes, just like that." I close my eyes as Jace starts to fuck me enthusiastically.

"Don't close those pretty eyes. You need to watch what your naughty security guard is doing." Jace's mouth drifts down to my tits and nudges my dress away, exposing my nipples. He latches onto one as he drives himself in and out, his dick touching all the right places inside of me.

I open my eyes, and I just about come on the spot when I see that Riku has his cock in hand and is using my panties to get himself off. My moans get louder, and Jace gives my nipple a bite before he pulls back and starts talking dirty.

"Riku, man, you should feel this. She's so hot and tight, and she's fucking gushing. She loves watching you use her panties like that. What about you? Don't you wish your dick was where mine is?"

It's too much, and that last thrust tips me right over the edge. "Fuck yes, Jace!" The scream rips from my mouth as my pussy convulses around his length. He groans and thrusts a couple more times before he loses it too.

"Oh god, it's so tight. Your pussy is fucking milking me. That feels amazing." And with that last little bit of dirty talk, I watch Riku come in my panties, making sure not to spill a bit or make a mess on the floor.

The elevator smells like sex, and the sounds of all three of us breathing raggedly is louder than the piped-in music. I rest my head against Jace's shoulder, trying to catch my breath. When I tap him on the shoulder to pull out and let me down, I groan at the pain in my ass from sitting on the rail. He chuckles and helps me straighten myself out, and when I finally look at Riku again, any evidence of what just happened is gone. My panties must be in his pocket, and his cock is tucked back into his pants. He's standing stiff as a board and won't look at either of us.

Jace grimaces. "Fuck, I'm sorry. I thought he was totally into it," he quietly apologizes, and I shrug.

"I'll talk to him after breakfast," I reassure him as he hits the emergency stop button once more to get us going.

"I can't wait for our dinner tonight." Alex leans back in his chair and drinks his chai latte as I continue to shovel scrambled eggs into my mouth. The chef makes them with something spicy and these thick pieces of sourdough bread. They're delicious, and just what I needed after my morning workout.

"Me neither." Jace smiles and looks a lot more relaxed than he had when Shane and I first came down.

Just as I finish my mouthful to answer, I see Alex's face pale, and his grip on his latte cup tightens considerably.

"Hello, love, fancy meeting you here." The English accent sends a shiver down my spine, and I know instantly who it is. A hand caresses my shoulder, and when I look up, Ashton is grinning down at me. He gives me a peck on the lips before moving around to Alex's side of the table and giving him one too. "Hello, duckie, it's been a while." Ashton has stunned Alex into silence, I think. He waves hello to Shane and Jace. "Good morning, I'm Ashton."

Shane stands up and holds out a hand. "Hi, Shane Silvers. I've heard a lot about you." Ash raises an eyebrow in surprise but takes his hand.

"I bet," Ashton says somewhat wryly, looking at

Alex. Jace stands and introduces himself as well. Once that's out of the way, he loses the smug grin. "I was wondering if I could have a word with Jacinta for a moment."

"Anything you have to say to me you can say in front of these guys." His eyebrows jump in surprise, and his eyes narrow as he looks around the table. Alex reaches for my hand, and comprehension dawns on the lord's face.

"Ah, okay, do you mind if I join you then?" He puts his hand on a chair as I look around the alfresco area, judging if anyone is within hearing distance. Luckily, the very nature of the hotel makes it so there is hardly anyone around, so I feel comfortable discussing private things with Ash.

"Sure, why don't you grab a coffee from the buffet or something to eat?" I suggest, and he heads off, giving us a moment alone.

"Are you okay with this?" I ask Alex, and he squeezes my hand.

"Yeah, I'm kind of curious about what he has to say, but give me a moment, please." Shane nods at his long-term partner with so much love in his eyes, then Alex gets up and follows after Ashton.

"You're not jealous?" Jace asks, leaning forward.

Shane shakes his head, picking up my hand and giving it a kiss. "Not at all. I'm secure in my relationship with Alex, and I also know he's never stopped loving Ashton. It would be good for him to get some closure."

I lean in and kiss him on the cheek. "Well, let's see if we can get some for him." We watch on as they have a whispered but somewhat dramatic conversation, none of us hiding our interest. I'm not sure what's said, but when they return, they're both frowning. Alex sits back down next to me while Ashton takes the seat between him and Jace.

We wait as he gets started on his food, but I can see Jace is just about ready to implode with impatience. Hiding my smile, I get this started. "What is it you wanted to talk to me about?"

He swallows and takes a sip of his beverage before clearing his throat. "I wanted to thank you again for what you did for me the other night. You have no idea what it means to me."

"It's fine. I would have helped any friend like that. But I don't understand why you're here just to say that."

"The day that story broke, my grandmother reached out to me. For the first time that I can ever remember, she *praised* me for my actions."

My mouth drops open in surprise, and Alex snorts.

"The dragon lady congratulated you on getting head in the closet at a club?"

"Well, no. She reamed me out for that, but the fact that it was Jacinta at my feet made all the difference. She congratulated me, then suggested I knock you up so you would have no choice but to marry me." The only reason I continue hearing him out is that there's nothing positive in his voice. He sounds like he's ashamed to even be saying these words out loud, which makes me decide that I need to give him a chance instead of running as far as I can as quickly as possible.

"Fuck off, she didn't!" Jace obviously doesn't believe it either.

"Oh no, I can assure you that's exactly what she said. You're wealthy, and you have a title. In her eyes, you're a catch. She wants me to lock you down quick smart." He sounds embarrassed as he explains the reasons why. Gone is the cocky, smug British aristocrat, and in his place is an unsure guy in his late twenties.

"What I want to ask you is if you would pretend for a few months for me. Be seen in public and on my arm. It would really take some pressure off of me." His words are so similar to what Hope suggested that I'm speechless for a moment, and although I already explained this plan to the guys, they are quick to voice their opinions again now, but I shut that down. Of course their opinions matter to me, but I also have questions. Why is this man practically begging me to help him out?

"Why do you let her dictate your life? We all know you're bisexual, but you pretend to be straight for your grandmother. It can't be your title because you have that already. From what I understand, there isn't much wealth left. I'm sure we would all appreciate an explanation."

Ashton closes his eyes and sighs deeply before opening them again. "You're right. I do owe you an explanation, and I most definitely owe you one." He's looking at Alex now, and I can see regret in his eyes. "Maybe I should have told you sooner, but it wasn't going to change anything. I was never going to be allowed to live my life like I want to." He sounds so heartbroken, and there's even the shimmer of tears in Alex's eyes. Shane reaches out and takes his hand, giving it a squeeze.

"I have a sister."

Chapter Twenty-Six

Jacinta

Alex gasps, the sound full of some pent-up hurt. "You never told me that!"

"She's a half-sister. Before he died, my dad knocked up a maid during a drunken binge. I don't think it was quite consensual, but Grandmother paid the maid to carry it to term then hand her over. I was fourteen when Edie was born, and I loved her to bits. I helped out with her as much as I could when I was home from boarding school. Much like me, Edith was raised by nannies. She and I were all we had. Dad was a drunken asshole who would smack me around, and I swore I would never let him raise a hand to her. Not that I had to worry. He tripped and fell down the stairs at our estate, breaking his neck in the fall, drunk as usual." Ash pauses and takes another sip of his drink as I absorb everything he's told me so far. He hasn't really given me a reason for the whole closet thing yet.

"When I came out to my grandmother as bisexual, she was horrified. She wouldn't have that shame on the family name, so she ordered me to stay in the closet. I argued with her about it, but she said that if I came out as bi, I would be disowned, and she would marry Edie off to the first wealthy man who wanted a title as soon as she possibly could. Edie is fourteen, so that means for the next four years, I have to stay firmly in the closet so that my grandmother doesn't follow through with what she threatened."

"But that's not legal in the UK!" I argue.

"But it is here in some states, no matter how taboo, and she wouldn't hesitate to come over here if she had to. She's Edie's legal guardian. I tried to get guardianship, but my first try was unsuccessful, and she said if I tried again, she has the name of a nice, wealthy Arab man who would gladly take Edie off her hands."

"Holy fuck," Jace breathes out.

"That's why I let you go. I love you, Alex, but I love my little sister more, and I couldn't give you what you needed while also keeping her safe." Ash's eyes plead him to forgive him, and I see Alex melt.

"Why didn't you tell me? I would have understood."

Ash smiles sadly. "I know you would have, but I didn't want that for you. You have so much love to give, and you deserve someone who could give you just as much and shout it to the world. It looks like you've found just that."

Wow. My eyes slide to Shane, who's wearing a contemplative frown, and I feel a little of Nana's matchmaking urge stir inside me.

"I appreciate you explaining everything." Ash flinches, finally tearing those heartbroken eyes of his away from Alex. "I'll be honest… I was going to make an appointment to see you and ask you to do much the same thing for me."

"You were? Why?" He sounds as surprised as I was when he asked me. I chuckle.

"I guess it's my turn to explain." I tell him everything about the hostile company takeover plans, including the unhappy shareholders and the fact that Cole hatched a plan to take the heat of Neighpalm Industries and put it solely on me.

A myriad of expressions show on his face as he listens, but by the end, he's smiling widely. "Should I get you an engagement ring to seal the deal?" he jokes.

"Just remember, in public, it's you and me, but behind closed doors, I'm with these guys, and I won't stop that. What I'm about to do isn't fair to them, but they're being very gracious in understanding how important my family is to me. And you need to remember to keep your dalliances private too. I will not be made a fool of if you get caught in a closet. I will happily announce our split and leave you to deal with the fallout." I don't mince words, because as much as he doesn't want to lose his sister, he's careless with himself, as the other day proved. "Pick your partners wisely, Ashton, because you have a lot more to lose than I do. And I'm having dinner with these guys tonight. I'm not going to change that. I'll send you a list of my upcoming engagements, and we'll coordinate, okay?"

"Yes, of course, and thank you. I'll leave you be now. It was nice meeting the two of you." He smiles at Shane and Jace. "And it was good seeing you again, Alex. You're looking well, and I can tell you're happy. It's all I ever wanted."

With that last remark, Ashton leaves us.

"Are you okay?" Shane asks Alex once he's out of hearing.

"I don't know." Shane reaches over and wraps his arms around our boyfriend.

"It will be okay. Everything will work out just fine," Shane assures him, but why do I think those words are actually a little more loaded than they seem?

I leave the guys since Shane has work to do and Alex and Jace are doing a snorkeling cruise. They invited me along, but after Harlow's mishap when she was here, I decide I don't want to risk anything. Hope and I have plans to go to the spa, so once we finish up our breakfast, we all go our separate ways.

Riku follows me to the elevator, and we both step in to head back up to my room. I was so distracted by Ashton and his drama, I had forgotten what happened just before he arrived, but stepping back into the elevator causes the memory to wash over me, and I find myself biting my lip, not wanting to look at Riku. I'm almost a hundred percent sure that Jace and I were over the line, not to mention me and Shane last night, and I owe him a big apology.

"Listen, I… um… I'm sorry about before, and last night. It wasn't fair of us to do what we did in front of you. I don't want you to think you're being pressured into anything. I'm not going to lie though. I find you sexy as fuck, and I really enjoy spending time with you. Both Shane and Jace noticed, but I think they also forget that I'm a job for you, that you're here to protect me, and I shouldn't be dragging you into any sex games. That's a kind of sexual harassment, and for that I'm truly sorry. I'll speak to them about it." There's so much regret running through me at the moment, not to mention embarrassment. I mean, it looked like he was into it, he could have said no, but we really didn't give him a choice.

RIKU

It takes a moment for Jacinta's words to sink in, and when they finally register, it's everything I've been wrestling over in my mind. I was worried that the guys had done the same thing to her, not asking for consent before doing all of those things in front of me. To hear her say she's attracted to me is like a punch in the gut. I've been sick with guilt about getting myself off while watching her and Jace fuck. Her cum-covered panties are still in my pocket, and my dick has been semi-hard since. Watching Jace drive into Jacinta like he had and the wanton way she had thrown her head back, reveling in the sensations, was intoxicating, and there was just no way I could stop myself from doing what I did.

Her opening the doorway into this conversation jolts me into action, and I step into her, crowding her back against the wall, trapping her with my arms.

"I want you like I've never wanted anything in

my life. I wanted it to be me thrusting my dick into your tight pussy, feeling you gush all over it. I wanted my mouth on your tits just like Shane had them last night. I wanted my face glistening with the proof that I was making you feel good. I want it all, so do not think for one moment that I wasn't into it. Do not for one moment feel guilty because I could have stopped you. I just didn't want to. In fact, I wanted to join so badly it took all of my willpower to sit back and watch. But I'm your body-guard, and I worry that I'll be compromised when feelings get involved. And I say when, not if, Jacinta, because you are the kind of girl that a man has feel-ings for. You're not a throwaway or a convenient excuse to release a little tension. I'm distracted by the way you smile, the mischievous glint in your eyes when you tease your boyfriends, the fire in them when you argue with Cole, the sexy shake of your ass as you walk in front of me. I should be taking myself off your rotation and replacing myself with someone else."

She shakes her head, ready to argue, but I rest a finger over her mouth. "But I'm not going to. I'm in deep, and although I may be distracted, these feel-ings make me even more invested in keeping you safe. I want to hear you moan my name, feel you writhe beneath me. I want to feel you strangle my cock with your pussy, and most of all, I want to spend time with you, talking about books and movies and going to dinner. You can't do any of that if you're hurt, and I don't trust anyone else with your safety, so you're stuck with me."

I take her lips with mine, gently at first, but the minute her hands grip my shirt and pull me tighter against her, it becomes feverish. Groaning, I thrust into her mouth with my tongue, entwining them in an erotic dance. Her softness melts into my body as she becomes pliant in my arms. I want to throw my head back and roar like an animal, the primal feelings inside of me desperate to get out, but I feel the elevator slow, and for now, we need to be discreet. So I untangle her hands and pull away with one last soft kiss. Her breathing is shallow and ragged as the door opens to her floor.

There's a couple waiting to get on, so I put my hand on her back. "After you, Ms. Summers," I say professionally. Her eyes sparkle with desire, but she smiles serenely.

"Thank you, Riku." She steps out, and I follow, allowing the couple to enter. I hear the door close behind us as we walk to her room.

"Oh, I do like it when you call me Ms. Summers," she says under her breath.

"Your wish is my command, Ms. Summers." I smother the smug grin that wants to break out across my lips and keep my face professional. *I can do this.* Last night and today are hardly the first time things like that have happened while on a job. But this is the first time I've been personally invested. It's going to be hard to keep my hands to myself, but luckily for me, Jacinta is a fairly easy client.

Let's hope that doesn't change.

Chapter Twenty-Seven

Jacinta

I'm feeling relaxed and beautiful after my spa treatments with Hope. We had a nice time talking about all the people that attended the opening, and I told her about my date with Shane. I didn't share any sex details or fill her in on my meeting with Ashton because although our employees are paid to be discreet, they can't help but overhear what I'm saying while doing our treatments.

I leave the spa on my own. I told Riku to take some time off while I was at the spa, letting him know when I got back to my room. I mean, I couldn't be safer in a hotel owned by my family, right?

On my way back to my room, I run into Cole in the elevator. I hadn't seen him since the flight, and I avoided him during the opening party. But he was so busy doing the PR thing, it was an easy task.

"Oh, hey," I say, surprised as I step in the elevator to go back to my room to change. Hope was meeting Dad, the girls, and Nana and Poppy for dinner at their hotel, and Harlow is still in sex seclusion with the boys. It's lucky she's already knocked up, or she'd be pregnant six times over.

"Jacinta. Hi. This is good timing, actually. I wanted to see if you and Ashton Lavington had spoken yet." He pushes the button, and the doors close. I notice he's selected the same floor as me. I hadn't realized he was up there too.

"Ah, yeah. I have, actually. Funnily enough, he approached me." I tell him about our conversation, leaving out all the details about him and Alex since that's none of his business, but I do tell him why Ashton asked me to do what we're doing.

"That's horrible. Has he spoken to a lawyer about things?" Cole sounds disgusted by the fact that Ash's grandmother is threatening him with his little sister's life, so to speak.

"I think that although there may not be a lot of money left, she has a lot of sway in society." I'd also wondered about how Ash can afford to live the lavish lifestyle he does if the family funds have dwindled that badly. I have to ask him when I see him next. I should know everything, right?

"Well, it works well for us then. This is a much better plan than the one I had, but I admit I was desperate," he says ruefully. "I probably should have talked with Hope to start with. I just didn't want to fuck up my first big obstacle on the job." Wow, Cole actually sounds vulnerable and unsure, and I kind of like this side of him. But within a flash, it's gone, and he's all business again. "Now, you know you're going to have to keep your relationship with the other three secret for now. We can't have you looking like a slut."

And I'm back to wanting to kick him in the balls.

"Fuck you, Cole. Does Harlow look like a slut? What about Dad, Emma, and Molly? Huh? Just because it's different doesn't make it any less." Thankfully, the elevator stops. I don't even care that it's on another floor. I storm out and leave him sputtering pathetic excuses behind me. I'll take the stairs so I don't have to spend any more time with that infuriating man.

COLE

I reel back as Jacinta spits fire at me. I can't control the way my dick leaps in my pants at seeing her all wound up. It's spectacular, and all I want to do is put my hands all over her to tame the wild beast.

Of course, I didn't actually mean it how it came out, but that's exactly how the tabloids and people like Camilla Carlos would portray her. I'm still trying to come up with an excuse as the door opens on the wrong floor and she storms out. A bemused-looking couple gets in, and it's only then that I realize that Riku isn't around. Where is her shadow anyway? I can't let Jacinta wander around on her own, so I stick my hand in the door to stop it from closing and follow her out.

How do I keep putting my foot in my mouth? This isn't like me. I'm professional. If you want to make it in the big business of the PR world, you need to have a way with words. It's the reason I am where I am now. I'm also pretty good with the ladies. I was married to a supermodel, for fuck's sake. I have to have done something right. But I just keep getting it wrong with Jacinta. Sure, at first it was because I made assumptions that I discovered simply aren't true, but now there's just something about her, something that makes me want to see her lashing out in anger. I never want to see her sad, scared, and upset, so I go out of my way to make sure she's not.

I follow Jacinta, and she slams the door to the stairs open, muttering under her breath, the sound echoing off the concrete stairwell as she climbs the couple of levels to her room.

She's so preoccupied by her anger, she obviously doesn't hear me, and she also isn't watching where she's going. She misses a step and stumbles, teetering at an odd angle. I rush up behind her and put my hand on her back, stopping her from falling. She squeals and turns around and gives me a shove. Because I'm not quite balanced, I proceed to tumble backward. The shock on her face as I roll down thankfully only a few steps is photo worthy.

My back smashes onto a step, and I curl my body inward to minimize any more damage, but I'm groaning in pain when I finally come to a stop at the landing.

"Oh my god, Cole. Are you alright? You scared the shit out of me, and I just reacted." She hurries down the step to where I've landed. She runs her hands all over my body, I'm assuming checking for broken bones or bleeding, and suddenly my pain isn't so bad.

"Oh, oh," I moan as she runs her hands over my pelvis.

"Holy shit, you might have broken something. Stay still while I call an ambulance," she orders, digging in her pocket for her phone.

"Just a little lower," I mumble, and her hands shift down before freezing when her hand brushes against my rapidly hardening erection.

"You fucking pig," she growls and smacks me before standing up. I chuckle, groaning as I pull myself to my feet.

"Sorry, I couldn't help myself. You were so worried. I didn't know you cared so much," I tell her, brushing off and assessing my injuries. There are some bumps, and I know I'm going to have some bruises, but I'm mostly fine.

"I don't, but Spencer would have been really upset if his dad was hurt, and I felt guilty that it was my fault." She won't meet my eyes before she whirls around and continues back up the stairs. A soft feeling deep in my heart warms at her words. The fact that she thought about my son, worrying about me for his sake, is a huge eye opener. How did I ever think this woman was superficial and self-involved? She's nothing like that at all. She's kind, caring, and thoughtful. Man, I've fucked up so badly.

"Jacinta. Hey, Jacinta, wait for me!" I call as she pulls the door open at her floor and storms down to her room. "Please, I'm sorry!" I sound desperate even to my own ears. She stops and turns around just as my phone rings.

"Shit." I pull it out of my pocket and see it's a FaceTime call from Spencer. I can't reject this. I swipe to accept it, and she rolls her eyes and swings around again.

"Hey, buddy, how are you?" She stops in her tracks.

"Daddy. Hi, I miss you! What are you doing? Did you go surfing? Did you see a volcano? Did you see a dolphin?" He peppers me with questions, not allowing me to answer one before he's on to the next. Chuckling, I keep walking toward Jacinta.

"Where are you, Daddy? Is that the hotel? Can I see your room?"

"I'm not near my room at the moment," I tell him when he finally catches a breath.

"Well, whose room is that?" he asks, pointing to the door behind me.

"I'm not sure, buddy. Lots of people stay at the hotel." Spencer's lip drops and starts to quiver, and my heart rate picks up. Fuck, now he's sad.

"But I wanted to see your room! I want to see where you slept. Who tucks you in and kisses you goodnight like Mommy does for me?"

"Hey, buddy, what's brought this on? Is Mommy around?" I ask, frowning. Hayden lets Spencer have her phone to call me, and she lets him do it in private in case there are things he wants to talk to me about.

"Well, I have Mommy, and Mommy had Soloman tucking her in last night, and I wanted to know who does it for you."

Soloman is Hayden's new boyfriend. He's not a bad guy, but I hadn't realized they'd evolved to sleepovers. Jacinta can't help her chuckle when she hears Hayden's excuse for him catching a man in her bed. Damn, I wish she'd been more discreet.

"Who's that, Daddy?" Spencer has big ears, so he doesn't miss much. "Is someone with you? Can I say hi?" He moves the phone around like it's going to help him, not realizing it's my phone that needs to move. While he's out of the picture, I look at

Jacinta, silently asking if she's okay for me to show him.

She nods, and I flip the screen around. "It's my work friend, Jacinta."

Spencer beams as she waves at him. "Oh, it's the pretty lady with the goldfish. Hi, pretty lady! Are you tucking my daddy and giving him a kiss goodnight?" Spence puts his face right up to the screen, and Jacinta giggles.

"No, buddy, Jacinta and I are just walking back to our rooms together." He pouts once more and looks like he's about to argue my case. "Spence, when I get back to my room, how about we read a story before you go to bed? It's four in the afternoon, which makes it about seven in California, so it's just about your bedtime."

"Can Jazzy read it to me?" he asks, and I have a moment of panic.

"I'm going out to dinner tonight with some friends," she tells him, and we watch the tears well in his eyes. Poor baby must be so tired. "Oh, no, no, don't cry. How about I read you a quick one, then Daddy can read you another?" she suggests, and he's all smiles again. Sneaky little bugger.

"Yes, please." He bounces up and down with excitement.

"Okay, hang on, buddy. Let me open the door to my room."

"Pass me to Jazzy! I want to ask her some questions," he says, so I hand her the phone before digging in my pocket for my key card.

"Have you seen a dolphin? Did you go swimming? What about a volcano?" I smile as I swipe my card.

"No, I didn't do any of those things, but did you know my sister has baby tigers?" We walk into my room as she drops that bombshell on my three-year-old son. The call is silent for a moment before he starts squealing.

"Can I see them? Daddy, I want to see the baby tigers!"

"Now you've done it," I whisper out of the side of my mouth, and she cringes and mouths, "Sorry."

"I'll send you some video footage that I have on my phone, and when we get back, we'll arrange for your daddy to bring you out to our place to have a look. Sound good?"

"Yes! Yes! Yes!" he shouts with glee, bouncing the phone around as I grab my kindle off the bed.

"Go get your kindle, buddy, so we can read a story, okay?" He puts the phone down and runs away.

"Thank you for doing this. I really appreciate it," I tell Jacinta.

"I wouldn't punish a kid for what his father says or does," she says a little coldly, and I flinch.

Shit, she's still mad. I mean, I don't blame her, but I was kind of hoping Spence had softened her a bit.

"I'm back! I want to hear the one about the rainbow fish," he demands, so I switch on my kindle and find the book before passing it over to Jacinta. She looks around the room for somewhere to sit before heading over to the sitting area. I set up the phone on the little stand I have specifically for this, and Spence does the same on his end.

Hopefully, I'll get a chance to speak to Jacinta once Spence hangs up.

Chapter Twenty-Eight

Jacinta

Dinner with the guys is magical, especially since they insist Riku join us at the table instead of hovering to the side. The wine and conversation flow naturally between the five of us, and never once is there an awkward pause where we run out of things to talk about. The food is superb, but we skip dessert in favor of a walk along the beach. The breeze off the ocean is cool, so Shane strips off his jacket and wraps it around my shoulders.

"I was prepared this time," he whispers in my ear before winking at Riku. I laugh as I peel off my heels and hook them through my finger before we walk down the steps and onto the sand.

The sound of the water lapping gently along the shore overshadows the traffic back on the street.

The beach is mostly deserted this late at night. One or two other couples are strolling around, but everyone is keeping their distance from one another.

"Are you ready for your show next week, Jace?" I tuck my arm into his as we walk along the beach. Shane and Alex are behind us in much the same position, and Riku is walking with them. Usually, I would have all this information, but I've stayed away from the warehouse where everything gets made. I didn't want to interfere or micromanage him. He should be able to enjoy the rush of his first show without me hanging over his shoulder. Not to mention I've been busy with Willow Castle and socializing.

"Mostly. All the models have been chosen, and we've had fittings. There are one or two last-minute designs that I still need to make, which is what we'll rush to do this week. Everything is being shipped down to NOLA on Wednesday, and Emma, Molly, and I are flying down too."

"Are you excited?" I ask, thinking back to my first show. I was so nervous, I puked in the bathrooms while I was dressing them.

"I'm so freaking nervous. I'm worried people are going to hate it."

I squeeze his arm, knowing there's no real way to cure the nerves. He'll feel better once the show is over and he sees what a success he's going to be. "Trust that Nana, Molly, Emma, and I wouldn't let that happen. The three of them helped pick the designs to go into the show, and they all have fabulous taste. I've never seen Molly in anything that isn't on point fashion wise, and Nana is practically a style icon. Now that Emma isn't playing caretaker, she's been enjoying dressing up for work too."

"I know you're right, but I really want it to go well."

"It will. People will be talking about your debut for years to come! I bet you're going to be inundated with requests to design for the red carpet. Your dresses are reminiscent of old Hollywood glamor, and they're fabulous. I've lined up Selena Cross to come see you before the premiere of her new film. She's a pain in the ass, but she'll showcase your designs beautifully. And my friend Evie will want a Jace Hardy original when her next movie releases too."

"Evie?"

"Yeah, Evangeline Masters. She's about to start filming a vampire movie. It's called *Newly Undead in Dark River*. It's a mix of sexy and funny, and believe it or not, the main character has a harem of men. Dec optioned it up when he and the guys started dating Harlow. He wants to try to normalize those kinds of relationships, and what better way to do it than through mainstream media?"

He stops and demands, "Pinch me," all of a sudden. I'm confused for a moment, but Riku walks up and does as he asked.

"Ow! Shit. Did you have to do it so hard?" He rubs at the spot that Riku grabbed.

"Now you know you're not dreaming for sure, right?" He laughs, and the rest of us join in while Jace continues to grumble.

"When are you going down to NOLA?" Alex calls out as we keep walking.

"Probably not until Friday evening. I've got engagements all week." I turn my head to look at him while I'm talking, so I catch his frown.

"Is Ash going with you to them?"

I pull Jace to a stop, forcing the others to stop or risk running into us. I turn so we're now all in a circle.

"Are you okay with that? I won't do it if it upsets you."

He waves his free hand. "I'm fine, or I will be. I'm still trying to reconcile the truth with my heart-broken assumptions. No, I won't stop you from helping your family out."

"Okay, but promise me, and this goes for all of you" —I meet each one of their eyes, including Riku's— "if you have problems with it at any stage, we need to talk about it. The press is going to make assumptions and speculate, and the three of you will probably read some of that rubbish. If you feel like you can't deal with it, let me know, and I'll call it off. We'll find another way to appease the share-holders."

They all murmur their agreement as the breeze

picks up off the ocean, and I start to shiver despite Shane's coat.

"Come on. There's an awesome ice cream parlor not far from the hotel. We can get some to go, and I'll let you lick it from my body." Alex pulls away from Shane and runs toward me. He bends down and throws me over his shoulder. The squeal that leaves my lips seems to echo over the ocean as he runs up the beach to where we left the car. Shane's, Jace's, and Riku's laughter follow us up the steps.

When we get back to the hotel with our ice cream, the guys leave me and Alex at the elevator, claiming they want to get a drink at the bar. I'd seen the four of them having a quiet powwow while I was deciding what flavor I wanted, so I guess they must have been making plans.

"That's okay. I'll go up and help Jacinta put all of this in the freezer." Alex waves the bag with the ice cream, and the guys just roll their eyes good-naturedly and wave goodbye.

The ride up is quiet, with Alex chewing on his lip as I fumble around for something to say. Why the fuck am I so awkward right now? I'm usually good at flirting, but all of a sudden, I feel as shy as a virgin on prom night. I try drastically hard to think of something to say, but I've got nothing. The sexual tension floating between us is just too thick.

"So…" I begin, but I trail off, fumbling around. I sigh with relief and rush out when the elevator door opens. I hear Alex chuckle close behind me as I beeline for my door and get it open. Alex steps past me, his body rubbing deliciously against mine, and I squash a small moan that wants to break free. When my eyes meet his gorgeous green ones, I see the heat and desire in them, and I know he feels the same way.

I let the door close behind me as he walks over to the kitchen and sticks all but one tub of ice cream in it. He reaches into a drawer and pulls out a spoon, then, with the tub in hand, saunters back to me. "Come on."

He grabs me by the hand and leads me to the balcony doors before pushing them open and stepping out. I shiver as the cool breeze off the ocean whips around us, but Alex just flicks the switch on the overhead heating, and the balcony starts to warm up. Together, we walk to the canopied daybed on the veranda. Pulling back the gauzy curtains, he helps me into it before passing me the tub of ice cream and the spoon.

"I'll be right back," he tells me, then leaves me in the darkened hideaway, only the ambient light from outside letting me see anything. I use my phone to look around the space, and when I find a switch, I flick it on. Twinkling party lights brighten up the entire area, giving it a warm, romantic elegance.

It doesn't take long for Alex to return with a bottle of champagne and the duvet from my bed. He climbs through the curtains, letting them fall closed behind him, and I watch in bemusement as he fusses around, setting up a little nest. He fluffs the cushions at the top of the bed and places the ice cream, champagne, and glasses on a little side table built into the space. Finally, he fluffs out the blanket and looks around with a satisfied grin.

He pours us both a glass of champagne. Handing me one, he holds his up.

"To exciting new beginnings." He clinks his glass against mine and tosses his champagne back in one gulp. Not to be outdone, I do the same, and he quickly pours us another. "To all of us making a go of it." That glass goes down as fast as the last, and we're both giggling when he takes the glass back and tosses them off the side of the bed. Thankfully, I don't hear anything break. He then gets on his hands and knees and crawls over to me, not stopping until he has me flat on my back, giggling as he tickles me.

"Finally got you all to myself! You have no idea how long I've dreamed of this." His whole body surrounds me as he bends down and takes my mouth with his. It starts off soft and caressing, but it becomes demanding as he grinds his body into mine, my thighs dropping open so I can get the delicious friction right where I need it. When we pull apart, we're both breathing heavily, and his eyes are hooded with desire.

He sits up and drags me with him before lifting the hem of my dress up and over my head, tossing it away. His eyes drink in my lingerie-clad body, his hands skimming over my skin as he reverently strokes it. "Look at this pale, milky skin. I've been dying to get my hands and tongue on it." He takes one of my lace-covered nipples into his mouth. I gasp and throw my head back as he uses his tongue to lick before engulfing it in his mouth and sucking.

"Let's get rid of all of this, as pretty as it is." His voice is low and husky, and he makes quick work of my underwear so that I'm lying completely naked before him. "Gorgeous!" Again, he runs his hands over me lightly and gently, like he wants to map my body under his hands. His hands drift to my thighs, and he pushes them apart. I feel my cheeks heat as he stares down at my pussy, his gaze intense. The anticipation that's building in my body curls my toes until I start to squirm under his scrutiny. A mischievous grin spreads over his lips, and he gives me a quick kiss, reaching for the ice cream that's next to us.

"Patience, I've dreamed of this for so long, and I don't plan on rushing it." He pries open the lid and scoops out some of the cold, creamy treat before painting my body with it. I squeak with how cold it is against my overheated flesh, but I start to pant when he paints my sensitive parts with it—first across my belly then each nipple. He lowers his head, and I feel his tongue swipe across the first path that has started to melt and run down my sides. He licks and sucks, and I squirm beneath his ministrations, the slide of his tongue made rougher by something in the ice cream.

"Hmm, delicious, mint chocolate chip has always been my favorite, but now I'm never going to be able to look at it again without getting hard." He licks and sucks the ice cream from my nipples, the rock-hard peaks throbbing by the time he's done, and I thrash my head back and reach my hand down to put some pressure on my clit, which throbs in time with them.

"Uh-uh," Alex scolds with another low chuckle. "We're getting to that bit now." He pulls my hands away, and the next thing I feel is cold ice cream on my clit.

"Oh my god," I moan, my hands fisting the fabric beneath me as my body coils tight with anticipation. Thankfully, Alex doesn't make me wait. His hot mouth latches around my ice-cream-covered clit, and he sucks hard. My back arches as I simultaneously try to escape and get more of the exquisite sensation. His hands are like vises on my thighs, holding them apart as he fucks my pussy with his tongue. He's everywhere, overstimulating me until I'm a sobbing, begging mess.

"Please, Alex, I need more!" I cry out, hoping that the balconies surrounding us are unoccupied.

He slides two fingers deep into my channel and slowly pumps them in, returning his tongue to my clit, circling it and flicking it over the sensitive bud. My body tightens as I feel my orgasm just out of reach. He has me balancing perfectly on the edge, giving me just enough pressure to feel good but not enough to send me tumbling over. My hands reach for his hair, and I grab hold as I try to create more friction, grinding my pussy into his mouth, but he just chuckles and pulls away. Before I can protest, he's climbing up my body, placing little kisses all over my feverish skin, then locking his mouth to mine in another breath stealing kiss. It's all lips, tongue, and teeth, biting and sucking, and it's all I can do to fist my fingers in his silk shirt and enjoy the ride.

Finally, he pulls away, and I fumble with the buttons, needing to feel his skin against mine. I'm too frustrated with this shit, so I just grab hold of either edge and yank. Buttons pop, and Alex's mouth drops open in surprise before he shrugs out of it. My hands go to his belt buckle, but I can't make it work. I whine in disappointment, having given up any semblance of pretending I'm not desperate.

"Hush, baby, I've got you," he coos, then he proceeds to shed the rest of his clothing until he's as naked as I am, his tan, golden skin a complete contrast to my paleness. I run my hands over his lean, muscled body, reaching down to take his steel hard cock in my hand. I fist it, pumping up and down, and his precum leaks out, giving me a little lubrication to make the slide smoother. Soon, he stops my hand with his.

"If you keep doing that, I'm going to embarrass myself." He pulls my hand away, and I feel him press his hard dick against my core as I raise my hips in invitation. He lifts one of my legs over his hip and thrusts deep, forcing his way into my tight channel, and we both groan as he seats himself fully.

"Oh yes." I sigh as I feel his body shudder, and my core wraps itself tightly around his throbbing cock.

"Oh wow, so good and wet and hot," he pants out, his eyes squeezed tight like he's trying to get himself under control. He stays there for what feels like forever, but eventually, he starts to move. His eyes open as he pulls almost fully out before slamming back in. He does this a couple of times before angling his body over mine. This time, when he thrusts in, his cock hits just the right spot, and a low, guttural moan leaves my mouth.

"Oh yeah, your moans make balls ache," he mutters as he sets a rhythm that has him hitting that spot every time. He winds my body back up until it's coiled tightly on the precipice of orgasm.

"Going to empty my balls deep into your body,

going to paint your womb with my cum. I want my babies growing inside your body. Going to fuck you so many times my cum is going to be leaking down your thighs." My hands caress his shoulders as I wrap my legs around his waist, needing to feel him surround me, his dirty words triggering something deep inside of me. He takes a nipple into his mouth, and with his next thrust, he bites down. I fly off the edge, my mind splintering, and ride the sensations, his dirty praise pushing all the right buttons. "Good girl, milk my cock. Your pussy feels so good squeezing me so tight." After a couple more thrusts, Alex loses it, and I feel his body shudder as he fills me with his cum. I know I should be worried that we didn't use protection, but I'm covered by birth control, and there's something primal and sexy about being filled by him.

His mouth finds mine as we both recover from the aftershocks of our orgasms. His body gets heavy as he relaxes into the kiss. Eventually, he sighs and pulls away, but instead of disappearing, he shuffles back down to my pussy and runs his fingers in the cum that's leaking out. He shoves his fingers deep into my pussy, stroking up to hit my G-spot once more. Overly sensitive, I cry out in complaint, but he hushes me.

"Shhh, just pushing my cum back into you. It's fucking sexy knowing that I'm in your body." He gently licks my clit, cleaning up my release as he continues to pump his fingers in and out. It starts off as too much, and I want to push his head away, but soon enough, it feels good. Alex manages to wring out one more orgasm, pushing his cum back into my body the entire time. Finally, I shudder and push him away.

"No more," I beg, and he crawls back to me, pecking me on the mouth.

"You did so good, my princess. Your pussy looks so pretty full of my cum."

"You've got a filthy mouth," I tell him, feeling exhausted, and he just grins.

"I can't wait for us to fill you up. I can't wait to know what your pussy feels like when you're full of Shane's and Jace's cum too."

I groan when he pushes his hard cock back into my body again. "Come on, baby, give me one more," he coaxes, and he builds me up into another orgasm with those long, languid strokes. I lose track of time as my mind drifts with all the sensations, the feel of his skin on mine, his dirty whispers in my ears, his hands plucking at my nipples before one drifts lower to my clit. This orgasm builds a lot slower, and it isn't as powerful as the first two. When it does hit me, it's like a gentle roll flowing through my body, my head going back as a guttural moan leaves my mouth.

"Alex!"

"Good girl," he whispers against my mouth before he speeds up, fucking me into the cushions below. My orgasm continues to move through my body, and I'm oversensitive and begging him to stop when I finally feel him shudder again.

I must pass out, because when I come to, we're wrapped in blankets, snuggled next to one another, and Alex's fingers are still deep in my cunt.

"What are you doing?" I ask sleepily, and he looks a little sheepish.

"Making sure my cum doesn't go anywhere."

"You do know I'm on birth control, right? I wouldn't have done what we just did without it." His face shutters for a minute, dare I say looking disappointed, before he nods.

"I guessed as much, but it doesn't hurt to practice."

"Do you want babies, Alex?"

He nods, no shame in his gaze at all. "Yes, and I want you to be their mother."

A warm feeling flows through me at his honesty, but before I can say anything, he removes his fingers and climbs off the bed. "Come on. Let's go have a shower, and I'll wash you."

He reaches over and scoops me up bridal style before running us inside. I squeal, wrapping my arms around him, hoping that no one is around to see us both naked.

Once we're clean, he carries me back out to the daybed. Pulling the curtains closed behind us, we snuggle under the blankets. He gathers me in his arms and presses a kiss to my head, then I fall asleep to the sound of the ocean waves, Alex's deep breathing, and thoughts of blue-eyed, blond-haired babies being carried around by their doting father.

Life is pretty much perfect at the moment. I just wish I could bottle it up and keep it the same, but I know that's not possible, so I'm going to make the most of it while I can.

Don't stress! I know I kind of left you hanging but Superficial Girl Part 2 will be out very shortly. Keep an eye on my Facebook group for the announcement. I'll make it live as soon as it's ready.

Thank you for reading!
I hope you enjoyed the book. It would be super awesome if you could leave a review wherever you bought it, because I love to hear what you thought of the story.

Want to keep up to date with new books coming soon? Sign up to my newsletter here
Newsletter

Another way to do that is to join me Facebook group. I drop teasers and giveaways in there all the time. Here's the link
Lexie's Ladygarden

Visit my webpage and check out reading orders and what else I've written.
www.lexiewinston.com

Acknowledgments

I really enjoyed writing Jacinta's story. Originally I was just going to leave it to Jace, Alex and Shane in her harem but the characters of Riku, Ashton and Cole had a mind of their own. They basically forced themselves onto the pages. I hope you are liking them as much as I did. I know I've kind of put Jacinta through the wringer but she couldn't have an easy happily ever after. Stay tune for Part 2 which I will release live as soon as it's through editing and formatting. I'll announce it in my Facebook group.

Thank you to all the normal crew this book wouldn't be possible without you all.

Michelle for your invaluable editing.

Jess for squeezing me in for a proofread.

Emma for all the late night and early morning chats.

My alpha and beta teams for being super awesome
as usual.

Grace for being my emotional support human,
talking me down off the ledge and smacking me
around when I need it.

Thank you to everyone who reviews and
recommends it and thank you to all of you who
take the chance and preorder the next one as soon
as you've finished the last. You guys are the reason I
can keep writing this story.
Until next time. Happy Reading
Xoxo

Lexie

Coming Late 2022

For so long now I've been a solo operative, not having to worry about anyone but my target and myself. I even have a code name that is whispered throughout the underworld.

The Phantom.

And people know to be scared if they get on my radar.

But the director of the secret agency I work for is also my dad, and I'm still his little girl despite how many kills I have under my belt. He's decided that I need to have a team to back me up.

I strongly disagree.

But we made a deal. If he wins, I have to join a team of his choosing and work a sex trafficking case with them, leaving the Phantom to retire. But if I win, he never brings it up again and I get to stay a ghost.

I'm going to hand this team their ass, because the Phantom is not a team player

Get it now